CUCKOO

"It's been a long time since I've read a novel that is such a compulsive read. The pages skim by and Wright handles the tension and mystery with the skill of a seasoned pro."

HORROR WORLD

"A plot as wild as this could have easily spun out of control, but Wright holds the reins tight. His dexterity is dazzling."

HELLNOTES

"It is impossible to get through a white-knuckle reading of this chilling blend of science fiction and horror without building up a headful of questions. The irresistible urge to "figure things out" is going to meet up with the immovable wall of a complex, constantly surprising plot. Wright's vision would seem too abstract to control, but he is the master of this nightmare from start to finish. "

SF SITE

"Haunting and frightening, Cuckoo is a clever blend of mystery and horror with just a taste of science fiction for spice."

FOREWORD MAGAZINE

Previously published 1999 by Hard Shell Word Factory, and 2002 by
Razorblade Press.

Copyright © 2011 Richard Wright

Cover design by snowangels.org

ISBN: 1463762038
ISBN-13: 978-1463762032

Cuckoo

RICHARD WRIGHT

RICHARD WRIGHT

DEDICATION

I wrote this book in 1997, fourteen years back. A lot of people have come, and a lot of people have gone. This revised edition of *Cuckoo* is for Kirsty, who bought it last time round as a cunning prelude to marrying me. Ladies everywhere should note that buying a man's novel and actually reading it is an excellent way to hasten wedding bells.

ACKNOWLEDGMENTS

This is a book with history. With each new life it's developed, there have been more people to thank. So, in no particular order, sincere thanks to Natasha Di Michele, Mark Williamson, Emma Buckle, Annie MacPherson, Mary Z. Wolf, Dirk M. Wolf, Darren Floyd, all at Borders Glasgow (RIP) circa 2000, Emma Barnes, Kirsty, and Eva. There are others. If you know who you are, then take it as read.

RICHARD WRIGHT

1 PERSPICACITY

Black clouds of nothing slowly evaporate. His mind is clearing. Bright, stabbing lights of consciousness pierce and illuminate. There is awareness. With awareness comes hell.

Burning? He cannot feel his skin. It is there, he knows, yet he has no experience of it. Awareness and nothing more, not yet. This is very much worse than pain, for now there is anticipation. He knows what his body is suffering, knows too that before very long he will have to step without this place where his mind hides, this haven of absent sensation. Content in his protective shell, he wishes only that the awareness would go away.

Awareness of stripping, searing and scalding. Awareness of pain without physical confirmation. An abstract section of his mind decides that this is good, for if he truly felt the pain he would be mad, dead even. Is this not the preferable position to be in? Not mad? Not dead?

But now he can appreciate, in an abstract fashion, the agonies being heaped upon his body. First the burning. Unsure at which point during the process he has awakened, he is still dimly aware that he is in a much worse condition than the first stage. So perhaps the initial burning has been and gone, and he is beyond the point where his skin reddens.

Lobsters. He remembers a restaurant where there had been lobsters. Picking one, blue and living, from a tank, he had joked in bad taste, praying that she was not a vegetarian. She had laughed. She had laughed again when it came back red. Scalded. Had his mind fled back to when he was six, when he too had been scalded? Just his arm, a spilt cup of coffee, but it had hurt. It had hurt for a long time.

He wonders now what it will be like to be scalded until he is dead.

2 SCALDED LOBSTER

She gave an inane giggle, and he knew he finally had her. A panicked thought had cavorted through his head when he selected his lobster, making the *I've got the hots for you* comedy gambit as he did. After all, she had yet to order. Perhaps she was vegetarian. Or vegan. Or whatever the hell you were that forbade you to eat lobster. He held such Templars of Virtue in utter contempt. When asked his own views on vegetarianism he fell back on the Omnivorous Justification.

"Aren't we descended from a line of omnivores? Even chimpanzees hunt for meat every now and then. Need it to supplement their vegetarian intake or they wither and die. Now either God or Evolution, depending on your outlook on universal design, organised things that way. I can't see why we should thwart the grand plan."

In truth he simply had a sneaking suspicion that vegetarians were weaker than he was. Something suffered and bled to fill your plate? So be it. He was a modern man, and fine with that.

Fortunately she had laughed. A little too hard, in fact. Those pre-dinner drinks (and she certainly could drink) had not been wasted. Now she was attempting to look deeply into his eyes from across the smooth oak table, valiantly battling an alcohol inspired stupor to do so. Awarding her full marks for effort, he swivelled round to see if his meal was any closer to arriving. A sudden contact with his groin caused him to jerk back with a sharp intake of breath. Her foot had made a too solid and unsubtle connection with his crotch, and while he appreciated the sentiment, her bodily coordination left something to be desired.

A pity, but she would still serve.

If she managed to get through dinner. Perhaps he had been a little too generous with the pre-dinner refreshments. Now he had to get her from the restaurant to the hotel while she still clung to the last useful relics of consciousness, which meant denying her further alcohol without wrecking her ego. Tricky, for the third bottle of wine was still half full.

Fortunately he had a plan. He would beat her to it, and feel better about the whole infidelity issue into the bargain.

He had, of course, spent many hours rationalising his affair away. Often elaborate and unlikely, these justifications did little to ease his guilt, existing only to give him a mental framework in which to operate, a series of patterns he could follow that felt less random than the callous truth. For example, it was not that he had no love for his wife, but that he happened to love Georgina as well. What gave society the right to choose which was the more valid of the two? Was he not doing the better thing by both of them? After all, his wife remained blissfully unaware of the situation, therefore had no cause to suffer. Georgina seemed perfectly content with her role as mistress, so must be happy with her own position in the scheme of things. It was simple and fair.

There were others reasonings as well. Amongst his favourites was the supposition that he was actually doing this for the *sake* of his marriage. Depression had recently scored serious marks in the serenity of his home. Office problems, most notably the complete inability of his employer to recognise Greg's contribution to the smooth running of the operation, had taken a heavy toll on his marital relationship. It preoccupied him continually. Was it his fault that no one appreciated his efforts?

No, said his wife, *of course not*. Jennifer was a good woman, but in the end she had proven ineffectual. She had made efforts, there could be no question of that. Affection, a shoulder to cry on, an ear to rant in.

It had not been enough.

Since the outset of the affair however, things had taken a marked swing for the better. His confidence returned, and his home life grew more tolerable. *You see*, he would say to himself, *I knew what I was doing all along*.

Baited by this self-satisfaction, his cynicism often pointed out that he had been involved in a one-night stand that had grown out of control with unpredictable speed. Dismissal was his usual response to this, though he knew it to be the utter truth. Depressed by the hard facts of his life, he had been flattered by Georgina's evident interest. It was as cold and simple as that.

So when she made that first pass at him three months ago his ego said yes. The real Gregory had naturally baulked at the idea. The real Gregory had gone back to his nice semi-detached home in Wimbledon, sat down for dinner with his adoring wife, then taken her upstairs to make loving love to her in their pastel blue bedroom. His ego, on the other hand, had taken Georgina out to a parking lot and fucked her hard against a wall. Approving of this second scenario, his body had stayed to join in.

So while the real Gregory had been hypothetically nuzzling his wife in the comfort of his home, his ego and body had occupied themselves elsewhere. Was that his fault?

No, answered his conscience, *of course not. Nor will it be so the next time. Or the time after that. Or the many times after that when you take her to quiet car parks and flatter your ego.*

In an elaborate effort to salvage a moral position, his conscience had opted to fall in love with his slut. This was, to his rational mind, patently ridiculous. He hardly knew her (unless he were allowed to include practical attributes such as the five points on the back of her shoulder and neck that made her gasp and cry). Questions relating to her favourite colour, or songs which made her nostalgic, or even whether she had ever felt a wild urge to run in the rain, would all have drawn a blank.

Of his wife Jennifer he could answer all of these questions. Red, *Sympathy For The Devil,* and yes, respectively. He was definitely in love with Jennifer. He must be, because he was married to her.

Puzzling this state of affairs, his conscience had decided that things were amiss. If he were not in love with Georgina, then the affair defined him as a fundamentally bad person. Yet how could he claim to be in love with a woman who he knew so little about? Hence, this Friday evening, this restaurant, and that lobster. The occasion had been a long time coming; nearly a full three months filled with London car parks, drives to the country, and hurried encounters at her flat. But he was finally doing it. Sort of.

Enthusiasm was hardly the problem. He had leaped at the opportunity to establish a retrospective justification for three months of lustful infidelity. For her part, Georgina had been delighted at the idea of dinner at a nice restaurant. Viewed from her perspective she had now become more than an outlet for his sex drive. She had become a *romantic* outlet for his sex drive. It was, to her, love's young dream.

Would that he were so young, he thought, glancing desperately at one of the Italian waiters. Thirty-two to her twenty-one. Superficially, this did not seem a big gap, but he had allowed himself to dwell on it too long. She would have been seven when he was eighteen, schoolyard skipping while he was having clumsy sex in the back of cars. It made him feel pedophiliac.

No relief was due from the waiter, who seemed happy allowing his customers to endure the discomfort of forced conversation. Greg would have to continue battling his way through the problems that had manifested as he and George talked. Differing interests. He tried to recall when he had stopped paying attention to music. She had discussed too many bands as he nodded away his ignorance with attempted interest. Her favourite colour had been black, her favourite song was something from some TV talent contest, and she had already run wildly through the rain. Naked. At a festival. He was out of his depth.

Fortunately, she had wasted no time in getting drunk, knocking some of the rough edges from the shape of the evening ahead. Smile lots, enjoy the food, go back to the hotel, and finally talk in a language they both understood.

But, pricked his conscience, *only because you are in love with her. It is terribly important to remember that you are in love with her.*

Deciding to have stern words with his subconscious later on, he put the traitor thought to the back of his head. Casting his eyes over the vision sitting opposite him was enough to divert him from all such cynicism. Her own eyes flicked drunkenly over his shoulder as the red-shirted waiter arrived with the lobster.

Which had been blue.

Which had been living.

Things began to go wrong then, without warning. Unfamiliar pressures took root beneath his ribs, building like a breath held too long. His chest jerked in shallow, spasmodic little bursts as it tried to alleviate the phantom forces accumulating there. Shunting his efforts aside, the pain refused to ease. An urge to howl built in him as the swollen nothing shot upwards from torso to head, gagging him as it slammed past his larynx.

Then his mind jumped, and the world followed.

Staring up at the table, little Greg listened to the voice of his mother drift in from the hallway as she answered the telephone. She sounded upset.

The mind of a six-year-old is not the most sophisticated machine on the planet. Many things were happening which Greg had no way of understanding. He had yet to grasp the concept of death, so would not have understood that his mother was being told of the tragic demise of her sister. In fact, being an only child, he had only the most cursory understanding of what a sister actually was.

What the unsophisticated six-year-old mind has no difficulty understanding is the concept of upset. Greg was often upset. When he fell and grazed his knee he got upset. When he got separated from his mother at the park, he got upset. When he was not allowed to stay up late he got *especially* upset. His mother had always tried to make things better for him at those times. He wanted to make her feel better too.

Gregory did not know that caffeine is an addictive, mood-altering drug. All he knew was that whenever his mother was upset, even if only a little bit, she drank a cup of hot coffee. Like the one sitting on the table. It was a black, sour-tasting substance, which he knew because his mother had once let him try some from the bottom of her cup. Though secretly revolted by the flavour, he had pretended to like it because he understood that this was a grown-up drink, and he had desperately wanted to be a grown-up. He was trying to be grown-up then, by making his mother feel better.

Reaching up, he curled his tiny fingers around the handle of the cup, pulling it towards him. It offered no resistance.

A howl went up, terror and surprise splitting the air as freshly boiled coffee burned into his skin. He would never know the fear that hammered through his mother at that moment. He would never understand how scared she was, death being so close to her thoughts. All he knew was that on the day his mother had been upset he had hurt himself trying to help. In return she had bent him over and slapped him for fifteen minutes, releasing tears to match his own with every blow delivered. Perhaps his head would someday understand why this had happened so, but his heart never would.

And his mind jumped back. Georgina was laughing, and he knew he looked awful. Lasting no more than thirty seconds, his daydream had left him clammy and white. The waiter's face confirmed how decidedly unwell he looked. The bright red lobster, which he had been staring down at, gazed back at him with mournful eyes. Sitting there, wondering whether vegetarianism might not be underrated after all, he heard Georgina's voice float through her giggles.

"I'm glad we did this, babe. I think we're really starting to get to know each other, you know?"

To Greg's relief, his plan proceeded smoothly after that. Georgina had been given the opportunity to drink less than a glass of the remaining wine, and he had got himself good and drunk. Putting the episode in the restaurant down to a cocktail of nerves and the alcohol already consumed, he had succeeded in keeping his mistress entertained throughout the meal, even managing to eat most of the damned lobster. On calling for the bill he was delighted to find the cost of the evening to be very reasonable.

Leaving his car outside the restaurant - in two days he would be furious to find a parking ticket awaiting his return - he had hailed a cab to take them to the hotel. Very sensible. Very mid thirties. Was this the man who had once driven from Cardiff to London under the influence of a bottle of Jim Beam? Why did he feel so old with her? Middle age was a long way from turning its shrivelled gaze in his direction. When she wasn't around he felt barely grown-up.

He instantly regretted his choice of words, for they heralded the Return of the Scalded Lobster and the Childhood Burn. It sounded like some cheap B-movie, the type he and Jennifer so enjoyed curling up in front of together.

Deciding not to think of his childhood, lobsters, and especially not Jennifer, Greg searched for something else to occupy him. Glancing at Georgina, he saw that the vibrations of the taxi had sent her to sleep. Not a problem, he would correct that at the hotel. A good thought. Relaxing slightly, he wallowed in the prospect of the evening before him. Golden curls reaching down to her waist. Muscular legs. Small and delicate breasts. An almost constant pout. Georgina was a striking woman. Better, she was *his* striking woman, at least until morning.

Upon reaching the Ramkin Hotel he bestowed a generous tip on the driver, who drove away happier than he had arrived. Greg felt fine, having done a worthy thing. Some of his good fortune had been shared and life was dandy.

Opening the building's glass doors for Georgina, he paid close attention to her reactions. The hotel was not, in the strictest sense, extravagant. Being forced to pay in cash, for Jennifer was a stickler for checking over credit card and bank statements, he had been unable to afford the luxury he wanted. It was still a nice place though, and he hoped that Georgina would be suitably impressed.

His hopes were consolidated. She was *very* impressed, in an inebriated sort of way. Her mouth hung open, her eyes telling stories of fairy princesses whisked away by shining knights. Liking himself in that role, he marched over the smart red of the carpet. Drunk as he was, he fancied himself an impressive figure as he approached the reception. Despite his unimposing height, he was far from unfit, and Jennifer was always reassuring him that he possessed a convincing charisma. Directing a powerful gaze at the receptionist, he declared his arrival.

"Johnson. Mr and Mrs." An alias for the evening, paranoia being ever at his heels. He was quite proud of the clarity of speech he managed. Gregory Summers was a man who could hold his liquor.

"I'm sorry sir, but we don't have a booking under that name."

Greg's mind took some moments to catch up with this announcement. Things had begun to go wrong again. "But...but I booked it this afternoon. In person."

From the look plastered across the face of the young man, Greg's clarity of speech had all but vanished. Salvaging what remained of his dignity, he tried again. The response he received was curt and to the point.

"I'm sorry, but you're not listed in the book. Are you sure this is the right hotel?"

Yes, damn it, drunk he was, but not that drunk. He paused. No, he was positive it was the Ramkin he had booked, even paying in advance. Besides, how could he embarrass himself in front of Georgina by admitting he might be wrong? Deciding he had no choice but to bluff, he attempted a steely expression.

"You're certain. Nothing under Johnson?" The clerk shook his head. "Very well, have you any other rooms for the evening?" They did, and he paid the extra money, informing the young man that he would be having strong words with the manager in the morning.

Leading the way to the lift, he looked back at his companion before breathing a grateful sigh of relief. If he was any judge of character, and he liked to think this was the case, Georgina had been impressed by his firm handling of the matter. Quite right too. Greg Summers was also a man who could handle a tough situation. Now she knew it. His missing reservation could even be a blessing on the entertainments ahead. Nothing a woman likes more than a show of strength, he thought.

Odd thing about the reservation though.

Damned odd.

3 MASKS

The observer watches him burn. She wonders, as he writhes and thrashes, if he is aware of making these physical movements. A slit smile breaches the mask of her face. At least he is now awake. She knows this, can see it. His eyes have not opened, nor has he made a sound to indicate his arrival at consciousness, yet she is aware of him. She reaches deep within him to touch his soul, sees the lobster and the hotel. Of course, her own memories of these events are still fresh. She does not need to see. She needs to feel. She does so.

So naïve when she found him, so full of grief. She had known then, as she knows now, that he was to be the one. It will be a long time before she finds another with his potency. In her own unique way she will miss him when he fades, for together they have explored far, wandering through passions he could once have only imagined. Can he ever appreciate what he is to her?

But he will wither now. She will be alone again. This is not, in itself, something she seeks. Rather it is the price, a tax without which her future would grow desolate indeed.

So many times now. So much suffering. A spark ignites in her soul as she thinks this thought. Yes, so very much suffering. Such worthy pain.

She reaches in again to find...

4 PAINTWORK

Blisters in the paintwork of the door revealed the hotel for what it was. A front. A sham. Gregory fought back his disappointment. On the outside of the office the wood was varnished and clean. *Good*, he had thought, *now we are getting somewhere. Here be managers.*

Invigorated by his fine night, he had been up early to speak with someone regarding the confusion of the previous day. Georgina had distracted him briefly. Twice, in fact. Both of them excellent and enjoyable distractions in their own right. Now she had gone home to her flat, leaving him a refund to collect.

The manager of the Ramkin Hotel, Mr Carlisle, met him in the foyer. He had seemed an efficient and orderly type. Upright, brisk, he stood a clear four inches taller than Greg, his blonde hair brushed tightly over his head to form a small ponytail. An angular face held the promise of a penetrating mind. *Mr Carlisle and I*, Greg had decided, *can communicate. We are That Sort Of Person.*

So he had thought. Now that he had been escorted to the grotty inner sanctum which passed for an office, the sham of Mr Carlisle was also exposed. As soon as the door had closed he lounged into the chair behind the desk, removed some tobacco from the pocket of his immaculately pressed suit, and proceeded to roll a cigarette.

"Mr Johnson, is it not? Please take a seat. Do you smoke?"

Ignoring the offer, Greg looked around. Only one extra seat was to be found in the room. Moulded from orange plastic, now extremely weathered, it made him think of garish city bus stations. Suppressing a full-blown scowl, he contented himself with furrowing his brow — a sure signal of his disapproval. Lifting the monstrosity with his fingertips, he placed it firmly opposite the hotel manager. As expected, it was not comfortable. Nothing in the room was. A collection of mismatched junk and discarded scraps. Even the sunlight filtered through the blinds halfheartedly, as though it too would rather be anywhere but within that office.

Obviously amused by the reaction of his customer, Mr Carlisle tried to hide his smile behind the inhalation of another lungful of carcinogens. When he spoke up a thick cloud of toxins blew from his lips.

"Very well. I am rather busy at the moment, as you can appreciate, so we'll keep this as brief as possible. You would like a refund?"

This was somewhat blunter than Greg had prepared for, and he found himself taken aback.

"Ah...yes, that about sums it up. I made a booking, along with an advance payment, yesterday afternoon. Your staff denied all knowledge of this when I arrived last night."

"So I've been told. You paid in person?"

"I did."

"And you signed the register upon payment?"

"That's right."

"Hm. Then perhaps you could explain to me why your signature can't be found in any of the records for yesterday afternoon?"

Gregory was stopped dead by the man's sheer effrontery. Was that really going to be his defence? How dare he insinuate that Greg Summers was the type of...

Summers?

An unpleasant thought reared up, and his insides churned. What if he had booked under his real name? It was possible. Rushing in during his lunch hour the previous day he had intended to sign the name Johnson, but flustered as he was, he could have made the mistake without realising it.

Time to change his approach.

"Would it be possible for me to check your register? I'm sure this is all a misunderstanding, and..."

"You're more than welcome to peruse the sheets for yesterday Mr Johnson, but I feel it should be pointed out to you that I am not a foolish man, nor am I in the habit of employing fools." Carlisle's face was as cold as his words. "My staff informs me that you did not book a room here yesterday. Ergo, you did not. However, should you care to wait here for a moment, I shall bring you the proof you so obviously need to refresh your memory." Reverting to the upright individual who had met him in the foyer, the manager took a last draw on his cigarette, stubbed it in an overflowing glass ashtray, then marched out of the office.

Greg knew he had signed that book. Last night, he had been a little confused, with the alcohol trying to convince him that he might have wandered into the wrong hotel. But in the light of a sober morning he knew this wasn't the case. He was in the right place, he was sure of it. So why did the rest of the world insist otherwise?

By this point he was prepared to abandon the whole idea of a refund. A night of pleasure was what he had sought, and that was what he had received. Georgina possessed an inhuman imagination, not to mention impossible physical stamina, when it came to matters of sex. Previous rushed encounters had only hinted at what she was capable of, given a whole night and a double bed. Never having been inclined towards the unusual, the gusto with which he had approached handcuffs and a blindfold shocked him.

Of course he resented paying double for the use of the room, but ultimately the experience had proven worthwhile. It was now curiosity that pinned him to his bus station chair. Mr Carlisle could be as smug as he chose, but for his own peace of mind Greg needed to know what had gone wrong.

Hearing the door close behind him, he realised with a start that Carlisle was back in the office. In his hands he bore a distinctive leather-bound register. Gold lilt, a red ribbon marking the page, the top right-hand corner bent out of shape. Yes, that was the document he had signed yesterday, he would swear on it.

As he took it in his hands, before the book was even opened, Carlisle's superior smile had already told him what he would find. He was correct. No Mr Johnson.

But no Summers either.

Running his finger down the page he found the precise time-slot he had filled in. A Mrs L. Harris was signed securely in his place. There was no correcting fluid, no doctoring of the letters, no obvious means of erasing his name. To all intents and purposes this woman had signed in a blank space.

Confused as it already was, his mind resisted the jump, wrestling it down in the effort to suppress it. Reality became a hazy, far away thing as wars raged in his head and chest, each battle stinging him as a physical hurt. When Mr Carlisle took a step back from him, shock scrawled across his face, Greg could not be sure if it was real or imagined.

And his mind did not simply jump. It leapt.

Understanding came late for Greg. Thirteen years old. That was when he finally comprehended the day of the coffee scald. Looking down at the still body of his mother, he found that he too wanted to hit something. Someone.

Worm food, he thought. *My mother has become worm food. When she is buried they will feast.* With the church-quiet murmur of mourners all around him he wondered if, should he pull back on her eyelids, he would find her eyes still intact. Eyes are the mirrors of the soul, or so he had read somewhere. Where would her eyes take him, if he gazed too long into them? What would he see reflected back at him? He nearly did it then, so easy would it be to just reach out and peel her worm food eyelids apart.

Over rehearsed explanations had spilled from the lips of his father. It was not, of course, Greg's fault that this tragedy was visiting upon them. She had been troubled, had never fully recovered from the death of her sister. Stress had been the cause; nobody had reason to suffer for her suicide. Especially not little Gregory.

So often had this been expressed that he had begun to doubt there was any substance to the platitude. Contemplating the words of his father, he thought the truth obvious.

Question: what causes stress?

Answer: other people.

Question: what person had she spent more time with than any other?

Answer: Gregory. Her son. Her murderer.

Wishing her happiness with her worms, he turned aside. In many ways it was easier on him than anybody could guess. After accepting that he was a murderer, by default a bad person, the pain and suffering he should have endured were easily dismissed. Grief was for the good, an elite grouping in which he no longer belonged.

For some reason his face hurt...

"Mr Johnson? Mr Johnson?"

Hurt. His face hurt. As he surfaced through varying levels of consciousness he realised that this was because somebody was hitting him. Rolling instinctively to his feet, he lashed blindly in the direction of his assailant. Connecting firmly with the Carlisle's jaw, he sent the man spinning across his chipboard desk. Coming to rest, Carlisle sat up, clutching his chin with a look of almost childish shock.

As Greg stared across the room, his crouched body a reflection of the adrenaline-tensed frame of the other man, his impression was of two wild beasts circling each other before some fierce territorial battle. Neither wished to make the first move as neither were sure they could win the final conflict.

Grinning at the absurdity, he put his hands up in a placatory gesture of submission.

Carlisle shook his head and allowed himself a nervous smile. "Hardly the best way to get your refund. You passed out. I was trying to revive you."

"By hitting me? Thank god you never went into medicine."

"Indeed. I think I saw it on *Grey's Anatomy*. Always works for him."

All the tension had been beaten from the conversation. Greg felt too exhausted to maintain his stubbornness.

"Did you really sign in here yesterday Mr Johnson?"

"I really did. Where the name Harris now appears."

"And is your name really Johnson?"

An awkward pause threatened to eliminate the tentative salubrity which had taken the men. Anxious to avoid further conflict, Greg put a final end to the lie.

"No. My name is Summers. Greg Summers. I wasn't here with my wife."

Another pause, one which filled Greg with stifling trepidation. For three months a fear of this moment, this admittance, had tortured him daily. Judgement was about to be levelled and he knew too well that he would be found wanting. Annoyed and surprised at himself, he found tears forming. Shaking with the effort of covering his feelings, he welcomed the plastic chair as he sank back onto it.

Then Carlisle relaxed, a genuine smile breaking across his thin lips.

"In that case I owe you an apology and a drink. Will you join me in the bar? Perhaps we can work out just what is going on."

All in all, Alex Carlisle was far better company than first impressions had indicated. Smiling over the top of his glass, Greg was surprised at how much he was enjoying the first real conversation he had engaged in for days. The cause of the smile was Alex's umpteenth apology.

"I admit I was a little hostile, but the only two members of staff working reception yesterday are people I know very well. They'd never heard of you before last night. It wasn't even that we were busy yesterday, especially not for a Friday."

"I know, you said." For some time now the discussion had been weaving elaborate circles around the subject of the missing signature. "Several times, in fact. But I was definitely here. Summers or Johnson, I must have signed something."

Confession, it seemed, really was good for the soul. As soon as the first drink was downed, at the too early hour of one in the afternoon, Greg had told the whole story of his affair. Hesitant at first, but later showing an openness he had not known himself capable of, he had given a detailed account of his life as an adulterer. Alex had been a generous and willing listener. He also had a blunt and refreshing way of stating the facts.

"But sign you did not. I hate to ask again, but you are *sure*?"

"That it was this hotel I signed into. Yes, I'm sure." Since they had entered the bar he had been trying to think of a way to verify this. Carlisle believed him, for which he was grateful, but he needed to give the man some hard evidence. Something which nobody, including himself, could question.

Only then did the obvious occur to him, and he almost laughed. Alex raised an angular eyebrow as Greg rushed to explain.

"Look, I know this isn't proof in itself, I could easily have put it there as part of my elaborate fraud, but I noted it on my phone so I wouldn't forget to make the reservation."

New Year's Eve. His present from Jennifer. She had been extremely annoyed that he had nothing to give her in return, but the gift she offered him was a cherished one. Encased in a real leather cover, replete with the earthy smell of newly tanned hide, the smartphone went everywhere with him.

Pulling it from his jacket pocket, he slid his fingers across the screen, opening up his schedule for the previous day. Beckoning Alex over, he held it up so they could each see the backlit screen.

Both men stared in bemusement at a display notifying the owner of a lunch meeting with somebody called Stewart, the previous day at half past one. There was nothing else. Greg looked up at Alex. Alex looked back. Then both men burst into laughter.

A drunken hysteria raced to take Greg, lifting him from worry to place him right next to Alex in a world of honest astonishment. An even more surreal thought struck him. Between giggles, he squeezed the observation out.

"I don't even know anyone called Stewart."

Five hours later, Greg was in Alex Carlisle's West End flat. Both men were extremely drunk.

"It's a very, very nice flat," said Greg, ignoring the feeling that he had already said this many, many times. It was a splendid flat and any such repetition was justified. Stylish black suede furnishings on a cream carpet. Very simple, very plain. The walls were adorned with equally simple black framed posters from recent cinema releases. The only vaguely colourful fixture in the room was the drinks cabinet. Greg had been right all along, he and Alex could communicate very well indeed. As a self-demonstration he communicated his desire for another scotch.

"Coming your way. Never let it be said that Alex Carlisle leaves his customers dissatisfied."

Another whiskey was duly presented to a grateful customer.

"So Mr Johnso...Summers?" Greg nodded vaguely. "Mr Summers. Have you often seduced young women in my hotel?"

"Frequently. The bed in room twenty-four squeaks appallingly."

Laughter again. Healthy, genuine laughter that scrubbed Greg clean of the grime from weeks of anxiety. Lies he had hated telling, truths he had been unable to share – none of them were important at that moment. He wished he had known this man for longer.

"I had best get that seen to then." Alex was scrolling through Greg's smartphone. Extraordinarily, what would once have been impertinence was now nothing more sinister than a friend's idle curiosity.

"This Stewart, whom you don't know, has been spending an awful lot of time with you recently."

"Lucky him. I hope he had a more memorable experience of it than I did."

Memory.

Stewart.

A soaring red ball.

Pain.

Shaking his head, he decided that the alcohol was affecting him more than he had thought.

"Greg? Are you all right? You're not going to have another fit, are you?"

A weak smile calmed his host, and Greg looked round for the door. *It must be here somewhere*, he considered. *I walked through it barely two hours ago.* Locating a suitable looking rectangle in the wall, he tried to stand.

"Fresh air," he mumbled. "Back in a tick."

Robert grinned, waved him towards the door, then glanced down at the phone in his hand. Greg was still battling for balance when Alex looked up again. He looked puzzled.

"Greg." He hesitated, looking once more at the little book to make sure he had read it correctly. "This isn't your phone."

At which point, Greg passed out.

5 DRAINING

Stage Two. Game over. The thought flickers through his head; to deny it is a strain. Not game over. Not yet. Not by any means.

He wants to open his eyes, very much.

A laugh bounces electrically along his synapses, though whether it ever reaches his lungs is impossible for him to know. He has no need to open his eyes. He feels the lids bubbling and blistering to nothing. If he waits just a little while longer his eyes will be open forever. And what will be reflected there? Where will his soul go when the process is complete?

His awareness expands abruptly. Floating? Of course he has been floating, this is already known to him. But it is so hard to hold his mind, so difficult to prevent the memories from guiding him to other places. Who is he?

Floating. And now he is sinking. If he focuses very hard on the raw mess which was once his auditory track he can hear gurgling. He knows this is bad. This is the outside world and he does not want to go there.

But his awareness does now contain the outside world, he cannot help this. He is sinking. Physically sinking. If he could remember how to use his arms and legs he would try to swim. He cannot, and does not.

Now his back burns worse, very much worse, than before. Something is wrong. Chill heat is searing his body, stroking organs and muscles with icy fingers. As it reaches his head, as his brain tightens at the onslaught, he realises what is happening.

His body is resting on cold metal. Millions of raw nerves, bereft of protective skin, are pressed against the sheet steel at the bottom of the tank. Each nerve stabs blunt icicles into his mind.

He notices the gurgling again. With a sob he will never know he has given, he realises that the tank is being filled for Stage Three. Welcoming the now familiar burning, his relief allows the memories to take him.

6 COMPLEX SPIRALS

Questions. As he floated towards consciousness he knew that there were questions. He was given no chance to recall what they might be. Before he even opened his eyes the world started to spin. Groaning audibly, an almost welcome sign that he was still alive, he recognised the sensation. Not, he decided, the worst hangover he had ever suffered, but certainly deserving of medals as a close contender. Risking all, he cracked open his eyes, only to find that the world was indeed executing complex spirals about his head.

An amused voice informed him that he was not alone in his suffering.

"You too, eh? There's a pot of coffee on the table."

Sitting up, an action that his churning stomach strongly disapproved of, he saw the man slouched over the black armchair opposite him. Carlisle. Alex Carlisle. Details from the previous night filtered back into his mind. It appeared he had slept on the settee. Aromatic coffee smells played over his nostrils, and he decided that there were more immediate priorities than his dishevelled appearance.

"A coffee would be very much appreciated. Thanks." Ignoring his rebelling equilibrium, he staggered across to the small coffee table in the corner. As he reached for the chrome cafetière standing there, his gaze fell upon a small leather case perched next to it. The phone. Greg reeled with the returning memories, questions shaking him as they flooded home.

Several hours and four strong coffees later, he was driving his blue Ford Focus home. Finding the parking ticket on his window had driven his confusion into anger, and now he seethed. Each dragging mile between Central London and Wimbledon only fuelled his rage.

Alex had told him that it was not his phone. At first Greg had refused to believe it, calmly informing his new friend that it had been a New Year gift from his wife. The obvious thing would have been to look at the phone itself, but to his surprise he had been too scared. Inexplicable alarm bells were howling through his subconscious.

After several moments hesitation he had flipped open the cover of the case. In clear bold print, much like his own, was scribed the name Richard Jameson. An address and contact number were also provided.

Combined with the ill effects of the hangover, this new shock forced him to sit firmly back on the couch. Richard Jameson. Not a name he could place, though it was still somehow familiar to him. At the back of his mind, beyond where he could reach, a thought was desperate to make itself heard.

Too confused to consider how to proceed, it had taken Alex to suggest ringing the number in the contact list labelled 'Home' and finding out who Jameson was first hand. Dazed as Greg was, Alex had even made the initial call himself. There had been no answer. Several times over the course of the morning they had tried that number. Nobody answered those calls either.

Over this time Greg had chained together a terrifying theory. Without question he had a phone identical to the one now sitting on the passenger seat of his car, right down to the choice of cover. So he must have picked it up somewhere believing it was his. Yet the only time the thing ever left his person was his home. So that was where he had picked up this one. Jameson must have left his own phone in Greg's house, probably somewhere Greg could have collected it without thinking the location unusual. Somewhere like his bedroom. Beside the bed. Where he left his own phone each night, the alarm primed for the morning. Richard Jameson had been in his bedroom.

Jennifer was having an affair.

Not once had he considered that his wife could be doing to him exactly what he was doing to her with Georgina. Now it was obvious. Over recent months he had assumed that their relationship had become smoother because of the confidence his own infidelity had given him. But why should she not also be enjoying the self-assurance which came from such secret liaisons?

He felt a fool, and he was furious. Of course, the hypocrisy in his anger had already occurred to him, but he could not fight down his rage. Jennifer was still away for a long weekend with her cousin - a story that he now found extremely dubious - giving him the ideal opportunity to check her things. Go through her private belongings. Examine everything she held secret.

A stab of shame lanced him, the tears that stung his eyes almost driving him from the road. Adrenaline prevented an accident, his reflexes automatically focusing his attention back on the A3, but his thoughts continued apace.

How could he invade her privacy like that? What if he was wrong? Richard Jameson could be a client who had left his phone at the office, or perhaps Greg could have picked it up somewhere else after all. But he could think of nothing to do except check the validity of his suspicions. It was small consolation to believe that Jennifer would respond in similar fashion if she had suspicions about Georgina.

With his heart a live thing in his throat, he approached the turn-off to Fontside Avenue. Standing at the far end of the street, his house was a place of sudden nightmare, full of hidden secrets and horrors. Worst among them was the concrete possibility of a life without Jennifer, mistrust shattering their relationship. For the first time in his life he had no idea what he would find beyond the outer shell of his house. Never before had he considered home to be anything other than a place to run to when life abused you. Now it was somewhere to run *from*. Threatened by the simple thought of opening his front door, he turned the corner and pulled up several driveways short of his own.

Resting his head on the steering wheel, he forced himself to breathe deeply. Over several minutes, he managed to cage the anxiety in his chest, coaxing and pleading with it until he could think with something approaching clarity.

A car passed him. Looking up, he witnessed a BMW 3 cruising into his driveway. Gazing on, incredulous, he watched Jennifer, dressed in the clingy blue summer dress he had given her for her birthday, climb from the passenger seat. From the other side of the car emerged a tall man. Long brown hair hung loose about his shoulders. Muscles curved the shape of his T-shirt and jeans.

Jameson.

Tears finally erupted from him, his internal cage no longer able to contain the growth of the beast it housed. For all his certainty while he had been driving, the final confirmation was agony to accept. Screams built in his chest, squeezing living tendrils around his lungs, but he refused to release them. Knowing what his next step must be, accepting a little of what lay before him, he let himself cry until he was exhausted.

Half an hour passed, then an hour. With each moment a fresh seed of grief flowered within him, growing a garden of pain as beautiful as it was lethal. When there was nothing left in him, his tears began to dry up. Opening a window, he heaved great lungfuls of fresh air, trying to alleviate the tightness which lingered in his chest. When he felt as human as he thought was possible, he readied himself to confront what was happening.

He would walk in on them. As simple as that. It was all he could think to do. Unable to see past the point of catching her during her infidelity, he had no way of planning any further. But he could do that much at least.

As he opened the car door the world took on a strange and remote quality, the details of the world surrounding him made intense and painful. Brilliant scarlet shone from his Focus as he turned from it to move towards his home. Shrubs in his front lawn, which he had planted months ago, had a new gleam, a jade vibrancy that bespoke the life within. Aeons passed during the journey to the front door. Familiar glass panels caught his eye to make him wonder why he had never noticed their crystalline, near religious, beauty. Removing his keys from his pocket he found himself marvelling at the metallic textures of their infinite, microscopic scratches and dents. He eased the front door key into the lock and twisted it to one side.

His world snapped back to normal as fury twistered through him. The key would not turn. Jennifer had changed the locks.

Acceptance and disbelief battled for control of his responses as laden moments thudded by. She had barred him from his own home. There had to be a rational explanation. She could not abandon the last six years of their life together

RICHARD WRIGHT

with such casual disregard. Something was seriously awry, he just didn't know what it was yet.

One sure way to discover the answer presented itself to him, and he reached out to press the doorbell. Pausing only momentarily, his finger seeming in that second to hope that Greg might change his mind, the deed was done.

Footsteps running downstairs. Jennifer calling out, in her sweet honey-husky voice, "Just a minute." Keys rattling in the lock.

The door opened. Jennifer stood there, wrapped in her white towelling robe. Blue eyes, pure and shining, looked up at him and he was lost. Incapable of doing more than stare at her, tears welled again in his eyes. Auburn hair, cut into a bob, bounced in the breeze as her too large, beautiful lips pursed in a frown.

Almost choking on the strength of the word, he managed to force out her name.

"Jennifer."

"Yes?" How could she be so calm when she held his heart in her eyes?

"Jennifer?"

"Yes, Jennifer Summers. Do I know you? My husband is upstairs, if you want to speak to him?"

Snatching out, he grabbed her wrists. "Husband! Jen, what the hell are you doing?" Pushing her back, he took them both into the house, still holding tight to her. Then he stopped. He felt his jaw drop.

Green carpet, cream wallpaper with pale green flowers, a varnished teak banister; these were what had occupied his hallway two days ago. Now everything had changed. As he stood there, limp, his mind completely failed to acknowledge the details around him. The alterations were so large that he could not accept them all at once. All he perceived were colours. Pastel blue, darker blues accompanying them. His light, summery hallway, the entrance to his home, was a suddenly cold and claustrophobic place.

In his battle to credit this new and alien location he almost failed to hear Jennifer screaming.

"Greg! Gregory!"

"What?" She sounded like she was in pain, and he realised how tightly he was holding her wrists. Letting go, he was about to reassure her when he realised that she wasn't looking at him. Her head was turned to look up the stairs, at the longhaired man he had seen earlier, now bounding down towards them with concern and fury in his eyes.

"Greg! Get him away from me!" She was talking to Jameson. Calling him Greg.

With a nimble hop over the banister (now a dark oak, Greg realised, as slow motion once more imposed itself on his world) the stranger landed beside him, looping one arm around his neck and yanking backwards. Shrieking messages of pain, the muscles of his shoulders and upper torso followed the movement, forcing him to step away from his wife and slamming him against the chest of the taller man.

Panic gripped Greg and he reacted on instinct, smashing his head up and back. Warm damp in his hair, along with the loosening of the arm that held him, told of his success. Whirling around, he saw blood streaming from his attacker's nose, spurting violently in the desire to abandon its host. To make certain he had delivered his intended message he lashed out again, this time with his fist. His knuckles sent him a bright distress flare as they connected with the already splintered bones of the man's nose, but the resulting howl of agony made his own hurt worthwhile. Whimpering, Jameson staggered against the wall, hands covering his ruined face. Unwilling to just leave him crouching there, Greg lifted his foot back to finish the job. A desperate shout exploded behind him.

"Leave him alone you bastard!"

Even as he turned he could hear the rush of air. The golf club that Jennifer was swinging at him came as no real surprise.

It never got the chance to connect. Every cell in his head suddenly wanted to expand against the walls of his skull. Collapsing, he was barely aware of the golf club swishing harmlessly through space that had only moments ago contained his head. Nor did he notice how very deeply it embedded itself in the wall across from him. On a very peripheral level he acknowledged the blood that suddenly fountained from his ears and poured down from his nostrils. Was he crying again, or was there blood seeping from his eyes too?

Like a bird suddenly released from a lifetime of captivity, his mind soared outwards.

On an elaborately beautiful day, when he was twenty-two years old, he met Jennifer for the first time. His final year at University had been a hard one, but he had good reason not to regret his decision to all but abandon his social life while studying. Graduation day. Receiving his first class masters degree.

While waiting for his turn to shake the hand of the principal, the traditional final acknowledgement of the degree award, he found himself talking to the girl next to him. Jennifer Sharpe. Although he already knew her as a face around the faculty, they had never spoken, yet they had connected with an immediacy that shocked them both. At the end of the ceremony they had gone for drinks and Greg, never previously a romantic man, bowled her from her feet. After many more drinks, several clubs, and a taxi ride to her flat, she and Greg made clumsy, wonderful love on her single bed.

Lying in bed that night, Greg spent a full two hours just watching her sleep. All he could think was that this was the most beautiful thing in the world, a cyclic repetition of fact that both soothed and excited him. Never in his life had he been exposed to someone who burned like she did, and he knew he could never lose her.

Her back curved elegantly to her neck, lightly muscled yet unmistakably feminine, almost feline. Everything in him wanted to stroke it as she slept, but he was too afraid of waking this glorious woman, of shattering the spell she had woven through simple slumber. So he contented himself with listening to her breathe, drinking in the scent of cooling sweat from her body as it mixed with heady perfume. It was a scent he would remember forever.

Coppery smell. Blood. Jennifer smells of blood? No, it was his blood. As his mind settled once more into the present, he realised he was covered in his own blood. His jacket and shirt were drenched, and his arms were cramped. Looking around, he was almost pleased to find himself back in his altered hallway. But something differed from his recent memory, and he strained to think what it could be. Cramp? That was it. His arms were tied behind his back.

He was lying on the stairway, and found that his ankles had also been bound. A voice near the telephone drew his attention.

"...appreciate it. Thanks."

Slightly muffled, coming as it did from behind the handkerchief held over the man's nose, the voice belonged to Jameson. Hanging up, he turned towards Greg.

"You're awake. Good. Do you understand what I'm saying?" Greg nodded, confused by the question. "Okay. By rights I should have called the police to have you arrested. You assaulted Jennifer and gave me a bloody good clobbering into the bargain. But I didn't. I don't know who you are, my friend, but you're obviously seriously unwell. I've never seen anything like what just happened to you. You...exploded. That's the only way I can think to describe it." He smiled humourlessly. "It's going to take forever to get the blood out of the carpet. Anyway, I've called you an ambulance. It should be here in about ten minutes. Did you get all that?"

Again Greg nodded. But he had a question to ask. One all-important question, and he had to ask it of this man, who had answered to his name. "What is happening to me?"

Confused, the man shook his head. "You're asking the wrong guy. Wait until the paramedics gets here."

Not enough, he had to know more. Perhaps he was ill, possibly delusional, but he needed to find out what had become of his wife. His life. "No. I mean...who are you? Where is my wife?"

"Your wife?"

It all made a horrible, sudden sense. This man did not know who Greg was. Perhaps he had believed she was single all along. Guilt flooded him as he looked into the mangled shape that was once Jameson's face.

"I'm sorry, so sorry. She never told you. She's married." A look of shock passed over Jameson's face, and Greg knew he had been right. "To me. Greg Summers. This is my house. Jennifer is my wife. You don't belong here." *Good*, he thought to himself. *Simple statements. I can keep hold of simple statements.*

Jameson's eyes turned hard. Speaking with a slow, careful rhythm, as though to a small child, he changed the whole of Greg's existence with cold candour. "Listen, and try to concentrate on what I say. I am Gregory Summers. I've lived in this house for three years. I met Jennifer when I was twenty-two, and she's been my wife for six years."

Greg's face was an open display of the incomprehension raging within. The man claiming his name seemed to feel for him.

"Look, do you have a wallet?"

"In...in my car. The glove compartment."

"I'll be back in a minute. The Focus, yes?"

As Greg nodded, he teetered. Was this other man confused? Why was he trying to convince Greg that he was not Greg? Again and again the same question revolved through his mind, repetitive and compelling. What the hell was going on?

Clicking shut, the latch on the doorway told him that Jameson had returned. In his hand was a wallet Greg recognised as his own. Picking through it, Jameson found the driving licence and read it aloud.

"Your name is Richard Jameson. You live in a flat at Manorfield Place. Recognise it?" Mute, Greg shook his head. It must be a trick.

"You still don't believe me?" Sighing, as though he was becoming bored destabilising Greg's entire life, he went through to the front room.

When he returned he carried a framed picture that Greg knew very well. His wedding photograph. Jen loved that dress, and found an excuse to wear it each year on their anniversary. Even her smile was exactly as he remembered it. Yet the photo was now fundamentally different. Standing in his place, in almost exactly the same pose Greg recalled assuming, was this other man. Jameson. Summers.

It was all true.

Greg screamed.

7 GRATIFICATION

Like a hot white light, the power flows through her. Though more than halfway through her meal, she knew she had left it almost too long since the last. But now it is done. Nerves that were dead flare back to life, drowning her in a tidal wave of sensation. Every cell in her body explodes with euphoria, pleasure clinging to her insides like sticky debris. Each touch of the breeze on her skin lends her a tremble of delight.

Through fluttering eyelids she watches the tank refill for Stage Three. In doing so she rejoices that her suspicions have proven correct. Her victim is not just potent, he is laden. She wonders faintly if he has family, if there are more like him to sup from, then remembers. No, there will be no more culling from that clan. But this one is proving ample to satisfy her appetites. She extends her tongue, licking her perfect lips in anticipation.

She is stronger than she has been for months. The hunt itself has been rewarding on many levels, for he ran far sooner than the others. Before him she had been unaware of the added trauma caused by prolonging the endgame. She will note it, and incorporate it in the future.

As the sensations fade she is almost too dazed to continue the delve. Knowing that she has missed a brief portion of the event disappoints her, but it is ultimately worthwhile. Allowing her orgasming senses to clear a little, she slips smoothly back into the specimen.

8 REBIRTH

"One a day, after a meal, and you'll feel like a new man."

A new man. The irony was not lost on him. Not Gregory Summers at all, but Richard Jameson.

After seeing the altered wedding photograph he had screamed for fully half an hour, had been screaming still when the ambulance arrived. Once at the hospital the staff had been forced to sedate him, dumping him into restless unconsciousness for the remainder of the day.

On awakening he had been subjected to over a dozen tests, all of which proved inconclusive. Nothing, as far as the medical staff could ascertain, was wrong with him. In the end they had kept him in a second night, he suspected because they could think of nothing else to do, then released him on Tuesday morning when further tests also failed to identify a problem. The pills they gave him were simple antidepressants, prescribed to do nothing more than prevent a level of excitement that could trigger another attack. Needing all of his faculties about him, Greg had no intention of taking them.

It was difficult to consider his potential illness with any sense of urgency. Next to everything else which was happening around him it was little more than an inconvenience, a problem for the long term which faded away beneath the din of the screaming short term. For example, he was now free to leave hospital and return to his life. Except that he had no idea which life he was supposed to be returning to. One thing was for certain - he could not go home. Whatever was happening, it had been made clear that he was unwelcome there. Which left him with nothing. No one.

Except Richard Jameson, the person he was supposed to be.

He pulled his phone from his pocket. Looking at it was pain, for it brought thoughts of Jennifer to the fore, but he swallowed angst and opened the cover to see the label on the reverse. Again he was struck by how similar the handwriting was to his own. Of course, he realised, it was meant to *be* his own. There was an address. Unfamiliar, yes, but somewhere to go, to start. It was time to take an active role in the weirdness surrounding him.

Hailing a taxi took almost ten minutes, but he was too preoccupied to notice the delay. As soon as one pulled up he jumped in.

"Seven Manorfield Place, please."

As the journey progressed, anxiety started to well in him again. It was easier than last time though. At least this was a fear of the unknown. Never again would he have cause to fear the known, for he would never again be able to trust in it. As with all bad movies he expected, at any moment, to wake up from this bewildering nightmare. *Of course you are Gregory Summers*, he told himself. *Who else could you be?* From the back of his mind, subverting the confidence he was trying to establish, a voice gave him the answer. *Richard Jameson.*

"I don't even know the man!" Greg only realised he had spoken aloud when the driver turned to glance at him.

"Sorry mate?"

"Nothing, sorry, thinking aloud." The cabbie returned his attention to the radio.

Cursing under his breath, Greg realised he had not been watching the route they were taking. Being unfamiliar with Central London, he had wanted to keep an eye out for any landmarks he might recognise, for future reference. At present he was almost certain they were driving through the Docklands. Every now and again he thought he saw Canary Wharf towering over the district, and he kept getting flashes of the river between buildings.

Slowing to a halt, the driver checked the cost of the journey.

"Thirteen pounds sixty, mate."

"We're here?"

"Manorfield Place, innit?"

Greg was amazed. Somewhere at the back of his mind he had been supposing that he would end up in some dingy little flat hanging over a shop somewhere. It fitted with the erosion of his life that his fake address be a pale shadow of his real one.

But this...Christ, this was the Docklands! You couldn't ask to live in a more exclusive area of London. The taxi was parked outside an extremely impressive set of riverside apartments. He checked his phone cover, confirming the address. It was correct.

"Look mate, you getting out, yeah?" The cabbie was losing patience with his confused passenger.

"Yes, of course." He quickly counted out the money for the fare, added a tip, and climbed from the vehicle. As the taxi drove off, he sneaked another look into his wallet. For the first time, he realised how much money he was carrying. Christ, there were hundred pound notes packed in there. He couldn't remember the last time he had held a crisp new hundred.

Dazed, he walked up the path to the apartment block. It was a lovely area, landscaped trees, small lawns, and flower beds dividing Manorfield Place from similar high-rise blocks. Gulls flapped and whirled over the Thames, ducking and rising among the sleek modern buildings littering the Isle of Dogs. He felt humbled as he approached the glass doors. A uniformed doorman looked up as he entered, and Greg felt radiant guilt flush across his face. After all, he was an intruder there. Before he could stammer out an apology, the doorman beamed at him.

"Mr Jameson! Haven't seen you for a good few days sir." It took a moment before Greg realised he was supposed to be Jameson. Then it took a moment more to suspend his disbelief that a stranger had recognised him as such.

"Yes, um, business I'm afraid." Sceptical, the doorman eyed his crumpled suit.

"So I see sir."

Greg smiled in a way he hoped would suggest that both he and the doorman were men of the world, then strolled towards the stairs. Praying that his flat was not on the ground floor, he started to climb.

"Feel like the exercise, is it sir? Floor six kills me every time."

Again Greg grinned a tight grin, then continued his climb. At the first floor he stopped to wait for the elevator.

A strong, ersatz Victorian feel predominated the interior of the building, comforting and rich. Even the elevator doors were wood clad. Greg shook his head. Surely he would remember living somewhere like this. It merely confirmed his theory that it was the rest of the world, as opposed to himself, which had gone mad.

With a polite little chime the elevator doors opened. Greg stepped inside, relieved to find himself alone. Easy enough to bluff a bored doorman, but what if he bumped into a neighbour whom he was supposed to be good friends with? Sighing his confusion, he pushed the button for floor six.

As the doors slid back he found himself stepping into a corridor with only two doors. Wandering along the plush red carpet, he had no difficulty ascertaining which flat was his. A brass plaque bore Jameson's name in large round letters.

A brief surge of fear zigzagged through him. In that moment of clarity he saw what he was doing, and it scared him. He was so close to accepting that he was Richard Jameson, not Greg Summers. Thinking of the flat as his own was tempting, and he was very nearly succumbing to the temptation of claiming a life, any life, as his own. Everyone else was so sure that he was this man Jameson, so why not he? It was as though he were being guided into a new identity, the lure being a considerable one. In the past few days he had been relieved of his home, his wife, his very self. In truth, having somewhere else to go was as comforting as it was confusing. Jameson certainly appeared a promising identity to slip into, for anyone who could live somewhere like Manorfield Place had made an ostentatious success of life. Perhaps far more so than Greg Summers.

All that prevented him from leaping body and soul into the illusion was his own bafflement. The incredulous scenario could not be so easily accepted, his practical nature assured that. Greg Summers was not a man to be fooled around with.

But still, that subversive part of his mind insisted that Richard Jameson might be.

Pushing the fear to one side, he promised himself that acceptance would not happen. In entering this flat he was doing nothing more than exposing a piece of the puzzle that was this whole deception. Until he knew who was playing this game he would be unable to confront them. To find out who this might be he must accede to the rules for a little longer. All the rules indicated that he temporarily assume the identity of Richard Jameson.

More secure with this interpretation of his actions, he fished his keys from his pocket. Nervous, for if the keys did not fit here he would have no other plan of action to follow, he placed them in the lock. They turned. *This is it*, he thought. *I am taking affirmative action*.

With the trepidation palpable, he pushed open the door. His step, affirmative or otherwise, took him into a world he could only have imagined a week before. In his most arrogant moments he had fantasised about living this lifestyle. He was not walking into an apartment; this was a damned penthouse.

Open plan in design, the main living space was huge. Stumbling vaguely through the door, he was astounded by the luxury that surrounded him. Sparsely decorated, the room still shone decadence.

Against one wall was an enormous bookshelf, packed full of hardback works. Running his eyes across the spines, he was impressed by how well read Jameson was. Fiction and non-fiction, esoteric tomes sitting next to commercially successful works. Plays, novels, poetry, biographies, philosophy, science. Greg was not an unlearned man, but his reading tastes had never developed further than what the critics labelled sensationalist trash. Ranged in front of him was the dream collection of the literati. Whether for show or pleasure, Jameson was a collector.

Turning away from the impressive ensemble of titles, Greg surveyed the rest of the room. A massive widescreen television and Blu-ray, both top of the range, remote control models wired into a high-end surround sound set-up. More shelves, this time stacked with DVDs and Blu-ray discs as culturally diverse as the books. Next to the windows, which stretched from ceiling to floor across the entire outside wall, sat a desk which was obviously a workspace. On it sat an Apple laptop, various pieces of hardware and a printer. He could only assume that these were as expensive as the rest of the flat indicated.

Furniture was sparse, consisting only of a deep green futon next to the bookcase, with matching beanbags opposite the television. So deep was the pile carpet that he felt a childish urge to take off his shoes and socks so that he could walk barefoot through it.

Collapsing on the futon, he shook his head in astonishment. Why would anybody set up so elaborate a deception as had occupied him over the last few days, only to expect him to accept this as his own? According to his opponent, and this was how he had begun to think of the manipulator he assumed to be behind these events, he was loaded. A millionaire, to be living this lifestyle. There had to be a catch, something to make him despair as previous events had. Where the hell was it?

At least Jennifer was not the opponent he sought. While in hospital he had toyed with the idea that this could be a cruel revenge on her part, perhaps sparked off by her stumbling across some careless indication that he was having an affair. Though knowing this to be elaborate and unlikely, it still sounded better than the other fantastical ideas his head created in the search for illumination. In his heart though, he had known that Jennifer could never be so creative and vindictive. Now he had the additional satisfaction of knowing that her budget could not have stretched so far as to hire this place for even a day. Besides, what sense was there in punishing him by immersing him in luxury? Her involvement in all this must surely be that of a dupe, convinced to go along with whatever insane scheme had twisted his life apart.

CUCKOO

Convinced by who? He had sufficient self-awareness to know that he was unlikely to have the proverbial 'powerful enemies'. He and his life were too mundane to have attracted attention from any hostile quarter. Even in his humble insurance job he was well liked and respected.

Still wondering, he resolved to explore the rest of the apartment. Four doors led off from the room he was sitting in. The first he tried, set into the bookcase wall, was nothing more than an extended closet. Dozens of coats and suits, all of the finest quality, hung above rows of shoes. As large as his hallway back home, the space was carpeted with the same pile as the main room and was easily walked into. A large mirror was set into the far wall. Greg was relieved to find his own image staring back at him, for at least he still looked the same man he remembered from last week. Shaking his head again, he closed the door. Investigating a closet for clues seemed a little too ludicrous, even given his current circumstances.

The second door in what he thought of as the reading wall led into a kitchen. Fully fitted with what looked like a rich oak finish, the space was a model of culinary efficiency. Everything had a place, and was arranged with a utilitarian economy that Greg simply did not possess. Every modern appliance was available, and the corner of the room was fitted with a pull out table and stool. Jameson was obviously a solitary eater, although the nature of the room indicated that cookery was an act he enjoyed. Nothing appealed to Greg less, but he could appreciate the elegance of the idea.

This room was also quickly abandoned. He would have a closer look later, but was fairly certain that the answer to his problems did not lurk amongst knife racks and espresso machines.

Also impressive, and just as unforthcoming, was the bathroom. Set into the floor was a tub almost large enough to qualify as a pool, with a toilet and bidet in the far corner of the room, and a walk in shower standing separate beside them. Shaving equipment and expensive toiletries were neatly arranged next to another huge mirror. Jameson was something of a narcissist.

Again this was given but a glance before his investigation moved on, leaving him just one door to open. It led into the bedroom. Here, at last, were the shocks Greg had been waiting for. Before he even noticed the four poster double bed, or the antique mirror, or the mahogany cupboards and drawers, his attention was drawn to the framed photographs which adorned the walls

Greg was depicted in each one, alongside an assortment of people he had never met. One showed him with his arm around the shoulder of an unfamiliar man, another was a school photograph full of faces he didn't know. Scrutinising this closely, he tried to find himself in the crowd. Sure enough, his boyhood self stared back at him from the second row of the formal, uniformed line up. Yet another photograph, this one as old as the school picture, showed him aged about ten, with a younger boy and a woman. Jameson's supposed mother and who?

After recent events Greg was becoming used to these little surprises, and the shock he felt vanished almost as swiftly as it arrived. Fakes of course, just as the wedding photograph had been faked, probably a simple Photoshop job. But still, they were extremely convincing, and he found it unnerving to see his image transposed onto these strange scenes. He assumed that was the point, and he congratulated his opponent on the intricacy with which the fraud had been arranged.

Just as he was ready to praise himself for dealing so smoothly with this new turn of events, a telephone rang.

After a moment of confusion, during which he had to remind himself that he was the one who was supposed to live here, the darted back to the living space. Several moments of frantic searching went by, and he eventually found the cordless phone on the second shelf of the bookcase, neatly propped next to *The God Delusion*.

Picking it up felt strange, as though he were some sort of intruder to this flat, but it was important to answer. Whoever was on the other end might hold a key Greg needed to open the mystery a little further.

"Hello. Gre...Richard here."

"Rich? Where the fuck have you been? I've been phoning for four days now. Decide to take a holiday and not tell anyone? You missed our Friday lunch for Christ's sake!" The venom of the verbal barrage shocked Greg from his complacency. Remembering the diary entry for Friday, he hazarded a guess at the identity of the caller.

"Stewart?"

"Who the hell else would it be? Jesus Rich, I've been worried sick. Where have you been?"

"It's...hard to explain. The last few days have been a bit of a blur."

Anger turned to concern. Stewart sounded genuinely worried. "Shit, sorry, I never thought. Are you okay? You haven't been hurt or anything? It's just..."

"I know, you were worried." Part of Greg wanted to lace his voice with sarcasm, but common sense told him to play along a little longer. "Look Stewart, I really am sorry, and I really can explain. What are you doing tomorrow?"

"Uh, there's a press conference in the morning to cover the launch of the DP5, but I'm free all afternoon."

"Perfect. Where shall we meet?"

"Usual?"

Quick thinking saved Greg, and he parried the question with pleasing ease. "No, I feel like a change."

"Fair enough. How about De Marco's then? It's the new Italian place off Oxford Street. Do you know it?" Indeed he did, he and Georgina had eaten there just a few nights ago.

"Sounds great. Around three then?"

"Sure. Just make sure you show up."

Greg forced what he hoped was a good-humoured chuckle. "I'll do my best. See you then." He hung up.

Breathing a deep, trembling sigh of relief, Greg gave himself the credit he thought he deserved. That had been handled well, and the meeting might finally provide some answers. Tomorrow morning could also be put to good use. For the evening before him though, he would make use of the facilities around him. After all, it would be a pity to waste the efforts that must have gone into the façade of 'his' penthouse, and after several days in the same set of clothes, he was in dire need of a bath.

9 SWEET, SAD WISHES

It knows itself to be nothing more than a tool, a device to further the activities of the mistress, but it is content with this fate. Minor damage has been repaired now, and it is better able to perform whatever tasks lie ahead. This pleases it, for existence is a tool to be made use of.

In her own way, the mistress loves it. In this too there is satisfaction. Only one regret gnaws at it. It cannot give the mistress what she truly needs, and she must go beyond it for that vital service. That is a compunction easily dealt with, for the function is far beyond the perimeters of even its greatest abilities.

It is curious, watching the mistress and the burning man, and wonders if it will ever be able to experience the unique relationship in which they are engaged. It supposes not, a knowledge that saddens it in small but tender ways. Lying dormant, knowing it is not needed at this present moment, it watches, waits, and wishes sweet sad wishes.

10 ERUPTION

Waking early, after sleeping better than he could have imagined, Greg discovered that the well-stocked kitchen provided ingredients for an indulgent fried breakfast. It was with some surprise that he realised how little he had eaten over the past few days.

Feeling healthier and happier for a decent meal, he left his temporary place of residence later that morning, managing a cheerful greeting to the doorman on the way out. Under his arm he carried a package containing two of the photographs from the bedroom wall. In his back pocket he carried his wallet, with which he planned to test an important theory. What he needed now was transport. A vague memory from the taxi drive of the previous day called out to him, and he turned left at the end of the path outside the building.

He was right. Not fifteen minutes walk from the apartment was a reassuringly expensive looking car hire store. Time to test his hypothesis. Walking in, he joined the short queue and waited for service.

"Yes sir, can I help you?" An attractive girl in her early twenties swung her attention his way.

"Probably. I need a car for a few days."

"Certainly sir. Have you seen our list of available vehicles?" She gestured at a poster on the wall, but Greg already knew what he wanted.

"Ford Focus. Blue, if you have it."

"Of course. If you'd like to fill in these forms I'll have your car brought around the front." Making short and discrete work of filling in Jameson's details from the documents in his wallet, he signed the car out for one week.

Then came the test. Having found a four digit number tucked into the back of his wallet, he could only pray it was what he thought. "I'll pay now, if I may? I'll cover any extras when I hand it in." Handing over Jameson's platinum American Express card, he tapped the number into the keypad, and held his breath.

The funds went through. While he had hoped they would, it still left him reeling. Jameson's wealth, at least some of it, was his to use. What kind of opponent would give him those kinds of resources?

Exasperated by the mixed signals he was receiving, he drove his new car into the city. He knew where he was going by heart, having memorised the route before he left. Parking proved problematic though, and he was forced to abandon his vehicle in a multi-storey car park some distance from his destination.

Forced to walk the rest of the way, he found himself less claustrophobic than he usually was in crowds. Normally he would have felt frustrated and uptight after only a few minutes of immersion in the throng, but new purpose had brought with it new tolerance. Taking positive steps to solve the mystery of his life had rejuvenated him. In his own eyes he was no longer the helpless victim.

Though claustrophobia left him mercifully untouched, he still felt strange and abstracted as he passed through the crowds. Knowing paranoia for what it was, he found it easy to dismiss his suspicions of the people around him. Where his gut wanted to cast each new face as a player in the conspiracy against him, his head was firm in discarding such notions. Still, he could not help wondering if he were the only one. Crazy as it was, he could not dismiss the idea that maybe, just maybe, he was experiencing an ordinary part of life, which everybody went through at some stage, but nobody ever spoke about. Twice he found himself wanting to grab somebody and demand of them, then and there, why they had never told him about this.

He restrained himself. He would have little chance of discovering the truth if he were to spend the rest of his days eating mush in a padded white cell.

Central London always had the disorientating effect of turning him about several times, but eventually he found his destination. Messop & Son Photographic Studios. The small shop front was discreet, and Greg felt reassured as he pushed open the door. It swung inwards, a small bell announcing his presence. A comfortable, if clinical, waiting area waited for him.

An old man, eccentric in a pair NHS prescription glasses, glanced up at him from behind the counter. Placing a wrinkled brown hand in one of the voluminous pockets of his white coat, he gave Greg a critical once over.

"Hm. How can I be of service sir? Let me guess. A wedding? No, no ring." Greg looked down in surprise, wondering when he had removed his wedding band. "Christening? Public function?" Stroking his thinning grey hair with the back of one hand, he waited for Greg to fill in the details.

"No, er, sorry." The old man, who he presumed was Mr Messop, raised a critical eyebrow.

"Not for you to apologise, hm? As long as I can be of assistance."

Taking the photographs from the envelope, Greg arranged them on the counter. "It's these I'm interested in."

"Are you indeed?" Messop bent attentively over them. "Fine work, very fine work. But, forgive me, these have already been developed. What do you wish me to do with them, hm? Reproductions perhaps?"

Greg smiled. "I need them examined. I think they're forgeries, but I'd like an expert confirmation to back me up." Messop's eyebrow, already raised, twitched a notch higher. Again, he bent low over the pictures.

"Forgeries, you say?"

"I believe so, yes."

"Well, who would have thought?" The man's eyes gleamed with pleasure. "Quite the challenge, hm? I'll look at them tonight. If you could come back tomorrow I'll give you an answer."

"So soon? Wonderful!" Greg was relieved. Part of him had thought the old man would dismiss him as a crank. "How much will that cost?"

"I think we'll settle that tomorrow, don't you think? We don't have a set price for this sort of service. It's a request we are rarely asked to fulfil."

"Rarely?"

"Never."

Greg grinned again. "Tomorrow then."

"Any time will do. Have a pleasant day."

Nodding his thanks, Greg left the shop. Wanting to laugh, he instead breathed great lungfuls of the city air. That had been easier than he thought. Once he had professional evidence verifying the nature of the conspiracy against him he would be able to consider the authorities as a means of settling the matter. It was a relief to think that somebody else might do the hard work for him.

He glanced at his watch. It was just past two, more than enough time to take a casual stroll to De Marco's and arrive early. It would not do for him to be late. If Stewart were there first then Greg would be forced to join him. Difficult, especially as Greg had no idea what the man looked like. If Greg was the one already seated then Stewart should have no difficulty in recognising him. Why should he? Nobody else seemed to. Pleased with his own cleverness, he set a brisk stride through the hordes of November shoppers.

Forty-five minutes later he was seated inside De Marco's, mineral water in hand, at a table facing the door. From where he sat he had a good view of the half-full restaurant, and was easily seen from the outside. It was better not to secrete himself in one of the more private alcoves, despite having several intense questions for this Stewart. Instead he wished to be in view of as many witnesses as possible in case of trouble.

Not knowing quite what to expect of this meeting was frustrating. Unable to make any firm plans, he would have to take a flexible approach. For all he knew, Stewart would buckle at the first challenge. Greg wasn't counting on it. He would have to fight for the answers he sought. Bracing himself, he waited.

It would have been easier if his imagination had not been trying to convince him that every man who came through the door recognised him. Twice now he had grinned at a complete stranger with an air of what he hoped was easy familiarity, only to be rewarded by blank stares and nervous nods. At least he could reassure himself that he was getting plenty of practise at this kind of deception. Sipping at his water, he decided that the best way forward was to ignore everybody who did not actually sit opposite him, and he turned his attention to the restaurant.

Traditionally decorated in an Italian style, the room was both comfortable and rustic. Greg felt fortunate that Stewart had chosen to meet there. It felt like he was on home territory.

Then Stewart did arrive, appearing so abruptly in the chair across the table that Greg jumped. Perhaps five years younger than he, this man had a lean muscularity about him that was both powerful and controlled. His neat, grey business suit hugged his figure as he sat. The easy smile he gave bespoke confidence.

Covering up his surprise at the sudden appearance, Greg tried to think of something to say. For some reason the man was familiar, though he could not say why. Perhaps it was something about the eyes. Reflecting on this, he made an opening gambit.

"Stewart." A nod accompanied the simple greeting.

For his part Stewart looked tense, his shoulders taut, his hands shaping words even before he spoke. "Oh, come on. Stewart? Have I pissed you off? Look, about last night, I'm sorry. I was angry, but only because I was concerned. It's not like you to just up and vanish like that." When Greg remained silent, Stewart became more anxious. "Cut me a break here Richie! I'm not going to chuck out three months of trying to get you to talk to me again, because you get your back up over a heated phone call!"

Greg made his decision. For now he would play along. "Look, calm down..." He made a guess, and stopped himself from holding his breath while he awaited the result. "...Stu." There was no reaction to that, so Greg went on. "I was a little annoyed, I admit. But everything's fine now. To be honest I was afraid you'd come in with a raging temper, furious that I left you in the lurch on Friday."

Stewart chuckled. "And I felt like I was standing outside the headmaster's office, waiting to be told off for swearing in class." Despite himself, Greg smiled. If he could only work out why this man was so damned familiar. He needed more information.

"Well, we're both forgiven then. Tell me about the launch." *Tell me about yourself. Tell me anything.*

"A success, I think. The media love it, and the bloggers are all over the thing, so word of mouth's off to a good start. With luck it'll be commercially available by the end of the month."

Greg didn't have the first idea what the man was talking about, so he took the safe approach. "Well done. You must be pleased."

"Hell yes, I could retire on this one. Not that I would, don't worry. You know I love coding this stuff."

"Good to hear."

"If I get my way, the next project will enhance the UI further. It's not as user friendly as it should be, given the extra year I asked for."

"Sounds exciting." Software. Computers. Not much to go on, but more than he had started with. "Did you come straight from the press conference?"

"Had to, it overran. Like I said, they couldn't get enough of the thing."

"Ha." Even to his own ears, his side of the conversation was becoming less and less convincing. There was nothing to be done about it. Until he got something he could use, he would have to keep nodding and smiling in the right places. Sooner or later though, Stewart was going to become suspicious. From the doubt already creeping into his eyes, it looked as though it would be sooner.

"Well don't look too ecstatic Rich, I'm only handing you the biggest market coup your company's ever had."

Greg couldn't help it. Before he had a chance to catch himself, his eyebrows shot up. He was supposed to own a computer company? "My..."

"Richard, this is bullshit. Why am I sitting here having both sides of this conversation? If something's wrong then have the good grace to bloody well tell me what it is. What's going on?"

Greg stared. Stewart wanted to know what was going on? The man was sitting opposite him, employed by some unknown authority to convince him that he was a software tycoon, and he had the temerity to ask the very question that had brought Greg there in the first place? It was sublime. Drawing a variety of responses from the diners around them, Greg began to laugh at the sheer idiocy of the situation. With tears sluicing down his cheeks, he barely noticed Stewart shaking his head.

"Oh. I get it. This is some kind of joke, right?" Again, the choice of words shook Greg's funny bone hard, and he had to grip the table to prevent himself from toppling off his chair. "Right. Laugh it up big brother. And when you finish you might want to tell me why I've become an object of such hilarity."

Greg started to bring himself back under control. Jesus, the guy was good. The look of stoic upset on his face was frighteningly authentic. Putting up a placatory hand, he prepared to try and salvage his own pretence. "Look Stewart..." It was at this point that his mind replayed the last snatch of conversation. He could feel his jaw slacken, causing his words to stammer over each other in sudden confusion. "My...brother?"

"Come on, what are you pulling here? Brother. You do remember what that is, don't you? Sibling. Fraternal relative. Kinsman. *Brother*. As in grew up together." Sarcasm laced his voice, but Greg ignored it. An uncontrollable heat welled within him, and it was no longer amused. Who were these people? It was as if they had been inside his head, removed his greatest fantasies, and laid them neatly on a platter before him. The apartment had been one thing. Who didn't sometimes dream of living a life where such luxury was available. The credit account and the new revelation of his owning a top software company had both followed that pattern, reinforcing the offer of his new life. But this was a final affront to his dignity. Growing up motherless from the age of thirteen had been a lonely nightmare. Through the years of solitary torture, one fantasy had given him succour. A family which loved him. Only when Jennifer entered his life did the loneliness recede. Now, having taken her away from him, they offered the only thing that might replace the security she provided. Violation slashed about his insides. How could they know?

Stewart began to speak again, but Greg lashed out, grabbing his wrist and silencing him.

"I do not yet know who you are or what you're doing, but it ends. Here. Tell me." Incomprehension flickered across Stewart's face, a concerned frown dominating his lips. Greg was having none of it. "Yes, yes. Very good. But mull this over, you bastard. I am not going to allow it."

"Richard, you're hurting my arm."

"And you've cut up my fucking *heart*. You aren't leaving here until I know how and why you're doing this, and if I have to pull your arm off at the elbow and beat the answers out of you with it, I will." Reinforcing the point, he tightened his grip further, noting with pleasure the pain it caused.

"This isn't funny anymore."

"You're right."

"Let go of my arm!"

Giving in to the rage, Greg yanked Stewart across the table and screamed into his face. "WHO ARE YOU!"

Which when his mind tried to jump. Now familiar pressures built inside his chest and head, swirling and pushing. Greg squeezed his eyes closed against the pain. *Not now*, he begged himself. *Please not now*. Aware of voices around him, hands on his arm, he fought against the jump with everything he could muster. To no avail. He could feel his mind begin to detach from the here and now. Struggling harder only sped the process.

Then he knew. He knew how to avoid it. Opening his eyes, not really seeing the cluster of onlookers or the waiter who was trying to pry his fingers from Stewart's wrist, he relaxed.

All the pressure, those terrible, pulsing forces which wanted to rip him apart, went away. Sighing relief, he released Stewart, a smile on his lips.

With no warning at all, he erupted. Blood surged from his nose and ears, pulsing out of him in a desperate bid for freedom. Acidic, scarlet tears poured from his eyes, while strange new pains bursting from his fingers made him look down. Blood trickled from beneath his fingernails too.

"Richard! RICHARD! Shit, will somebody call an ambulance!" The waiter vanished, presumably to make that call. Everybody else stood well back from the sprays of blood gouting from him. Even his newly found 'brother' moved a respectful distance away. A churning deep in his stomach told him that a new orifice was about to run red, but this didn't worry him. For the first time, he realised that he was in no serious pain. Granted, the bleeding parts felt like they had tiny needles jammed into them, but it was far from debilitating.

Again his stomach heaved. Rising shakily to his feet, he turned to Stewart. With one hand held before him he opened his mouth as though to say that everything was fine now, that the worst was over. Stewart stepped forward, and with a final convulsion, Greg sprayed crimson vomit over him.

Using the shock of the moment, relishing the obvious disgust with which Stewart leapt backwards, Greg turned and ran. As with his fingernails, his stomach felt as though a slender metal rod had pierced him through, but he ignored the pain and belted out of the restaurant.

Horrified faces turned to him on the street, but he avoided their gazes. Trying to remember his route from earlier, fighting all the time against waves of dizziness and nausea from the blood loss, he stumbled like a madman in what he hoped was the direction of the car park.

He was forced to stop once during his flight, to catch his breath and duck into a public toilet to wash up. Contradicting the theory that modern city dwellers have a reduced sense of public duty, several people had already tried to stop him and see if he was badly hurt. *Typical*, he had thought, *never a Good Samaritan around when you want one, then six come along at once*. A little firm persuasion sent them about their business.

As soon as he washed the drying blood from his hands and face he walked the rest of the journey at a brisk pace. Of course, the suit was ruined, but he had been provided with plenty of spares at the apartment.

Despite being only a little more informed from his meeting with Stewart, it felt good to be fighting back. For too long he had been passive in this affair. Now he was finally taking chances to solve it. It was the most thrilling thing he had ever done.

Running from the restaurant had been necessary. Once he lost his temper and grabbed Stewart the game was blown. There could have been any number of associates watching, but Greg had escaped nonetheless. A successful afternoon, for now they might be getting an idea that they had picked the wrong man to mess with.

As he entered the multi-storey car park, he was aware of several odd glances being thrown his way, but was confident that they were due to the state of his suit. He did not seem to have been followed to the car. Paying equal attention to the rest of his trip, he felt sure he was not being watched. *Why would they need to do that*, he realised, pulling his car into one of the residential parking spaces outside his block. *They know where I'm was going.*

Hurrying into the building, he was caught off-guard by the doorman, who rushed to block his way.

"Mr Jameson! Are you all right sir? Your suit…"

"Is covered with blood, I know." The man appeared to be concerned, and as Greg had yet to decide if he was involved in the conspiracy he chose to give him the benefit of the doubt. "The man sitting next to me at the restaurant had some sort of fit. Actually threw up blood. Stewart and I are wearing most of it."

"Is the gentleman all right?"

"Better all the time."

Looking relieved, the doorman stepped aside. Greg was about to walk by when a thought struck him. "Look, I'm a bit shaken up by the whole thing, so I'd like to get an early night. If I have visitors, anyone at all, you're not to send them up. Understand?"

"I'll send them on their way. It must have been very traumatic."

Greg stifled a laugh, thinking of Stewart's face. "It was. And thanks." That said, he headed for the lift.

Once back in the comfort of the apartment his energy fled him. Slumped in one of the voluminous beanbags, he lay perfectly still for nearly an hour. Only when the telephone rang did he start back to life.

Shooting across the room, his hand was on the receiver before he had time to think. Then he stopped. It would almost certainly be Stewart. What was left to say to the man? Did he really want to answer the call? Lifting the receiver, he spoke before the person on the opposite end had a chance to get a word in.

"Fuck you," he said, then switched off the phone.

Standing still, he felt exhaustion sweep over him. Thinking time, that was what he needed, preferably lying down somewhere warm. Feeling blank and lifeless, he stripped off his ruined clothes and ran himself a bath.

11 FRATERNITY

School was too terrifying a concept for Richard to contemplate that day. Thirteen years old and a regular truant, his problem was easily solved. He did not attend. Mr Rhodes, the tyrannical head of the English Department, had arranged to have one of his 'little chats' just before the lunch break. His hands still aching from the last time Rhodes had taken the cardboard cane to them, Richard was in no hurry to keep the appointment.

But what fun was skiving without company? Most days, Richie would have a host of friends to choose from in organising his adventures in absenteeism. That day, however, there had been no time. At first he had decided to be resolute, to face his fate with dignity. This state of mind lasted until he reached the end of the garden path. Resolve himself to being unable to clench his hands for a week? Was he out of his mind?

By then it was too late to organise anything with his friends. There was no chance to call anyone at home. Everyone would already be on their way to school. The opportunity to feign illness was already wasted, for his parents would never accept that the burgeoning teenager who strolled out of the door just moments ago had been struck down by a malignant virus before even reaching the street. He was left with just one choice. Stewart.

He didn't mind dropping his little brother off each day. The primary school was on the way to his high school, and it was a proud measure of responsibility that his mother would allow him custody of Stewart for the journey. Today though, he desired company far more than parental respect. Devious thoughts sprang to his mind as he turned to his brother.

"Stewart, I think today should be an adventure." Stewart looked at him as they crossed the road, face blank. "Today we are going to the park."

His brother's face lit up like a Christmas tree. "The adventure park, Richie? Please can we make it the adventure park?" The kid was at the wonderful age of seven; bright enough to take the bait, but not yet intuitive enough to question it.

"Aw, heck Stu. That would be a wonderful idea, but we don't have time. I just meant that, if we were quick, we might be able to stop at the kiddies park for five minutes. It's on the way." Stewart was crushed. For a moment Richard thought he might have pushed too hard, but his brother bounced back.

"We could be really quick?"

"Sorry Stu. But hang on..." Richard exaggerated the look of dawning realisation on his face to a ridiculous extreme. All that was missing was a disembodied light bulb flashing above his head. Stewart took the hint.

"What Richie? What is it?"

"Well, if you reeaaally want to go to the adventure park I don't see why we shouldn't. It would mean being naughty though. We'd have to take a day off school. Couldn't tell Mum or Dad. Might not be such a good idea."

"I promise I won't tell!"

Hook, line, sinker.

"You better not. Just remember that I'm only coming along to make sure you're all right. It's your idea."

"I won't get you into trouble. I'll tell them it's my fault if we're caught." Seeing the assenting look on Richard's face, he laughed and began to run in the direction of the adventure park. Richard jogged to keep up, grinning all the while. Kids were so easy.

By one o' clock Richard was bored. Lying next to the rope swing, he forced yet another smile of approval at the Tarzan-like antics of his brother.

"Did you see, Richie? Did you?" Nodding that he had indeed seen, he tried to will the next two hours to pass. Stewart had a boundless energy for the various rides scattered through the park, but Richard had managed only two hours of such enthusiasm before the novelty wore thin. Still, it had been his idea, so he had little right to complain. If only his brother would let him be for five minutes instead of seeking his constant approval for each new stunt he concocted.

An idea occurred to him, one which might buy him those precious moments of peace he desired. Rolling onto his stomach, he reached out for his schoolbag. It took a few moments of rummaging, but eventually he found it. Pulling the cricket ball free of the odds and ends that seemed to infest his bag, he shouted over to Stewart.

"Hey, do you fancy tossing a ball around for a while?" Stewart came haring over. Richard knew how this worked. Older brother worship meant that anything he suggested must be a good idea. Often irritating, for it sometimes seemed that Stewart had no original thoughts in his head, it occasionally proved useful. It was time to make the most of it.

"Okay, you go and stand over there, by those trees. When you're ready give me a shout." With a laugh, Stewart ran in the direction Richard had pointed. Stopping just short of a thick line of trees, he turned and waved.

"Right, here it comes." The first throw was an easy one, landing practically in his waiting brother's lap. Stewart managed to get his hands round it, though he winced a little at the force with which the solid ball smacked his skin.

"I got it Richie! Good catch, huh?"

"Not bad, shrimp. England squad next." Stewart giggled. "Chuck it back." The throw went wild, but it took him only a few steps to line himself up for it properly. A small hop secured it safely in his outstretched hand. Now for plan A.

"Good throw. You ready? It's coming back at you." He hurled it. With some pride he watched it sail over his brother's head, clear of even the luckiest catch, into the trees beyond. Stewart watched it go, then turned back.

"It's all right Richie, I'll get it." Turning, he launched himself into the undergrowth, which swallowed him in an instant.

Plan A was a success. Richard had watched the cricket ball, and was sure he could find it if he had to. Stewart, on the other hand, should end up blundering around in there for at least ten minutes. He threw himself to the ground.

Sprawling there, the afternoon sun heating his face, he congratulated himself on a successful skive. Before they went home he would brief Stewart on what he should say had happened at school that day. That should go pretty well; for all that he could be irritating at times, his little brother was smart for his age. Later he would use Dad's typewriter to forge the sick notes they would take to class tomorrow. He would even go into the primary school himself, most of the staff knew him pretty well by now, and explain in person why Stewart had been missing.

Engrossed as he was in this planning, the next events were surreal and out of context. At the very edge of his thinking he registered Stewart shouting.

"Watch this one Richie!" It seemed a long way away, probably because his brother was not expected to return for at least another five minutes. Slowly, he turned to face the direction of the trees. A red blur sailed towards him. With no time to move or respond, all he could do was watch the cricket ball smash into the side of his own face.

With a splash, Richard woke up. The water was still warm, which meant he had only been dozing for a few minutes. Good, with all his other problems the last thing he needed was to be found drowned in his own bathtub.

As always, the ball hitting his face was the last thing he remembered from the dream. In real life he had been knocked unconscious by the ball. It had been just his luck that the best throw Stewart ever tossed was the one he had been least likely to praise. His little brother had enough good sense to run and fetch help, finding a park attendant just along the path. Richard had been rushed to hospital, where it was determined that he was suffering nothing worse than a mild concussion.

When his mother and father had been called in they had been too relieved at finding their children in good health to make a fuss about them skipping school. What with Richard having concussion and Stewart getting the fright of his life, their father decided that more than enough punishment had been meted out already. It was still a story which amused them during the annual Christmas gathering, one his father took particular pains to relate to any and all guests who visited them.

Shaking his head, Richard got out of the bath, wrapped a towel around himself, and wandered to the mirror. Plugging in the hairdryer, he directed a blast of heat across his scalp.

His gaze met his reflection.

Dropping from his lifeless hand, the hairdryer caught briefly on its cord before the weight pulled the plug from the socket. It clattered to the floor.

Greg began to shiver violently. Sinking to his knees, he put his hands over his eyes and cried. How? How was it done? Another person had looked at him from that mirror.

For a few moments, before he had fully woken up, he had been Richard Jameson.

An hour later he felt better. Not much better, for he still couldn't stop himself from trembling, but better than in the bathroom. When it had happened. Knowing that he had to face up to the incident, he finished adding sugar to the cup of tea he had made. Someone had once told him that sweet tea was good for shock. He didn't want to think too carefully about who might have said that, for he didn't want to know whether they had been talking to Greg Summers or Richard Jameson at the time.

Brainwashing. It sounded like something from a science fiction movie, but nothing else fitted except for schizophrenia, multiple personality orders, and other dysfunctions. Even without the necessary psychiatric knowledge though, he was fairly certain that schizophrenia didn't come replete with luxury apartments, credit accounts, or families. No, this was all too material to be a delusion.

Which took him back to brainwashing. Somebody had planted a false memory in him. Just the one as far as he could tell, for he had spent the last hour scouring his mind for further reference to Jameson. All he found was the incident of the cricket ball. The most distressing thing, the reason he was still trembling, was that the memory now persisted. At the same time as he remembered burying his mother at the age of thirteen, he also remembered playing with his brother Stewart. On the very edge of that latter memory was the mother who had taken Jameson home from hospital. He could not recall her in the same way as he could the adventure park, but he had a vague knowledge of what had happened next, as though he had been told one. It gave him a headache. A heartache.

Attempting to take a swallow of the tea, his shaking hand spilled hot liquid on his arm. Wincing, he recalled the coffee scald when he was six, a precious, crystal memory that was his. Welcoming the pain on his skin, for it affirmed the past for him, he moved to the sink and let cool water soothe the burn.

Somehow, over the last few weeks, the false memory had been placed in him. He had no recollection of this happening, but he supposed that anybody capable of planting a memory would have no trouble in erasing another one. Christ, how long had these people been preparing him for this? In many ways though, he was now closer to the answer than ever. At least he now had a grasp of the mechanics that had lent such credence to their ploy. If they could brainwash him, they could also brainwash Jennifer. No wonder she had been so hostile towards him. Her traitor memories had cast him as a delusional maniac.

Perhaps he had also stumbled on a reason for the violent flashbacks he had been having. This was trickier to put together, and he moved through to the living space. Sipping his tea, he noticed that the trembling had stopped. Panic over, Greg Summers was back in charge.

Sitting at the desk by the window, he gazed at the river crawling by, allowing his thoughts to brush randomly over the problem of the fits. He had almost dismissed them as secondary to the main torment. As his life had been taken from him a piece at a time, his health had become a small consideration. What if it was a physical symptom of the same problem though, like the weeping nose which accompanied a cold? Better, what if it was actually some sort of immune response? Yes, that could be it. What if he was reacting against the false memory in some way? Perhaps the flashbacks were an attempt by his subconscious to reject the implant, a way for his mind to grasp at the real past and violently reassert it? After all, the very nature of the fits forced him to remember parts of his life with unusual clarity.

His subconscious was fighting fire with fire. They had placed lies in his head, and he had responded by vividly experiencing the truth.

Now if only he could find a way to switch them off. With luck the simple acceptance of what was happening might mean that his mind no longer needed to spring these reminders on him. It was unlikely though. They were more like an automatic response. He would have to be prepared for it happening again. At least he had found a way to stop himself from passing out, but the physical symptoms were still uncomfortable and messy. Perhaps, when he had time, he might pay for a hypnotist to try and undo some of the damage his enemies had wreaked.

Time was not a luxury he could enjoy yet. His clumsy attempts to threaten Stewart must have alerted his enemy to the fact that he was a potential troublemaker. If he had ascertained one thing for certain, it was that they were powerful. No casual hoodlum could be behind a scheme as elaborate as this. One look at the apartment he was sitting in was enough to confirm the expense of whatever operation he was victim of.

Could it even be the case that he was a specimen in some government experiment? The idea seemed preposterous at first, but on closer examination it became more plausible. In fact, it seemed the most likely explanation for an unlikely scenario. Who else would have such access to every aspect of his life? Who else could arrange a deception of this scale?

On the other hand, this was the age of post-millennial paranoia. All you had to do was switch on the television to see yet another show or movie wrapped around a conspiracy theory. People had an unnerving desire and ability to believe such things, but it was harder to dismiss them when he was living through one.

Raising his mug to his lips, he realised he had finished his tea. Time for action then. What Greg needed was hard evidence, or at least something to demonstrate reasonable suspicion. Tomorrow he would have confirmation that the photographs he had dropped off were false, but would that be enough to evidence anything? Probably not. He had to have more facts.

So, taking the brainwashing into consideration, who did he think was knowingly involved in the plot against him? Jennifer was ruled out, and Alex Carlisle was an innocent bystander who would never have been involved if Greg had not been so stubborn about having that refund. Stewart was less certain, but Greg could not dismiss the possibility that he too could be an unknowing dupe. No, of all the people who had been involved in his recent life there was only one who he could be certain was working against him.

The man his wife was sleeping with, who had stolen the life and name of Gregory Summers. That was where he would find his facts.

As a plan formed in his mind he chuckled at how preposterous a situation he was in. To acquire the information he needed, Greg was going to have to burgle his own home.

12 VISION

It is foolish of him to feel fear now, he accepts this as truth. After everything already done to his body any concern is misplaced, for concern implies action and resolution, and there is none available to him. Knowing it is irrational does not quell the terror, and he squeezes his already closed eyes tighter shut.

Were he on the outside he knows he would see little skin about his body. What remained would look tattered and red, would perhaps remind him of the bandages from some rancid Egyptian corpse. Even from the inside he knows that he will be unable to avoid seeing for much longer.

Throughout the process he has been aware of his eyelids. As the skin has been eaten away his perception has turned from deep red, through scarlet, to the near white he sees now. Across his eyes the last layers of flesh are damp tissues, close to dissolving completely.

In some unconscious way he realises that this will be the true beginning of his torment. White-hot lances of agony will replace his abstract awareness of pain. As long as he can close his eyes he is able to hide from the world. It is a hiding place that will soon be exposed.

She will be there watching, with her demure smile. He will look into her eyes for those few moments that he is still capable of sight and know he is seeing reflections of where he will be when he dies.

As he opens his mouth to scream and hot fluids sear the tender flesh of his throat, he feels the scars they burn through his lungs.

It begins. Light stabs into his brain as the first minuscule hole appears. Others follow it. With frightening speed, he finds himself looking through fleshy gauze. For each tiny pinprick made, a splash of fluid seeps gently against the ball of his eye. He remembers an experiment at school, the eyeball of a bull being dissected in front of the biology class. It had been a strong rubbery material, difficult to cut, but the fluid working on him will not shirk at the task before it. It does not care how long it takes about its penetrating business. It has time.

As his eyeballs burn he watches the remains of the lids vanish. As the last loose strips are sucked away by the slight current beyond, the world presents itself to him. Glass on all sides, and the fluid. Beyond that, in the larger world, she is watching. His golf ball eyeballs implore her to end this, to find someone else. She smiles.

His vision blackens once more. At the same time as he feels the explosive bursting of his eyeballs, the gelatinous black fluid within them flowing to join the other liquids of the tank, he is glad of the blindness this heralds.

He will never have to look on her again.

13 KEYS

It was two o' clock in the morning, and Greg stood opposite his house in Fontside Avenue, wondering what the hell had possessed him. Just seeing his home, with everything the word implied, had almost turned him back. Now he was standing there trying to instil in himself the will to proceed. Excuses wheeled through his head, each supplying sufficient reason alone for him to abandon this course of action. His long, dark coat flapped about him as he tried to rationalise them away.

Firstly, he had not the faintest idea how to break into a house. A search of Jameson's apartment had revealed nothing in the way of burglary tools, which was not the biggest surprise. The place could well have been littered with housebreaking equipment that he wouldn't recognise if he fell over it.

On the other hand, this was his own home, and he knew precisely how to get inside. The key under the back step, which he had placed there himself, had allowed him access on previous occasions when he had found himself locked out. Tonight would be no different.

What if he woke Jennifer up? She would be terrified of him, the man who loved her most in the world. Could he bear that? His heart said no, his head said yes. Yes, he would have to. When he had sorted this business out, when everything was over, she could be treated. She would remember. She would be grateful.

Shivering, he tried to tell himself that it was the cold wind, rather than the fear, which caused his muscles to shudder so. A car drove past the entrance to the avenue, and he flinched. Cursing his nerves, he fought for the elusive calm that would make his task easy. Walk in, look around, and walk out. Simple. They would probably never know he had visited. Glancing at his watch, he realised that he had been waiting for almost half an hour. It was now or never.

Taking a deep breath, he crossed the black tarmac river of the road. In the light of the orange street lamps the house looked forbidding, cold. No warm meal awaited his homecoming; no fond embrace would greet him as he entered. Putting such self-pity to the back of his mind, hating himself for indulging in the first place, he made his way round to the back of the house. Remembering the garden as the warm vista of life he had nurtured was difficult in the shroud of night. Shapes he had birthed were unfamiliar, making the place which was once his home into a new environment. An alien landscape. He shut his mind against that image too, and what it stood for. Time enough to reclaim his home later.

As silently as he could manage, he crouched down to the step that lay before the back door, prising it gently towards him. It gave no resistance. Slipping his hand beneath it, he felt his heart pound the beat of strained anticipation. He had never noticed how loud it sounded before. Looking round, he saw that the lights in the windows of the neighbouring houses stayed off. How could they ignore such commotion? His hand continued the search.

His fingers touched metal.

Blood rushed to his head, and for a moment he thought he might faint. One tiny metallic talisman had now committed him to this act. No more excuses. If it had not been there he could have turned around, lived with the fact that he had tried. Now he had no choice, and was surprised that he felt a little stronger for it. Knowing that it might not be possible to force entry had led to indecision and doubt. Now that was over.

Closing his fingers around the precious key, he withdrew it from beneath the stone step. Standing slowly, he faced the door. Previously it had been an ordinary wooden door. In his mind's eye it was now a gateway. He did not yet know what lay beyond it, but the token in his hand would allow him access. He slotted the key into the lock. It had been recently oiled, which he knew because he had done it himself, and slid smoothly back.

Pushing open the door, he stepped into the kitchen and closed it behind him. He had made little noise up to that point, and allowed himself a sigh of relief when he heard no sound to indicate that another might be awake and roaming. The darkness around him was a reassuring blanket capable of masking his presence from others; it was with regret that he reached for the small torch hanging from a cord around his neck. Flicking it on, he was almost surprised to find that the kitchen was as he had left it. After the earlier shock of his altered hallway he had somehow expected the whole house to be a strange new world.

He was not there to visit the kitchen though, and he creeped through the folding door that marked the entrance to the living room. There was something he wanted to check, though it was also not his main goal. He suspected that if there were anything useful to be found, it would be in his study upstairs, next to the bedroom where Jennifer slept with his enemy. He rejected this notion too, suppressing the rage it caused. There was nothing he could do except gather the evidence he would need to reverse this state of affairs.

The study was where he had kept his important documents and papers. His replacement would almost certainly do the same. Things there were safe from Jennifer's eyes, for it was the one room in the house that had been his and his alone.

Before visiting the study he had brief business in the living room. Shining his torch across the marble mantelpiece, he confirmed what he had suspected. Jennifer was as much a victim as he. Photographs on the shelf were as he remembered. The holiday to Spain, Jennifer's parents, their university graduation shots; all were present and accounted for. This could not have been for his benefit, for he knew it was only luck which had brought him as far into the house as the hallway. That mean they were there to convince Jennifer.

He sent a prayer heavenwards. Although it hurt him to know that these people had tampered with her mind, it was blessed relief to prove to himself that she was not a willing party to his torture.

Strengthened by this revelation, he eased into the hallway. Having lived there for three years, every creak and squeak was well known to him. Even in the dark it was child's play to move silently. Stepping along the passage, still the only room he had discovered to be altered, he noted with a pained smile that the dent the golf club had made in the wall was still there. If that had connected he might have been dead at the hands of the woman he loved.

Moving on, he reached the bottom of the stairs, and stopped. For the first time since he had entered the building he heard something other than his clamouring heart. Something just at the edge of his hearing. A tide of adrenaline made him lightheaded again, and he fumbled with the button that would turn off the torch. It went out and the dark embraced him.

Dropping to a crouch, Greg listened to the sound for some moments. It was a low, continuous noise, coming from upstairs. Slightly grating, it rose and fell with a haunting, familiar rhythm. A tear traced the edge of his nose as he realised what he was listening to. Jennifer. Snoring.

At the same time as blossoms of nostalgia burst his gut, he was struck by a bout of helpless mirth. Sitting still, he tried to contain his laughter, clutching the bannister, terrified that he would give himself away. He knew it was stress which provoked this reaction from him, his body deciding that it was better to laugh than cry. After a few moments, when the silent giggles subsided, he climbed to his feet. Every nerve felt strained to capacity, and his stomach ached from holding back the laughter. But nothing amusing existed in the prospect of the stairs.

Standing at the bottom, he gazed up to the darkness. He had never feared the night, but now he understood where such terrors came from. On the ground floor the dark was the simple black of night. Moonlight still seeped through windows, enhanced in places by the harsher glow of street lamps. Upstairs was another world. The hallway of the first floor had no windows, no light. It was the dark of creeping things. The black of hiding.

Well, he thought as he gathered himself, *it can bloody well hide me then*. Choosing not to use his torch, though he very much wanted to, he put a hesitant foot on the first step. By the eighth he was immersed in gloom. The snoring grew louder, and Greg had reason to fear this. Where the blackness would conceal an opponent from his sight, the snoring made it difficult to hear the tiny sounds which might still give him warning of their approach.

Ninth step.

Tenth step. Still darker, still louder. Greg knew that the deep breathing of his wife was only loud in isolation, but it seemed as if she was screaming her sighs at the silent house.

Eleventh step.

Twelfth step.

Thirteenth and final step.

The snoring stopped. Already taut nerves screamed at Greg as a deafening silence swamped his senses. A trap. All his instincts tried to talk to him at once. It was a trap, he had been lured upstairs by the welcoming sounds of his wife at peace, and now he was caught. Frozen in place, his legs refusing to implement the desire to run, all he could do was stand and wait. Expecting someone to leap on him at any second, he closed his eyes and trembled.

Hours tried to pass in this state. He had no idea how many minutes dragged themselves past before a new sound pierced his ears. Opening his eyes wide, he swept them through the dark, trying to spot movement. Then he understood that the noise was nothing more than the resumption of the snoring, altered in pitch and rhythm. Greg slumped. Jennifer must have turned over in her sleep, or perhaps woken before drifting off again. Glad that his legs had mutinied against the desire to flee, he took the final step onto the landing, wondering how burglars coped with the stress of breaking into a home.

Still recovering from his shock, trying hard not to shake, he sneaked past the bedroom, listening hard for anything more threatening than the sounds of deep sleep, and was gratified to hear nothing but that. Opposite the bedroom door was the bathroom. An unwelcome observation, for his bladder felt ready to burst through anxiety. He shuffled on. Past the guest bedroom, past the airing cupboard, to the door at the end of the short passage. Small distances had become outrageously enlarged in the dark. Though he knew he had travelled no more than a few feet from the stairs to the door, he felt the journey had taken forever.

Relieved, he reached out for the handle that would allow him passage to his destination. Finding it, he twisted and pushed.

The door held firm.

Anxious, he pushed a second time. No movement at all. The door was locked. It was a possibility that he had not allowed himself to consider. The second reason why the study was the safest place for his enemy to store documents away from the curious eyes of his wife was that it was the only internal door with a lock.

Fighting back tears of frustration, Greg stood helpless. The darkness around him had now ceased to be a concealing cloak, subtly altering itself into an externalisation of the emptiness within him. Staring blankly into it, he sought to find just the faintest glimmer of hope there. Nothing presented itself. Desolation and despair turned to anger. He was so close. Deep inside enemy territory, he was inches away from what he sought. On the other side of the door the unattainable study mocked his efforts. One key. That was all he needed.

Clarity swept through him. One key, which he knew where to find. A key he had always kept close by him. A key which lay in the top drawer of his dresser. In his bedroom. Could he walk into the room, retrieve the key and get back to the study without waking the pair who slept there? Could he bear to?

Again the fear. Knowing that he had little choice was small consolation, for the enemy had grown large in his imagination. He tried to remember that the last time they clashed it had been Greg who was victor in battle. Then he had been enraged, furious at the strange invasion of his life. Now he was on edge, mentally and physically exhausted. No competition. Worse, if he woke them Jennifer would see him, terror shining in her eyes, and Greg would feel his heart powder to nothing. Would he be able to strike the man she thought she was in love with?

Despite these thoughts, he knew he would do it. He had gone too far to throw everything away through cowardice. He would retrieve the key.

Releasing the handle, he turned his back on the sanctuary that had denied him. Like a man in a dream he waded back through the dark of the passage.

Guest bedroom. Airing cupboard. His bedroom.

Though he knew there was no one to see him, he felt foolish standing outside the door to his own room. Despite himself, he remembered being six again. Waiting outside his parents' room, not daring to enter because he knew his father did not believe in the monster he had heard in the closet.

A grunt from within shocked him back to his senses, but he knew it had only been the sound of a sleeping man. Jennifer snored on.

Now or never. His life was rapidly becoming governed by that single phrase.

Before he could talk himself out of it, he grabbed the round handle of the door and opened it. Now the snoring was a terrible sound, the monstrous cacophony of some terrible beast he dare not wake. Standing still, he propped open the door with a shaking hand, allowing time for his eyes to adjust to the faint light which crept past the heavy curtains. It was strange to see again, for he felt he had spent a lifetime in the dark of the hallway.

Now he could make out vague shapes in the room. The double bed protruded from the wall on his left, neatly bisecting the space. Though his mind wanted to fill in the details his eye could not pick out, he concentrated on what was actually before him. A black shape, nothing more. Two mounds huddled in the centre.

His wife, sleeping in the embrace of another man.

Unexpected fury pushed him into action, and he took an involuntary stride towards them. Fate saved him from his own foolishness, his foot catching something on the floor. Tangling about his ankles, it felt like a living thing was trying to unbalance him. He started to topple. Lashing blindly in the direction of the door, he caught himself on the handle. For a horrifying moment it was not enough. His body was too far forward, the strain too great for his inadequate muscles.

The consequence of failure was discovery.

Desperation gave him strength and he heaved, feeling the screams from his protesting arm. Then he was up.

Bile rose in his throat as fresh weakness took him, but he swallowed it down. Relieved now of the strain, he felt he had pulled every muscle in his left side.

It was a sacred pain. He hurt because he had succeeded.

Stirring in sleep, the larger mound turned towards Greg, who held himself still. If he should wake now...

The shape settled back to sleep, a regular breathing indicating that the slumber was deep and peaceful. Greg allowed himself to breathe again. Reaching down to his ankle, he felt for what had entangled him. Recognising the feel of silk, he allowed himself a moment to caress the dressing gown that he found. The peg on the back of the door, where Jennifer hung the garment, was loosely fixed. Greg had been meaning to tighten it for weeks, for the robe fell often to the floor. It must have tumbled down when he entered.

His anger had dissolved. Grateful for the muffling effects of the thick carpet he had laid last winter, he glided to the dresser at the foot of the bed. Crouching, he eased open the top drawer, being careful to support it as it came. He well knew how easily it could slip from the main unit. With one hand holding the bottom of the drawer, he felt with the other. Listening for any change in the double rhythm of the breathing behind him, twice stopping as the pitch or speed of the sounds altered, he picked through underwear until he found the key.

It was done. The key was in his hand and the drawer was closed. Holding tight, letting it bite into his hand, he moved back round the bed. Before leaving he picked the fallen dressing gown from the floor and hung it back on the peg. With his hand on the door, he turned back to the bed. Exhilaration at his accomplishment gave him a rush he could not ignore.

Murmuring under his breath, so low he could barely hear it himself, he addressed the larger of the two mounds. "Got you, you son of a bitch."

Then he was out.

His rising excitement causing his blood pressure to increase, he moved back to the study door. Laying a hand upon this final obstacle, he gave silent thanks to whatever guardian angels he possessed. Visualising the small brass key in his hand, he fumbled momentarily for the lock, then found it. The small click made him pause as the door unlocked, for it seemed explosive in the gloom. Only when he was satisfied that he had not disturbed the sleeping couple (and his mind retched as he thought the word 'couple') did he proceed with opening the door.

When he had stepped inside he locked it behind him. Being the only entrance to the room, anybody else wanting to enter would have to give themselves away long before they could be a threat. Of course, what he would do after receiving this warning was anybody's guess, but at least he couldn't be taken by surprise. Looking round, he conceded the need for the torch here. The strip blinds were firmly closed and the blackness was as thick as in the hallway. Finding the button, he focused the beam of light in front of him.

Only to find nothing there. That couldn't be right. Moving the beam from left to right, he reached for the main light switch. Knowing it to be unwise, but unable to understand what the torchlight was presenting him, he flicked it down.

Such was the change in brightness that he had to close his eyes for a moment. When he could open them again he blinked several times to ensure he was seeing correctly.

All the furniture had indeed gone, the room now being empty. What came as the bigger shock were the walls, or what now covered them. Pinned to the far wall were dozens and dozens of black and white photographs. These he inspected immediately, and was not surprised to find that he featured in many of them. Most were representations of him on the street or in his car. Two showed him in a bar. In all shots he was the focus, with everything around him blurred and hard to recognise. Only one was specific enough for him to place, for it showed him meeting Alex Carlisle in the foyer of the Ramkin Hotel a lifetime ago. They were shaking hands, Alex looking as upright as Greg remembered thinking at the time.

He was not the only one to feature in the photos. A quick count showed that there were five other men highlighted prominently, none in his company. Did that mean that these others had shared this fate? Could this wall really be a display of targets that had been chosen along with him? If so, where were they now? Scouring the exhibition, he tried to find a common factor that could link all of the men together. Two were dressed in business suits, one seemed to be a tramp of some sort, one wore a police uniform, and the final man might have been a teacher or lecturer, for he was wandering around a campus somewhere. The only similar thing was the age range, for all of the men looked somewhere in their early thirties. Apart from this they were from obviously different walks of life, with nothing to connect them.

Why those specific people? Why him?

Shocked by what he was seeing, he examined the wall to his left. Only then did he appreciate the scale of what was being done. A dozen charts were pinned up alongside one another, each headed by a different place name. On every one there was a list of numbers one to seven. Each number had a line through it in red marker pen. Dublin, Liverpool, Glasgow, Newcastle-upon-Tyne, Birmingham, Cardiff, Manchester, Edinburgh, Swansea, York, Aberdeen; all major population centres, all with seven numbers crossed neatly off. The last list, London, had only five numbers crossed through. The sixth, and he could only assume this was him, was as yet untouched. Which meant that whatever had begun with the erasure of his identity had yet to be completed.

Feeling sick to his stomach, he realised for the first time the fatal consequences this might indicate. Bile bit the back of his throat, and before he could stop himself he dropped to his knees and was threw up.

Kneeling there, staring at his own vomit, he wondered how desperate his situation was. He had come to the house of his own free will, placing himself deep within the lion's den. If he was right then his wife was currently curled next to a killer.

Feeling weak, he glanced up at the third wall. Seven large charts hung there, the first five displaying a series of numerical statistics. Greg did not know what any of them meant, although he thought they looked medical. All he knew for certain was that the sixth, his own, was blank. Whatever they did, they had yet to do it to him. At once hopeful and fearful, he climbed to his feet. They wanted to do something, but had not yet had the chance. Now the advantage was his, for he had what none of the other targets had possessed. Prior knowledge.

Eager for one last clue, just one indication of why he had been chosen as the sixth victim in London, he turned back to the photographs. A voice murmured from behind him.

"All my own work. Do you like them?"

14 HEAVEN

Eye contact. For a brief moment, just after his eyelids dissolve, he turns to meet her gaze. She imagines what he sees in her. A manipulator? A murderer? Or something deeper than that, at once both less and more than such simplistic human terms can describe. She is always astonished at how difficult it is to read an expression after the eyelids go. No matter what the specimen thinks or feels, the eyes are simple balls of white and colour. She finds the purity of this to be beautiful. The fully exposed eyeballs are a splendid contrast to the now tender red of the stripped down facial muscles. More than this, they show the true nature of the human condition. Wide-eyed wonder, shock, and pain.

She is almost disappointed when they burst.

Relief is what he feels at this, gratitude that he will never have to gaze on her again. This is to be expected. Everything she has meant to him during his ordeal has been forced into a new light in the past twelve hours. The effect is deliberate. She became his safe haven at the end, something for him to hold on to. Now he has been betrayed. She can imagine the distress this has caused, though she can also experience it in truer ways.

It will soon be time to drain the tank. A delicate, anticipatory quiver runs through her; a low moan slips across her lips. Forcing herself to remain perfectly still, checking that she is still firmly attached, she waits for heaven.

15 ANGLES

Greg turned round. Standing in the now open doorway, leaning against the frame with casual insolence, was the man who had stolen his life and his name. Held up for Greg to inspect was the original brass key to the door. Looking down at his own, he realised he had liberated a duplicate.

He looked back up, trying to meet his opponent's amused gaze without fear. What made it harder was that the man's face was unmarked. Despite the beating Greg had inflicted on him just days ago, there wasn't a hint of bruising to mar his tanned complexion. "Your work? You took the photos?"

The other slipped into the room, pushing the door closed behind him and putting an exaggerated finger to his lips. "Shhh. Don't want to wake the missus." Dismissing any risk Greg might pose, he turned his back and studied the pictures on the wall. "It takes a great deal of effort to set up something like this you know. A great deal of preparation. I wouldn't want you to think you were being treated with anything less than strictest professional standards."

Greg had difficulty accepting what he was hearing. It was just too surreal to be talking to somebody who admitted what was happening. Despite everything - the charts, the pictures, the very nature of what threatened him - he felt elated.

Looking down at the vomit on the floor, the man tutted his disapproval. "It seems that every time you visit I have to clean up after you."

Despite his serenity, Greg's was reply little more than a whisper. "Why?"

Surprised, the man looked up. "Do you really think I'm going to tell you? After all the effort it took me to shatter your life, you think I'll set it right for you in one night? Oh, you've done well, you deserve credit for that. Very few think to come here for information. Usually they end up on the streets or in a cell somewhere. A few have even been committed to various psychiatric wings. But not you. You're stronger than that. How much have you worked out? Please indulge me, I'm genuinely curious."

Greg knew he should run. Nothing stood between him and the doorway, he thought he stood a good chance of making it out, but he wanted this conversation, the chance to reach the bottom of the mystery. He gestured to the charts. "A dozen towns. Seven victims from each, all of who turned round one day to discover that nobody knew who they were. Family and friends all had their minds altered in some way..." A quick pause, for that sounded so much like bad science fiction even he didn't believe it. "They remember you as the man whose life you're destroying. Another identity is set up for your victim, complete with memories to support it, which he may or may not choose to accept. That's all I've got." He took a deep breath, wishing the man would indicate how right or wrong he was. Nothing was forthcoming. "I don't know what's next. Some sort of ritual murder, maybe. That wall," he pointed, "numbers the victims you've chosen in London. I'm the sixth and I haven't been crossed off because you haven't finished with me. When you have you'll choose a seventh, then move on to another town. How am I doing?"

For a long moment the other watched him. The corner of his mouth twitched upwards, a musical chuckle bursting through his lips. Greg cast a nervous look down the corridor, but there was no response from the bedroom. Jennifer was oblivious to the confrontation occurring just yards from where she slept. After some moments the merriment faded and the man spoke.

"I'm sorry, really I am. But you're so close in some respects, so far in others. Really, all you need to do is change the angle you're looking from and you'd have it." Another chuckle. "Still, that is rather the point. I just thought that, to get this far, you must have pieced it together. Never mind, it's an impressive theory."

Annoyed though he was by the ridicule he faced, Greg couldn't stem his curiosity. "So where am I wrong?"

"Oh no, I'm sorry my friend, but you don't get off that easily. You are becoming something of an wrinkle in our operation…"

Greg twitched. "You're not alone?"

A moment of silence.

"Very good. Yes. Well done, you're a fast one." All good humour had departed the man now, it had angered him to let slip even that small fragment of information. With the sudden absence of pleasantries the real danger of the situation imposed itself. Greg felt like he had stepped on a live wire. Every muscle in him screamed a desire to move in a separate direction. It was only indecision that anchored him. All at once he wanted to run, attack, and urinate where he stood.

Fixing his gaze again, the other man continued, his voice mesmerising.

"As I was saying, you have become visible. Your episode at the restaurant was high profile, and we cannot allow our activities to reach the public eye." He considered for a moment. "On the other hand, we aren't ready for you yet. There is so much you still have to suffer before your time."

Greg felt dizzy; the desire to run was overwhelming. He had to keep the man talking. "What are you going to do? Brainwash me again? Make me forget"' Hearing his voice as little more than a whine, he felt vulnerable and pathetic.

"And waste everything we've built up already? No, we haven't time to start again." He took a slow step forwards. "Perhaps it would be simplest to put you in storage. Not as strong a stimulus for your suffering, but not entirely ineffective."

Greg knew that this was his last chance. He didn't have the slightest idea what the man was talking about, except that it was bad and it was *now*. He ran to the door, flung it open and sprinted into the hallway.

Or tried to. Before he was two steps to the precious exit, an iron hand clamped about his wrist, yanking him back. As his feet lost contact with the floor, star-hot agonies told him his wrist was sprained. Landing painfully, still held tight, he was sure he was about to die. So fast, so strong. Was this the same man he had beaten senseless in the hallway downstairs?

"Now, now. So eager to leave after all your efforts to enter?" The voice was behind his ear, and he was sprawled too awkwardly to turn and face it. "No, better you stay here for a while. Consider yourself a houseguest." A click and the feel of cold metal around his sprained wrist were the signals of his captivity. Handcuffs. The other man began to drag him across the floor. The pain from his wrist increased tenfold, causing hectic black dots to dance in front of his eyes. As the other cuff closed firmly around the doorknob, he struggled to grip hold of his consciousness.

"Another valiant effort." His vision cleared, despite the fire still burning strong across his lower arm, as the other crouched before him. "Now then, you seem fairly certain that you're halfway to a Eureka moment regarding your predicament." Greg stared blankly at him. "Well, this is unacceptable to us I'm afraid. We can't have you believing yourself to be a sane and normal victim. You'd render yourself useless. So I'm going to show you something to make you reconsider your half-cocked notions and blundered theories. Watch closely now, I don't do repeat performances."

Greg watched.

And Greg screamed.

Two hours later he had stopped crying. Next to him, his second pool of vomit polluted the air with an acrid, eye-watering stench. His trousers were still damp from his lost bladder control, and his handcuffed arm had begun to cramp from hanging behind him.

It failed, he tried to tell himself, *and I am sane*. He knew this could not be true. What he had seen could not be real. Perhaps he had been brainwashed again, or had hallucinated the whole thing. Or maybe he was just mad. Whatever the case, enough of his rational mind remained to realise that he was deep in trouble. The door that he was now handcuffed to had been closed and locked, and the light was out. Through the blinds the dim grey of morning had begun to make itself known, but inside it was still dark.

He had to get out. Deciding not to think on what he had seen at the end of the conversation, he cast his mind beyond it, to where his torment had been discussed. *Had he not suffered enough?* What did the thing mean? Perhaps it was all part of the murder ritual, an inherent suffering before the actual demise of the victim.

Except, said his subversive subconscious, *you aren't dealing with a simple serial killer, are you Greg? You aren't even dealing with a human being.*

No. Such thoughts would be fully considered when he was out of this place. When he was safe. For now he would continue as though he was dealing with a simple madman. The irony of that made him chuckle, for psychotic killers would be preferable to what he was dealing with. Despite the hysterical edge to his humour, it made him feel almost normal again.

Shifting his weight, he realised how bad the cramp was when a stab of pain clamped his eyes shut. He let out a hiss. The first problem was his arm. Trying his hardest to block the pain, he twisted his body until his feet were beneath him. Moving before he could convince himself otherwise, he rose to his feet. Stiff muscles protested the action, his arm blazing under the abuse, but he was standing. Allowing his dizziness to pass, he used his free hand to rub life back into his dead one.

Feeling better for being upright, he considered his options. Before leaving, Jameson (*the thing*) had taken his key from him. Though the lock was not a particularly strong one, it would be suicide to think of breaking the door down. Everybody in the house would hear, and his escape attempt would be over before it began. Besides, the first problem had to be the handcuffs. With his left wrist securely bound to the doorknob, he was going nowhere. Checking the cuff about his wrist, he tried to find some give in it. Prising with his fingers, he tugged and pulled until the stabbing from his wrenched limb made him stop. Nothing. Only the key was going to open them. Even if his wrist were not horribly swollen, no amount of working on the cuff would free him.

Despair licked down his spine. He would wait there, 'on storage', until the thing returned. When it did so, and he was judged to have suffered an appropriate amount, it would kill him. Greg still didn't know why. Some of his theory had been accurate, or at least close to the truth, but what was missing? Where had he gone wrong? He had been told that looking at it from a different angle would reveal everything to him, but he had no idea what that might mean?

Looking from the wrong angle?

He lost all interest in theories and suppositions, and he focussed on the cuff. Not the one attached to his still swelling wrist, but the one around the doorknob. It was also too tight to slip off, but that might not be a problem. What he needed to see was the handle itself, where it was attached to the door. Hoping there was nobody in the hallway, he turned the flashlight on. It was as he remembered from fitting it, a plain brass knob inset in a rectangular base screwed into the wood of the door. A moment of hope, of private triumph, glided through him. It was possible, but he needed a screwdriver.

He didn't have one, and rummaged in his pocket for a suitable substitute. His keys were too large, his pen too fragile. He settled on a one-penny coin. Heart rattling his ribs, he kneeled next to the lock. Placing the torch in his mouth, he began work with his free hand.

The task was long and arduous. Several times he thought that the joints of his fingers might break with the strain as they pushed and twisted the penny anticlockwise. Perspiration made his grip loose, and each time he slipped he would nearly lose the coin as it flew from his grasp, but it never rolled beyond his reach. The work always began anew. One screw eventually came out, a small but precious achievement. It gave him hope for the second, which took longer to drop to the floor. Sore from the constant strain, his fingers grew numb, forcing him to stop for a few minutes. After allowing blood to flow back to the tired flesh, he continued. Saliva dripped from where he held the torch in his mouth, jaw muscles watering with fatigue. Release of the third screw brought with it elation, and it was with renewed vigour that he tackled the last.

Then Greg was staring at the fourth screw as it sat in his hand. He could hardly believe he had done it. Working quickly now, he disassembled the rest of the handle and removed the knob. As he slipped the cuff from the end of it, a sudden surge of energy blew through him.

Having never had his liberty taken from him before, Greg had not previously understood what freedom really meant. There was no time to enjoy it. Limping to the other side of the room, his flashlight now back in his hand, he looked over the pictures a final time. Taking the photograph of Carlisle and he meeting in the Ramkin, he folded it and placed it in his trouser pocket.

Checking himself over, he tried to assess his injuries. Only his wrist was seriously damaged, though his fingers throbbed and his back and legs sang bruising from when he had fallen during the struggle. Other than that he was exhausted and hungry. Two meals had been surrendered to various parts of the floor now, and he felt weak from lack of sustenance. He would only have one chance then. If he were caught a second time he would be finished. Having made a mistake once, his enemy would not be so casual the next time he confined Greg.

But escape was finally realistic. With the door locked there was only one means of leaving the room, and he pried apart two slats of the horizontal blinds across the window with his aching fingers to steal a look outside. Jerking his head back, for the morning light was bright enough to sting his tired eyes, he allowed himself a moment to adjust to the new dazzle. Looking again, he saw the street was empty. Good. The evening had begun with him taking on the role of burglar, and the last thing he needed was to be arrested as such when he was trying to leave. Fully opening the blinds, he fumbled with the window catch. It swung slowly open.

Relaxed footsteps beat from the hallway behind him, coming towards the study door. Hammering hard, his heart was suddenly his entire chest. First floor to ground. He could do it. He would have to land carefully, letting his knees absorb the shock of the fall. Swinging himself over the windowsill, he perched precariously. What if broke his leg, or even his back? What would he do then?

A key slid into the lock behind him and the time for doubt was over. Hearing the door open, Greg jumped.

It was over faster than he imagined. For less than a heartbeat the world flew upwards, blurring across his vision. Then the ground hit him. Air exploded from his lungs, the impact trying to sculpt two-dimensional shapes of his feet. For a confused instant he didn't know whether he was on the ground, or had just fallen backwards off the windowsill and into the room. With his head clearing, he rose to his aching feet. Without looking behind him he hobbled a cripple's pace across the lawn, towards his car.

He could see it at the end of the street, but couldn't manage more than a hobble. In his head, he tried to estimate where the thing might be by now. After it entered the room there would be a second or two of confusion before it turned and ran down the hallway. By now it must be at the bottom of the stairs, and his car was still too far away. The fall had been the final straw for his tired flesh.

Now it would be on the street behind him. After a moment's delay unlocking the front door, it would have sprinted down the drive after him. Greg could almost count off the approach in his head.

Ten seconds. Nine seconds. Greg reached his car, fumbled epileptically for his keys. Eight seconds. Seven seconds. Finding them, he shoved the first one directly into the lock. It shot in and he twisted. Six seconds. Five seconds. It wouldn't turn. Four seconds. He realised his mistake. Three seconds. This was his car. His real car. The keys to which were on a shelf in his fake apartment. His hire car was parked around the corner, near the entrance to the street. In his panic he had made for the first blue Focus he saw. Two seconds.

One second.

Greg whirled to face his incoming enemy. He was alone on the street.

He searched each garden for hidden figures, suspecting some trick, some new game. The avenue was empty. Only when he looked back to the study window did he see the face he sought. Disguised once more as the man Greg had first met, it stood in the study, nonchalant, unconcerned by the escape it had witnessed. Seeing Greg gaze upwards, it smiled and raised an arm in casual farewell.

Sickened by what the thing was, Greg turned and fled.

Closing the door of the apartment behind him, Greg allowed his aching body to relax. Feeling he could collapse at any moment, it was an effort to even turn the key in the lock. The beanbags in the corner called him forward, and with enormous relief he dropped onto one.

He had not been pursued. Despite his tired efforts to determine why, he couldn't see any logic to it. After the effort of catching and containing him, he had been certain that he would be pursued during his haphazard escape – he would have been easy enough prey. The only sound reason he could think of was that the enemy knew where he had fled. They could pick him up any time, for he had nowhere else to run. Perhaps that was why they had provided such a comfortable haven in the first place, so they always knew where he would be.

He had to leave. Staying was suicidal. He might as well just drive back to Wimbledon and hand himself over.

Yes, he would flee. In a moment. When his shattered body had recovered from his ordeal. A few seconds of recuperation were not too much to ask after all he had suffered.

Closing his eyes, he tumbled to a deep, troubled sleep.

16 SOFT TEARS

Smoke filled the room as he looked up at the enemy. The man was clear in his vision; other details were made hazy by grey light. He was talking, though Greg understood little of what was being said. Wisps of smoke distracted his attention as they drifted through the other's long, brown hair.

Only then did he realise where he was, and he recoiled in anticipation as the last words became clear.

"...don't do repeat performances."

He did not want to watch, nor did he know which part of him fixed terrified eyes on the the man's face. Strong, matinee handsome features, wavy brown hair. That was what he would see, would make himself see, for nothing else could be real. Telling himself this did not ease the iron fear that tightened around him.

At first the changes were subtle, almost unnoticeable. Healthy, tanned skin gradually whitened, becoming pallid and drawn. Sores, red and spreading, appeared at the corners of the mouth and eyes.

Spreading out. Spreading sickly.

Like some virulent disease, they grew over the rest of the skin, glistening red cracks cutting through whiteness. Flakes of healthy tissue dropped to the floor. A leper now, contagion reeked wetly from it as the condition worsened with the passing seconds.

Greg tried not to breathe, for the sudden fresh meat smell was suffocating and vile. Ripping his eyes from the face, he turned to his left and vomited until there was nothing left for his stomach to evacuate.

Though he wanted nothing less than to see, his head turned back, and he screamed. Where once had crouched a man, there now hulked a monstrosity. *It can't be true*, he thought, *it can't be real*.

Everything about the man was as before, with one singular exception. Not a square inch of skin remained on his body. The face he looked at was one of tendons and muscle, blue veins and slick fat standing prominent against the scarlet backdrop of flesh. No hair remained on the head, and the eyes were joke-shop wide. Staring at Greg.

The thing stood back, removing the mundane dressing gown to reveal the rest of its body in the same condition. Red muscles were taught across the ribs, the pounding heart beneath causing them to shudder and fall in time with the inhuman pulse. Intestines gleamed slickly from the abdomen, rubber-soft and writhing. Over the entire of the wet and stinking body flies landed, laid eggs, and drew sustenance.

It leaned close to him, foetid breath driving into his nostrils.

"Fear me."

Greg jolted awake, the scream stopping in his throat before it could sound out. It was becoming dark and he rushed to put the light on. How long had he been asleep? A glance at his watch told him nearly twelve hours.

Heading to the kitchen, he tried to clear his head of the nightmare memory. A cup of coffee helped, and he was soon able to think without the smothering grogginess of oversleep clouding his mind. He had slept for the entire day, yet no one had come to snatch him. Why? Were they waiting downstairs, eager for him to exit so they could pounce, or was a new game being played out?

The nightmare still haunted him, despite the other matters hollering for his attention. Acknowledging that it would not leave of its own accord, he resigned himself to thinking on it. Impossible though it seemed now, as he basked in the luxury of the apartment, the dream had been accurate, borne of memory not fantasy. That was what he believed he had seen, but what in the name of God was it? Nothing he had ever beheld looked like it, nor was there a fictional creature he could compare it to, yet it was real. How could he challenge something he did not understand, in a game with rules that had yet to be explained to him?

What he knew for certain was that it wanted something from him, needed his suffering. Everything he had been through was designed to heighten his emotional trauma – even being shown the creature's true appearance had been to that end. So what happened now? Wandering to the window, he took a cautious look at the car park far below. Nothing was out of place in the half-light. No strange cars, no lurking figures in the shadows. It was frustrating, for he did not know what they expected of him. If he could only work that out, start anticipating them instead of constantly reacting, he would stand a chance of getting ahead of them.

Think then, he thought as he sipped his coffee. *What would you expect yourself to do?* He had not yet taken the most obvious step in going to the authorities. He was being criminally manipulated by a creature that wanted to kill him, so of course he should go to the police. Studying the notion, he made up his mind. This was what was expected of him, so it was the last thing he could allow himself to do. Doubtless each of the five victims before him had sought help from official sources. None of them had survived.

So where could he go? Friends were ruled out. It was probable they had suffered the same fate as Jennifer. This left one choice, one acquaintance so recent that he might be outside their circle of influence.

Touching the photograph in his pocket, he allowed his hopes to ignite afresh as he remembered Alex.

Two hours later he was standing in the evening rain outside Carlisle's flat. On the ground next to him was the suitcase he had packed, for he did not plan to return to the flat again if he could help it. He pressed the buzzer a second time, praying that the hotel manager was in. A click sounded from the speaker, followed by Alex's weary voice.

"Hello." He sounded groggy. Greg had obviously woken him.

"Alex? It's Greg Summers. Can I come up?"

There was a puzzled pause. "Greg who?"

Greg's heart sank. Surely not Alex too?

"Oh, Greg! Sorry, I've just got out of bed. Hang on." The lock of the door buzzed open. "Come on up."

With a deep sigh of relief, Greg opened the door. He was right, whether too peripheral or just too recent, Alex had escaped the net after all.

At the second floor he turned onto the landing. Alex was standing by his door, jeans and a T-shirt hanging haphazardly over his wiry frame. He beckoned Greg inside his flat, concerned .

"Greg, you look terrible. What happened? Been in a fight?" The last question was a joke, but Greg could not help rising to it.

"Yes." He collapsed on one of the couches.

Alex's eyes widened in surprise. "Shit. Should I call the police? Where did it happen? Are you hurt?"

"Wait. Just hear me out. What I need, Alex, is for you to sit down and listen to me." Seeing the intent in his eyes, Alex nodded, sitting on the couch opposite Greg.

And Greg began to tell his story. Starting at the evening with Georgina, he laid out each moment as it had happened, leaving aside no detail he could remember. It took him nearly an hour to tell the tale, backtracking several times to amend points he had already made. Alex sat, attentive and silent, though all of it. At last he finished.

"I picked up some stuff and came here. It's one of the few places they don't seem to know much about yet." Alex stared at him, making no comment. "Well? Am I crazy? What do you think?"

Alex stood, a little wary, and rubbed his eyes. "What can I say? You were doing fine until the skin fell off the bloke who's sleeping with your wife. After that, yes, I pretty much decided you're an absolute bloody lunatic."

Greg felt momentous relief when he recognised a glint of humour in his friend's eye. "Don't mock. I'm having more than enough trouble with this as it is."

"Sorry." He looked sincere. "If it's any consolation, I'm pretty sure you believe all this."

Greg sank back in the couch. "Christ, I know *I* believe it. I believe everything I just told you. That might be the bloody problem."

Alex smiled again. "Right. Okay, I refuse to discuss this further without something fortifying in me. Drink?"

"God yes. Scotch with ice."

"A man of good taste. I'll join you in that." He walked over to the cabinet, poured the drinks, then returned and sat down. Handing Greg a scotch, he looked concerned when it all but vanished with the first swallow.

"Easy. Whatever's happening won't get easier to fathom if you're wasted."

"I know, I know. But that felt good." Grinning at Carlisle, he went and poured himself a second measure then returned. "Don't look so worried, I'll slow down." As he sat, he looked Alex straight in the eye and asked him outright. "Do you believe me?" |

Alex returned his gaze steadily, then glanced away. "I don't know Greg. You look like hell, which fits the story, but the rest of it? Conspiracy theories. Brainwashing and murder. Even hell-spawned demons. Seriously, you have to give me some help here. You sound sane enough, but I saw one of your fits, remember? If you really want my opinion, it looks more like a breakdown to me. Maybe something else you should get checked." He paused, struggling to say it. "Some tumours, Greg. Don't they cause hallucinations? Other illnesses. Schizophrenia. Alzheimer's. There's a comprehensive list of things that might fit what I'm seeing before we get close to actual conspiracies and demons."

Greg acceded the point. He hadn't expected to be taken on his word. Pulling the photograph from his pocket, he tossed it over. "This should do for a start."

Alex snatched the paper out of the air, looked at it for a moment, then let out a deep sigh. It was a photograph of the two of them meeting for the first time. "From that wall in your house?" Greg nodded. "You were being watched from as far back as that morning?"

"Before that, I think. At least the night before. I had my first fit in the restaurant before I went to the hotel."

Alex nodded. "There's more?"

Trying hard not to touch his swollen wrist, Greg pulled back the sleeves of his jacket and shirt to reveal the handcuffs which still hung from his arm. "There's these."

"Christ. You can't get them off?"

Greg shook his head. "Lock-picking ranks right up there with burglary as one of the skills I don't have. Every time I try to force them off, my wrist screams blue murder."

"I'll bet. Fine. I believe you. But I'm still holding court on fleshy beasts and brainwashing."

"I don't blame you." Then the big question, the whole reason he had presumed to come here. "Will you help me?'"
There was a moment of utter vacuum; it seemed to Greg that Alex had no idea what his answer would be. Then, staring into space, he nodded his head.

Four days of solitary pain crashed in on Greg, and he started to cry. He wasn't aware of Alex crossing to sit tentatively beside him, nor could he remember precisely when the larger man began to hold him. All he knew, as he lay like a newborn in his friend's arms, was that he was safe. After all the running, the struggles and revelations, he was finally safe. Making no attempt to hold back, he relished the chance to weep soft tears.

Alex allowed Greg to cry until he was certain that the nightmare had been, at least for the moment, subdued. Only when he felt that his new friend was holding together better did he go to make coffee.

Greg used the time to consider his next move. Lying back on the couch, he let his mind wander over the possibilities. They were few in number. He had an ally at last, the single thing that kept him from despair, but what new options did that open up? How was he better off than before?

Cigarette smoke drifted past his eyes as Alex took the seat opposite him again. A mug of steaming coffee was presented, and he sipped it, burning his lips in the process.

"Easy does it," warned Alex, "I'm not convinced I should be giving you any caffeine at all. You're stressed enough as it is."

Coffee. Burning. Strangely, those images felt as though they should be familiar to him. Unable to place why, he shook the thought from his head.

"Do you mind if I have a cigarette?"

Alex gave him a peculiar glance, then handed his pouch of tobacco over without a word. Deftly, Greg pulled loose a cigarette paper, then spread tobacco over it and rolled a narrow tube. Only when he was running his tongue along the glued edge of the paper did he realise what he was doing.

He stared at the object in his hand as though it might bite him, then lifted his head to look at Alex. The words were difficult, emerging as a breath. "I don't smoke."

"Thought not. I remember the look on your face when I lit up in my office. You rolled that like a pro, though"' Alex's brow furrowed. "Can we try something? Call it an experiment." Greg nodded. Putting out his own cigarette in the ashtray on the table, Alex pulled a lighter from his pocket. "Smoke it."

Part of Greg was repulsed at the thought. Even when he was a boy, he had never been tempted to indulge such stupidity. For as long as he could recall he had been aware of the dangers inherent in smoking, had always thought it a disgusting habit. As a child it had made him nauseous whenever he was in a room with somebody smoking. Now though, he was curious. Oddly, the thought revolted him less than it once had.

He nodded his ascent as he placed the cigarette in his mouth. Alex reached over with the lighter, sparked it aflame, and lit the tiny homemade.

Deciding that the experiment was useless if he entered it halfheartedly, Greg drew in deep. He expected to explode with a convulsive fit of coughing. He expected to feel sick. Neither happened. Instead, after a moment of mild lightheadedness, he realised he was enjoying the cigarette tremendously. Some of the tension left his body. Noticing the inquisitive cock of Alex's eyebrow, he answered the unspoken question. "It feels good. I can see why it's so addictive."

"This is your first cigarette?"

"Yes." He took another draw. "Just being around the smoke used to make me queasy."

Alex looked troubled. "Why did you ask for one?"

"I'm not sure, it was just an urge. I felt like having a cigarette." He realised what he was saying, knew it sounded foolish. "Isn't that how it starts?"

"I don't think so. It wasn't that way with me. Besides, think it through. You've never had a cigarette in your life, yet you have a sudden urge to smoke. Without even thinking about it you roll a perfect cigarette, a skill which takes time to perfect. Then you puff away on a strong, unfiltered tobacco that should, by rights, leave the smoking initiate retching and choking. It makes me wonder."

Greg realised precisely where the argument led. A chill broke over him, his suddenly clumsy movements causing him to drop the cigarette.

"It makes me wonder if Richard Jameson might be a smoker."

Picking the cigarette from the floor, Greg extinguished it in the ashtray. After the dream of the adventure park he had been sure that no other fragments of Jameson were to be found in him. Perhaps he had been looking in the wrong places. "I think, perhaps, he is." Exhaling, he reached for his coffee. And stopped short. "I forgot."

"Forgot what?" Alex was eager, the mystery snaring him. "You don't usually drink coffee either?"

Greg shook his head. "No, I've always drunk it. At least, I think I have." Could he be sure? "When I was very young I scalded myself with coffee. It terrified my mother and she slapped me. Whenever I burn myself it makes me think of that. Just one of those memories that sticks with you, I suppose."

"Joys of childhood, and all that."

"Except, just before I asked for a cigarette, I burned my lips on the coffee. I couldn't remember why it was significant. I knew it was, but I couldn't work out why." Fighting back a fresh surge of panic, he forced himself not to shout. "I couldn't place it, Alex. Do you know why? *Because it wasn't me trying!* I was Jameson again, like in the bathroom. Every time I relax, he forces his way in. I can't even tell when it's happening!"

"Okay, calm down. Panicking isn't going to help." Greg nodded, letting breaths of air soothe his rising anxiety. Seeing this, Alex continued. "I know it's distressing, but you have to stay calm. Before we do anything else we should get you cleaned up. And you can hardly leave the flat with those handcuffs dangling from your wrists. I don't know what we're going to do after that, but we'll work this out. I promise."

Greg knew what Alex was trying to do and appreciated it. Short term goals. At the moment it was too terrifying to consider the wider implications of the situation. It was easier to concentrate on what could be done then and there. He took another sip of coffee, clinging to his recovered memory, then nodded his agreement.

"Good. Wait here." Saying this, Alex picked up his jacket and keys, unlocked the front door and was gone.

Greg was left alone. Despite having woken up only a few hours ago, exhaustion from the telling of his tale crashed in on him. Minutes later, he was dozing quietly on the couch.

When Gregory Summers married Jennifer Sharpe, it was happiest and most terrifying day of his life. Despite drinking little the night before, he woke late and panicked. Dressing was a blur, all he later remembered was having to do it twice.

Had he not glanced briefly in the mirror before leaving he would have worn jeans and a T-shirt to the ceremony. Similarly, the drive to the church was a manic affair, verging on the suicidal. Once there, the torment continued. Waiting at the front, knowing in his heart that Jennifer wouldn't show, he was near tears when his bride strode through the doors. Vows were exchanged, words flowing from his mouth without the direct intervention of his mind. They kissed.

And the years of loneliness and isolation ended. He had a family. Somebody who loved him, whom he loved dearly in return.

People meeting him at the reception received little more than a dazed look and a beauteous smile. Nobody minded. *Shellshock*, they said to themselves, and this was not far from the truth.

The newlyweds honeymooned in Florida. Eager tourists, they made the most of the often tacky sights and attractions. Over those two wonderful weeks they shared themselves more willingly and truly than Greg could have imagined possible.

Panic-stricken shouts...

"Greg! Jesus, Greg!"

His eyes darted open, the fog of sleep dissipating in an instant. Alex was above him, shaking him awake. Reading the fear in the man's eyes, he looked around the room. Where were they? Had they found him?

Then he noticed the dampness of his clothes, felt the slickness on his face. Looking down at himself, he saw the cause of Alex's concern. His clothes, the settee, even the carpet - all now bore the familiar signs of one of his flashbacks. All were crimson with blood.

While he slept, he had exploded once more.

17 FADING

Eternity continues. This time, as the tank drains, it is only the sensation of sinking that alerts him to the fact. Nothing remains of the complex biological system that is the ear to tell him of any gurgling.

Sinking. Falling. Dropping. Then the pain. What must he look like now? Despite the shattering icicle stabs of sensation, too intense now to determine from which part of his body they scream, in his mind he comes close to a chuckle. He knows exactly what he looks like. The thing, the creature that fractured his life. There is no skin left on him, intuition tells him, only muscles and tendons. Blood and fat. It is even possible that his stripped body gleams redder than that other monster had been, but the globules of fat will be as white, the shudders of his heart as strong. For a while.

He wants to give up now. No life awaits him should he escape, not as he is now. He would spend the rest of his days in hospital, alone but for the nurses. Even they would turn away in sympathy and horror.

Now there is a new sensation, a fresh pressure sitting next to the pain. It builds in his torso, climbing slowly through grades of power until he feels sure he must expand to contain it. His awareness becomes dizzy, flashes of red illuminate his sightless brain.

He knows what it must be, this strange force. Upon draining, the fluid has been replaced with pure, sweet air. Which he can no longer breathe. Great swallows of the fluid have bubbled within him, eating his lungs away until nothing remains but the pool of grey mucus that must now slosh at the bottom of his chest cavity. The only things preventing his chest from collapsing are his still solid ribs.

Building, building, the pressure increases until he knows he must explode. The insignificant part of his existence that still recognises himself as individual grows smaller.

Fading?

Why is he?

Fading?

Away?

With a rush, the pressure recedes and he returns. He is not dead, and the sensation of rising, floating, is the only clue he needs to tell him why. The fluid which now refills the tank is keeping him alive, somehow replacing the function of his lungs to bring him oxygen.

For just long enough to make his death a slower sufferance.

18 DUBIETY

An hour later, Greg emerged from the bathroom. It had been a labour to bathe, loss of blood having again left him listless and without energy. To his alarm, he found himself becoming used to the sensation. Alex was sitting on the remaining clean couch, staring in open disbelief at the stained mess of its twin. Greg read his thoughts without difficulty. *So very much blood.*

When he had woken and realised the cause of panic, it had been the task of a few moments to calm his friend. All he had said was that this was nothing to worry about, at least compared to all the other things they had to worry about, and that he would explain when he was cleaned up.

The hot water of the bath had been soothing, soporific, and it had been a struggle to emerge from that enveloping comfort. His myriad aches - his sprained wrist, the sting of his feet - all became less debilitating in the penetrating heat. Eventually though, he could rest no longer. There were things to be done, even if he could not yet specify what they might be, and only he could do them.

"Alex?" The other man looked up, shock still in his eyes. "Are you all right?"

A brief and welcome smile flickered across Carlisle's lips. "You're asking about *my* health?"

Greg chuckled. It was strange, but in a funny way he had adjusted to accept these events. They no longer caused him such dismay and confusion. Still, he badly needed Alex's strength to maintain himself. Earlier the manager had been so controlled, so strong. What now sat before him was a man edging along a precipice. The reasoning behind the violent physical eruption he had borne witness to might be sufficient to calm him. Sitting next to Alex on the couch, Greg began his explanation.

"Okay, take a deep breath. This is what I think happens. Do you remember I told you about the fits earlier? How they've become steadily worse?"

"Of course. But I had no idea..."

Greg raised his hand to silence him. "Let me finish. The fit, if that's what you want to call it, which happened this evening sort of validates most of what I thought. The theory I was working with supposes that they're a method for my own memories to reassert themselves against the implants. We already know there may be more artificial memories in my head than I'm aware of, and I think that this particular fit was a reaction to the new ones which surfaced this evening."

"The cigarette episode?"

"Exactly. I don't think they're dangerous, just uncomfortable."

"I take your point Greg, but not dangerous? Take a look at the couch. How much blood do you see there? A pint? Two?"

"I know. Still, whatever doesn't kill you makes you stronger, isn't that what they say?" Alex gave him a sceptical look, then sighed.

"Do you know if any of your fellow brainwashees have these fits?"

Greg shook his head. "Not for certain, but if you want me to guess, then I don't think so. This might be something the creature hasn't come across before. I'm less susceptible to my new identity than others have been, and it doesn't know how to deal with that. It only dropped its disguise to shake me up, I think that was because the fits were stopping the brainwashing from having a severe enough effect."

"You weren't suffering enough."

"That's it. I don't know why it needs me to suffer in such specific ways, but it's significant enough for it to take extreme measures to make sure that I do."

Alex shook his head, though Greg was relieved to see that he had visibly relaxed. *Amazing*, he thought, *what the human mind can accept with a bit of nudging and rationalisation*. Now it was time to start thinking about the future. "So," he hazarded. "What next?"

Alex shook himself. "Well, first we're going to get those bloody handcuffs off you. After that you're going to do your damnedest to clean my couch."

During his brief excursion, which Greg was surprised to hear had only lasted an hour and half, Alex had made his way back to the hotel. Picking up a toolkit from the caretaker's office, he had driven back by way of a twenty-four hour garage and bought some paracetamol and bandages.

Greg took the pills dutifully. His sprained wrist had swollen to press firmly and painfully against the chill metal, and the constant throb which originated there was signal enough that taking the cuff off was going to hurt like hell.

He was right. Laying the arm across the coffee table, Alex took a hammer and chisel from the dusty bag on the floor. Carefully resting the tip of the chisel against the lock of the cuff, even this gentle pressure sending a light shock of pain through Greg's arm, he glanced at his kneeling friend.

"This will probably..."

"Hurt. I know. Hurry up, the suspense is…"

The hammer descended and Greg screamed, tears springing to his eyes. His arm was dipped in molten torment, but the sensation soon numbed to a mute ache.

"Oh, hush," Alex said. "The neighbours are going to think I'm murdering somebody in here."

Yes, thought Greg, *and what an accurate guess that would be*. Through gritted teeth he asked, "Is it off?"

"Not quite. One more good blow should do it, I think." Greg closed his eyes against the coming shock. Hot fire again drove into his flesh, boiling blood and tearing at nerves, and he bit his tongue to silence himself.

"It's off." For a moment he thought Alex was referring to his tongue, then he opened his eyes with relief. Pulling back his arm he saw, for the first time, how badly swollen the wrist actually was without steel to keep it in check. Black, blue and red blended to form a harsh kaleidoscope of pains. He felt faint.

"Could I…could I possibly have another paracetamol?"

"Certainly," Alex grinned. "And for being such a brave little trooper, you can be dismissed from all couch restoration duties until further notice." Greg replied with a wan smile.

After he had sunk another of the pills, they set about making sure the wrist was securely bandaged. Again, the pain was terrible, but the end result felt far stronger than before.

"Thanks," he told Alex, and meant it.

"No problem." His eyes twinkled. "A pleasure, in fact." His face turned serious before Greg could respond. "Now, to business. Fun though torturing you is, we're going to have to take a break and look to other things." Tired, the paracetamol beginning to take effect, Greg nodded drowsy agreement. Alex sat next to him. "I've been thinking," he said, "that there are two leads you haven't followed up yet." He made it sound like a bad police show. "Firstly, there are the photographs you handed over to authenticate."

Greg had completely forgotten about the eccentric developer he had intended to visit that day. "Good. And second?"

"The only person you've left completely out of the loop." He paused, meeting Greg's eyes. "Your lady friend from my hotel. Georgina."

The next day found Greg energised, in high spirits despite everything. Having rested well - if there had been nightmares then he did not remember them - he felt in good health. Only a dull throb from his wrist, which knifed out when he forgot himself and tried to use it, reminded him of the aches of previous days.

Alex was up before him, preparing a breakfast consisting mostly of cholesterol. They wolfed it down, greases relished as plans were made. It was decided that they should take Alex's car into town, leaving Greg's outside the flat. Wondering whether it was paranoiac to be making such elaborate precautions in the cold light of day, Greg in the end accepted that he had developed a healthy sense of fear over the past week. Safety had to be placed at the fore. They could well be grateful for the anonymity at a later point.

After breakfast they dressed, then made their way down to the car. Greg was relieved to see Alex casting eyes over the people in the street, assessing each, for it made him feel he was being less neurotic about the whole affair. Glancing round for himself, he noticed nothing out of place. Still, when the car door shut he was relieved to be away from even the potential of prying eyes.

Warmed by the morning sun, Alex's car was somnolent and comfortable. As it reversed from the residential car park, Greg felt his mind wander from what Alex had started to say.

Georgina. Alex was right of course, he hadn't given her a moment's thought since the Ramkin. He just couldn't see how she could be connected to recent events. Of course, she had been present for his first flashback, but that had to be coincidence, didn't it? Would they even bother to tamper with her memories, if they knew about her? Where other things which had been taken from his life were precious beyond measure, Georgina was...what? A distraction? A diversion from the tedium of his own existence? It was a gloomy realisation, but he knew that she was both. Certainly not significant enough to be used against him. It would be irritating to find that she had no memory of him, but nothing more than that.

It had been Alex who again pointed out the obvious. Greg's life had been tampered with on or soon before the day he had wandered into the Ramkin Hotel. Since that point everybody who should have known him considered him a stranger, and everybody else thought he was Richard Jameson. Except Georgina. She had dined with Greg Summers, and when his hotel booking vanished, it had still been Greg Summers who she spent the night with. When she departed the following morning, it had been Greg Summers she bade farewell to. They hoped that she would still be a reliable witness to his identity. If she had been overlooked by the enemy, if she still recognised Greg for who he was, she would be *proof*.

What they would then do with her testimony was another question, one that pained Greg in a very personal way. Should her tale ever be used then all the sordid details of his affair would be revealed. If it were possible to salvage Jennifer from the grip of the brainwashing, then it would be to this story that she returned. What would that do to them?

Absurd as it was, this was the most subtle and disturbing thing he had so far faced. Not terrifying in the same way as the creature had been, but striking in a deeper, more insidious way. All his battles to reclaim his identity were based on Jennifer being the reward if he succeeded. Would it be worth the struggle if she returned only to turn her back on him, tormenting him in her own way through abandonment and divorce? Even worse, could their marriage continue as a sterile, lifeless thing forever marred by his betrayal?

He would take the risk. If necessary, he would take any risk. Too much had happened for him to just withdraw from the battle, to flee the breathing nightmares that haunted and taunted him.

"...we going?" The end of the question intruded on his reverie. He flushed with embarrassment.

"Sorry," he replied. "Mind was wandering. What did you say?"

"I was just asking how we get there."

Greg thought about it. "I'm not sure. I walked there from a car park last time."

"Fine, we'll leave the car at my hotel. Will you be all right from there?" Alex was looking at the road, but his face was creased with concern. With a sigh, Greg realised this was going to happen every time his concentration lapsed. Alex was all too aware that he was dealing with a man having difficulty holding firm to his identity.

"I'll find it. And I really was just thinking."

Alex glanced across, surprised. "I'm that transparent?"

"In a word, yes."

"Sorry, I just can't help..."

Greg cut the apology short. "No offence taken. One us should be watching me. As I don't seem able to catch my personality swings until after the fact, it's up to you."

Alex nodded. "I'm honoured," he said.

It was an unnerving experience to be walking the city streets like a man with nothing to fear, though Greg knew his

paranoia stemmed more from Alex's elaborate precautions than any real sense of things amiss. Alex thought it important not to be seen in public together, which was a sensible enough thought given that the hotel manager was still Greg's only unseen card in whatever game he played. What had really set his imagination alight was Carlisle's secondary goal, to see if he could spot any pursuers. In trying to do that, he was tailing him on his walk, at a considerable distance.

Greg walked with as much purpose as he could, but it was like having an itch between the blades of his shoulders. Knowing Alex was following made him want to turn and see if he was still there, watching, keeping him safe.

His awareness of the people around him had grown exponentially. Not a minute passed without him thinking he had just caught a glimpse of the thing's human disguise.

The corner of his eye caught long brown hair blowing in the wind. He forced his head not to whip round and look.

Alex, did you see that? Was it him?

A tall man in jeans and a T-shirt brushed him at a traffic light.

Alex, he's found me! Are you watching?

Twice he found himself ready to break into a run and flee, just to get as far away as possible from where he was. Someplace safe, and enclosed, and protected, and warm, and secret and...

He was there. Messop and Son Photographic Studios. Sweat soaked the fabric of his shirt. He opened the door and stepped inside, turning as the door closed and the bell rang to look out of the window at the street. Nothing. People. Ordinary people completing their random errands, on an average day.

"Feeling the heat, hm? It's an uncommonly warm day for the time of year." Startled, Greg turned. Forcing a grin to open his face, he stepped up to the counter.

"Mr Messop, good morning." He wished he could power the croak from his voice, but the dry panic had yet to fade. "I called by a couple of days ago."

"Ah yes. The unusual service." For a moment Greg thought the old man might leave it at that, locking the two of them in uncomfortable eye contact, but then Messop turned his myopic, NHS-enhanced stare away and vanished into the back room. His voice drifted to reception.

"If you would care to wait a moment, I shall retrieve your photographs."

For the few minutes that Greg was left alone his panic returned tenfold. Glancing back at the door, he expected it to shatter inwards and reveal the tall, longhaired man. Or the skinless tormentor from his nightmare life.

The door was still closed when Messop returned.

"Hm. Did my best you understand. Interesting work, to be sure." Greg could no longer speak. He had already heard the facts in the developer's voice. Suddenly the room was very, very large and Greg very small.

Sitting in the transport café where he and Alex had agreed to meet, he avoided considering the implications of the morning. Alex would soon be there. Alex would know what it meant. He had become used to handing his life over to strangers. Only this last thought reached his face, placing there a lifeless smile. It flickered away, and anybody watching might doubt it had been there at all.

Within five minutes of him choosing a table and sitting, Alex arrived. Impassive, Greg watched him enter, seeing his friend grin as he surveyed the plastic cheerfulness of the place. Each garish colour in turn defied its fellows to complement it, forming a mutant rainbow of the room. The smell of frying proteins hung made his eyes water. Four other people sat in the café. A young couple feasted on plates of chips, while an elderly pair hunched two tables down from Greg, sipping from mugs of tea.

Alex pulled up a chair. "I certainly claim no expertise in the ways of espionage, but I think they're probably harmless." He caught Greg's eye then stopped, noting the blankness, seeing the nothing. "Greg..."

Raising a marionette-like hand, Greg stopped the question before it was asked. "You first," he said.

Alex paused, then nodded. "Fair enough. As far as I can tell, there was no one following you. I dropped a reasonable way back, so nobody should have associated me with you. Better safe than sorry." Again, he paused. When the question finally came it was gentle, almost tender. "You?"

Greg winced, for this was a moment he had dreaded since leaving the shop forty-five minutes earlier. Reaching inside his jacket pocket, he pulled forth the photos which had been returned to him, tossing them on the table as though glad to be rid of them.

"He couldn't find anything wrong with them."

Stunned, Alex sat back in his chair and stared out of the window. For a time they remained like that, two men sat opposite each other in a small café in the centre of London. The respectful silence hanging between them was tangible, a force field keeping the world away. Greg noticed, from the corner of his eye, a waitress come towards them to take an order. She came up short a few feet away, gazed at the two men, then turned and walked back to the counter, too aware of the moment to intrude.

When he could bear the silence no longer, he broke the spell. "Well?"

"Well what?"

"What does it mean?"

Alex looked back up, surprised. Studying Greg's face for a moment, his surprise grew to astonishment. "You mean you don't know?"

Greg shook his head, stubborn to the last. "Don't know what? This is hardly the time for games."

"Games? Christ." Again he searched Greg's face, perhaps looking for some glint of humour or misunderstanding. On discovering nothing, resignation collapsed over him. "You're in shock, or active denial. You know what this means and you're waiting for me to reassure you that it's not the case." He looked into Greg's eyes, sorrowful, then shook his head. "I'm not going to do that. I can't see how such pretence is going to hand us anything but more problems. So I'll be blunt. There is a very real chance that you are Richard Jameson."

Greg flinched. He knew he had heard the words, but was unable to decipher their meaning. He shook his head.

"I'm Gregory Summers."

"Listen to me. Listen carefully. These photographs are real. You've confirmed they show you as a young boy. You've had them authenticated. These photographs are your childhood."

"No. I'm Greg Summers."

Alex clenched a fist, frustrated. Picking up one of the photos, he turned it to face Greg. It showed him as a child, alongside his ersatz mother and brother. Speaking with increasing conviction, Alex ploughed on. "Explain this to me, then. Explain this photo. You have to consider the possibility that Richard Jameson is the original personality, and Greg Summers the impostor. Is that really less believable than anything you've told me?"

Greg was coming to life now, denial threading hot anger through his stomach. "Alex, I know you mean well, but I know who I am. The photo is confusing, but I'm still Greg Summers. Even the crazy old man who looked at it only said that any tampering was beyond his skill to detect. It doesn't mean he was right. Don't you see?" His voice was hissing now, sounding unhinged even to his own ears. *"This is what they want me to think!"* Closing his eyes, he tried to will himself calm. "You're reading too much into this."

"The tobacco." Now Alex was the one fighting to contain himself. "Greg, the tobacco."

Confused, he shook his head. "I don't..."

"We know Jameson smokes, yes? You wanted that cigarette, you enjoyed it. You smoked it easily, without coughing or feeling nauseous or any of the dozen symptoms I would expect of a first time smoker."

"Jameson's personality took over. We've covered this Alex, the brainwashing..."

"Your mind can be brainwashed. Your lungs, I suspect, can't. You didn't cough. I thought it was odd, but you were so sure you were Summers..."

Greg spoke like an automaton. "I am."

Hostility hung between them, palpable and bitter. Reading the surety in Alex's eyes pushed a race of thoughts through Greg's head. *I trust him,* he thought, *I know I trust him. Now he's taking their side, trying to confuse me. But I trust him. Nobody else has helped me. Nobody else has accepted me. Nobody else has let me cry. I trust him. Why is he doing this to me? Doesn't he know how close I am to losing myself? Can I prove myself to him? Can I...*

"Georgina," he said, and it was almost a gasp. Seeing the confusion on Alex's face, he continued, words tripping over each other in their quest to convince. "Please Alex, don't make up your mind yet. We stick with the plan. Let me talk to George. Let me find out who she's been sleeping with for three months. If she won't accept me as Greg then I swear I'll listen. But let me try. Please?"

To his eternal relief, Alex nodded. "Agreed. It can't hurt to have all the facts before we try to work this out. Just promise that if she doesn't tell you what you want to hear, you'll be open to this."

Grateful for the respite, feeling like a man on trial, Greg nodded. His treacherous subconscious, however, trembled in anticipation of the response Georgina might give.

In his heart, he already knew who she had dined with that day.

19 VERIFICATION

Georgina Hood had seduced Greg in a bar four doors down from his office. It was early evening and Greg, not normally a solitary drinker, had finished a hard day. Going straight home to Jennifer was a bad idea, recent experience had told him she would only become the focus of his frustrations, so a chance to shake off the stresses of the day was important. It was quiet inside, the afternoon mass having left for familial homes, the evening crowd still grooming and preparing for a night out. This left the brightly coloured bar, replete with neon lights, only a handful of patrons. Greg had stared into his second lager, finding the whole atmosphere annoying and pretentious.

Georgina approached him as he ordered his third drink. Tight jeans wrapped around graceful, muscular legs, and a tight T-shirt made an asset of her delicate breasts. What struck Greg most surely, however, was her hair. Blonde, naturally curled, and hanging loosely about her waist, it rippled with the tempo of her words. Sky blue eyes flashed above a mouth which contrived a pout to suit every emotion.

Small talk ensued, and then Greg had proceeded to buy her a drink. Several glasses later, more than he had ever intended to stay for, they were having frenzied sex against the back wall of the car park.

It need not have gone further than that. They had agreed to meet again in two days, but it had been the booze speaking. In the sober light of the following morning Greg could have dismissed the idea as foolish, but he did not. Excited by this vibrant young woman and her attraction to him, he kept the appointment.

Thus it began. At least, Greg hoped that was how it had begun. Despite his assurances to Alex, he was far along the road of doubt. There was no question that these memories were vivid and real to him, but he was no fool. The validity of his memory was the whole focus of his dilemma.

Driving to her flat, the weight of his situation bore more heavily on him than ever. This would be the final proof he needed to convince both he and Alex of his identity. The reality had hit home. He really could be Jameson.

A shudder took him as he glanced across at Alex. No help there. His friend was fixing his attention on the road ahead, trying to avoid further conversation until he had fulfilled his promise to meet Georgina. Greg regretted his hostility in the café, for Alex had only been trying to help. The very nature of the discussion had caused Greg's violent reaction. It questioned the very fundaments of his identity in ways he could not dismiss. As well as that, he resented that Alex had been the one to bring the topic up. The man who had done so much for him, supporting and helping him, taking him at his word time and again. When Alex doubted, it threatened what little security he had left. Raising the question had been for Greg's own good, but it had also been a rejection of sorts. Despite the short time they had known each other, perhaps because of the heightened circumstances they found themselves in, he had come to trust Alex, and his opinions counted for much.

Knowing now that his anger in the café had been misdirected, he felt easier in himself. After he had faced the next trial he would apologise, but that ordeal was fast approaching. Already the car was pulling into one of the parking spaces outside the flat where Georgina lived.

As the engine died there was a moment of intense silence between the two men. Neither looked at the other, but there nevertheless existed a communication between them. It was the silent, respectful support given to the terminally diseased. Both men now accepted the truth. Speaking to Georgina was just a formailty. Greg Summers would die in just a few minutes, never having existed. Richard Jameson would be born anew. The shiny sleek car in which they travelled was a substitute hearse.

Alex was first to intrude on the silence. "Well?"

Greg grunted, not wanting to stand up yet. If he stood first it would become obvious that he was shaking, and could not trust his legs to hold him. Yet it was his own funeral march they were playing. Gingerly, as though discovering for the first time how to walk, he stepped from the car.

Turning to face the flat, Greg wished that he believed in a god. It would be reassuring to trust his fate to a higher power. Until recently he had believed in only two things - the love he shared with Jennifer, and his own ability to survive whatever life threw his way. Those beliefs had both been savagely ripped from him.

Jennifer was gone.

He might not even exist.

That was the most frightening thing. He was more and more certain that, regardless his memories, he had until recently lived life as a man called Richard Jameson. If this were so then he had been Gregory for a matter of weeks, probably only days. That had been his entire life.

He ceased to care whether Jameson was the true identity or not. He was Summers now, inherently Summers. Summers was breathing the thick city air. Summers was terrified at the thought of knocking on the door of the flat. Summers. Not Jameson. If he reverted to Jameson, would it be like dying? Would the original man, once in control of his life again, be glad of Greg's passing? Whatever his faults, Greg could not believe himself so worthless that he should be so easily discarded. Whether he had existed for thirty-two hours or thirty-two years, he wanted to live.

The immensity of the thought set him shaking again, then Alex was beside him, lending his strength. Greg tried to smile, turning his attention back to the flat. She lived on the second floor of a two-storey house, Greg remembered that she shared the hall and stairway with an elderly couple on the ground floor. He had only met this pair in passing. During his very brief visits in the past there had been time for only the most physical of social activities.

Wondering if those days had ever been more than a sophisticated lie, he pushed open the gate and walked up the garden path. Allowing himself no pause, he knocked briskly on the door.

A horrible moment of déjà vu swamped him, and it took only a moment to realise why this was all so familiar. For a second after the door opened he actually saw Jennifer standing there, all recognition and warmth gone from her face.

It was not Jennifer who now stood in front of him. It was Georgina. The only similarity between the two faces, real and remembered, were the uncomprehending looks they wore. She didn't know him. Alex had been right. Her glare was the barrel of a chambered rifle. This was his execution.

"Greg? What the fuck are you doing here?"

All the strength flushed from his body. Sagging, he discovered that he had been holding his breath. Releasing it eased the pressure in his chest just as her words sealed away the doubt in his mind. Dizzy with relief, the world spinning around him, he could think of only one thing to say to this beautiful, redeeming angel. "I think I love you," he managed, before he passed out.

Shaking. Voices. Greg was becoming very familiar with the sensation of disembodied unreality that accompanied a sudden waking from blackness.

"Greg? Honey?" Georgina. A woman who loved him. Right then, that was worth waking up to. He cracked open his eyes. Above him was her bedroom ceiling, and it amused him to realise he had never seen it in daylight before. The single mattress on which he lay was familiar to him, though. He could almost smell the musk of sex in the air.

"Greg? Are you feeling better babe?" He let his head swing round to the side. Framed against the large bedroom window, she was haloed by the afternoon sun. His redeeming angel.

"Much better, thanks. How long?"

"Couple of hours, I think. You sure you're okay?"

"It was just...relief, I suppose. You have no idea how many reasons I have to thank you." Or perhaps she did. Her flickering, never still eyes reflected deeper concern. Still groggy, he lost the thought before he could ask about it.

"You suit your hair back." Had he really nothing more important than that to say? Still, he had never seen her with a ponytail. In fact he had never seen her in casual clothes. He supposed that she spent only a small part of her life dressed to impress him. She should have made less effort. The baggy blouse and torn jeans she wore were a refreshing, plain glamour. She was about to speak, but stopped. "Go on," he said.

"Okay," she had difficulty forming her question. "I've been talking to your friend Alex. He came out with some pretty weird shit."

"Ah." That was it, the thought he had lost.

"Is it true babe?" The dam broke. "Only I didn't know whether he was causing you trouble and I should phone the police or something. He frightened me Greg. I mean, when I say weird, I mean *weird*. I thought he might be, well, dangerous or something, and you've never mentioned him, and you both just show up like that." Her pout tried to perform fear, confusion, strength, and concern all in one moment. He decided that the only thing to do was kiss it, and did. It was a long kiss, velvet soft and passionately felt. As he pulled away, he was laughing.

"Do you know," he said, "I haven't felt this good in a long time." Still chuckling, he met her demure, puzzled stare. Trying hard not to think of the lean, graceful body beneath those loose folds of blouse, he decided to be blunt. "George, I don't know how much of the full story he told you, but I trust him. I'll take a guess and say yes. Every word he said was true."

Her expression was worth capturing on canvas.

They entered the living room together to find Alex waiting for them. He lounged in the moth-eaten settee sat squarely in the middle of the small room. As they walked, Greg saw Alex engrossed in a *Diagnosis: Murder* rerun.

His wry glance was noted, and Alex smiled his angular smile. "There was nothing else on," he explained, "and I needed to do something. I hope you've managed to convince the delightful Georgina that I'm not, in fact, utterly insane."

"I think we at least have the benefit of the doubt."

"Good. Well done. Now you might want to convince me too. I felt bloody silly telling her about your recent adventures."

"Adventures?" Greg took a seat next to him. "You make it sound like an Enid Blyton."

"Indeed. Five Have Fun With Brainwashing. Childhood classic."

Georgina giggled as she wandered across to her tiny kitchenette. "Does anyone want coffee?" Greg nodded, though Alex declined.

"How much did you tell her?" Greg asked while Georgina was busy.

"Everything I can remember. I told it from your point of view, hence being forced to question my sanity. Again."

Georgina arrived with the gratefully received coffee, pulling up a chair to seat herself. All eyes turned expectantly to Greg.

Feeling self-conscious, he ran through his ideas once more, trying to see if any were flawed. Being honest, he had to admit that they all were, but he could find few improvements to make at that point. The unofficial conference began. "I want to thank both of you, first." There was more to that than the words expressed, but now was not the time. "You've already done far more for me than I could possibly have asked. Now you can stop if you want." He inhaled deeply, for he was offering to relinquish a great deal. "I can't ask for more. I won't. Neither of you have any real idea of how much danger there is in this, but please believe that I do. I'm frightened. If you got hurt because of this it would damage me more than they ever could themselves."

They looked at him for a moment. Alex broke the stillness. "My choice to make though, isn't it?"

Twitches at the corner of Greg's mouth threatened a smile. "Well, yes. If you feel that you must burden my further adventures with your presence, then there's nothing I can do to stop you." The smile broke, Alex returned it.

Georgina was more hesitant. "Babe, I don't know. I'm not even sure how much of all this I believe." Greg raised his eyebrows, and she blushed. "I get you're in some kind of trouble, but aliens and mind control?"

She was worried that she might offend him with her scepticism, but she needn't have been. Greg knew full well how implausible his situation was. His reply was tender and firm. "Act, for the moment, as if it were all true. Everything. Pretend you doubt nothing you've heard, then base your decision on that."

Her eyes widened. She resembled a rabbit pinned to the road by fast approaching headlights. "Greg, it's scary." He nodded, and she continued. "But whatever trouble you're in, I want to help. I love you."

A variety of emotions competed for his attention; he wanted very much to kiss this brave, wonderful woman. For the first time, perhaps, he was seeing the person behind the make-up and lewd sex. Catching the look in his eyes, she gave him a smile both shy and aggressive with anticipation.

Alex coughed, and Greg broke the moment before it could develop.

"Right," he said, failing to cover his embarrassment. "Before I tell you what I want to do, we have to prove to Alex that I'm Greg Summers. It shouldn't be too difficult now." Alex was attentive, paying close heed to this new argument. Greg addressed him directly. "Do you remember, in Richard Jameson's diary, that he had a meeting with Stewart on the Friday I came to your hotel? Well, it was missed. But Stewart implied that it was a regular meeting, he mentioned nothing about Jameson having missed any others. The absence was supposed to be a new thing, I think." He paused to see if Alex was following the argument. His friend gestured him to go on.

"Well, I can't have attended any of those meetings as Jameson. Tell him why George."

She caught his glance and understood. "I've been having an...a relationship with Greg for the last three months."

"See? I've been *Summers* for at least three months. Richard, according to his brother, had only been missing for a few days." He held his breath, hoping that Alex would not find some hole, some vital flaw in his argument.

"There's Facebook, too," said George.

Greg turned to her, surprised, and then shocked at his own idiocy. "I haven't even looked. Bloody hell, Alex. Why didn't we check Facebook?" Alex shrugged, and they both turned to Georgina.

She looked from one to the other, nervous. "Babe, you unfriended me a week ago. I haven't heard from you since. That's why I was surprised to see you. I tried to friend you again, in case it was a glitch, but nobody with your name looked like you, and they'd all done the privacy thing, so I couldn't check them out properly."

Alex shook his head in wonder, as he pulled his own phone out. "Wait a second." Tapping the icon for his Facebook app, he searched Greg's name, and a column of images were displayed. A quick scan, a tap, and he brought up a picture. Reversing the phone, he showed it to Greg. "That him?" Greg nodded, the thing with the man's face, laughing, long hair tossed back. It made him sick, knowing the creature was able to masquerade as him online, to anyone in the world. Alex ran another search, and showed him the phone again. It was Greg's face now, and the name above it read 'Richard Jameson'. "Don't suppose you'd care to guess a password, would you?"

"Wouldn't know where to start."

"Fair enough." Alex looked again at the phone, then slipped it into his pocket. "They're thorough. Have to give them that."

"You believe me?"

Alex nodded. "You're Greg Summers. Which leaves us the mystery of the photos."

"Not much of a mystery. I'd be happy to guess that anybody with the technology to brainwash people might have the resources to produce faultless photographic composites." Alex nodded, not entirely happy with the answer but willing to concede the point for now.

"So," said George. "What now?"

What now indeed. The fight for his name had become a team effort, and he ventured his suggestion with a smile on his lips. "Now," he said in a conspiratorial whisper, "we kidnap my wife. We're going to abduct Jennifer Summers from her cosy home."

The silence was thunderous, and long. Alex just stared at him, mouth hanging open. Georgina refused to meet his eyes, her gaze panicking across the room as she considered the implications of the idea.

With unnerving timing, the phone rang. All three jumped in their seats, then laughed at each other's reactions. Smiling, Georgina rose to answer it. When she picked up the receiver however, her smile faded. Taking a step back, she dropped the telephone as though it had bitten her.

Greg snatched it up. Nothing, just the buzz of a closed line. Replacing it, he turned to his lover and caught her shoulders, meeting her frightened gaze, forcing himself to ask the question in a calm voice. "George, who was it?"

She shook her head. "I don't know, they didn't give a name."

"What did they say?"

Meeting his gaze again, Georgina seemed to draw strength from his eyes. "It was a message for you. He said that he knew where you were. That was it."

A startled coughing from Alex was the only response she received.

20 ABDUCTION

After a hasty departure from Georgina's flat, one marked mostly by paranoia and nerves, the rest of their plans were made at Alex's. It was still the only place Greg thought might have slipped past the guard of his enemies. When they had settled there, curtains drawn, he outlined his idea.

"Georgina, as far as the police will be concerned, is an unreliable witness. Our relationship was...well...a secret. There's only our word that it happened at all. There's no proof that she even knew me. The only person who can help me now is Jennifer."

Alex pointed out the obvious flaw. "Greg, she *believes* this other man is you. As she understands it, she's met you just once, when you knocked on her door, and that was hardly the best of introductions."

"I know. That's why we're going to kidnap her."

Despite their protests, Greg finally convinced them that the plan had merit. Jennifer would be abducted at some point when her ersatz husband was away from home. Once she had been brought back to the flat, Greg would try to find a way past her brainwashing in the hope that she might reach the same level of awareness as he. It was a slim chance, but also the only thing he could come up with that might work.

It would be painful, he knew. He clearly remembered her fear when he broke into the house. If she looked at him with terror in her eyes, his heart would break. It would be up to Alex and George to keep him strong

Of the two, it was Georgina who had most amazed him with her mettle. She must know that she was now fighting for the end of their relationship, but she had not wavered. Again, he was struck by how remarkable a woman he had involved himself with, and resolved to make the most of the time left to them.

After the plan had been settled and approved, it came time to designate roles. Despite Greg's protests, Georgina had been the one chosen to watch the house for the creature's departure. Alex had made the most sense of the decision.

"Calm down, he had soothed after Greg threatened to do it alone rather than endanger her. "It isn't that we have a lot of choice. We know for a fact that the creature owned photographs of me meeting you, and you can't stake the place out yourself. There's a chance that Georgina is a face it doesn't know." He was right, but it was the least satisfactory part of the plan. That left Alex and he to commit the abduction. It was a simple idea, but a one-shot only gambit. If it failed, the enemy would be forewarned. There would be no further opportunity to try the same thing.

Once Georgina had called them from her mobile, she would return to the flat by the quickest means and await their arrival. Meanwhile, Greg and Alex would drive to the house and snatch Jennifer.

Two major worries plagued Greg, the first of which was that the creature might return during the attempt. Secondly, this was no remote hideaway they were planning to raid. It was a house slap-bang in the middle of suburbia. Sleepy, yes.

But how far could they push their luck? It was unlikely that the creature would depart at night unless it had very good reason to do so, especially after Greg's last break-in, so they had to make the snatch during the day.

Risky, but there was no choice. The creature had already found them once. It could do so again. They were running out of time

Greg sat on the couch, glowering at the telephone. Georgina had been gone for four hours.

"Staring at it won't help," Alex told him for the third time.

"Neither will meaningless clichés," Greg snapped. Regretting it at once, he added, "I'm just worried about her, that's all. She's risking a lot by helping me. More than you understand. If you had only seen this thing…"

Alex sighed. "You've got to realise how hard it is to see through your eyes, Greg. If we took you all the way at face value we'd have to be insane."

"I know. I've put you in a position you can't even grasp."
Alex sat back in the chair. "I think it will be enough that we're up against anything at all. I'm no hero. I'm frightened. Whether I'm facing a demon or a serial killer is much the same to me."

Before he could continue, the telephone rang. Startled, his heart pounding next to his tonsils, Greg reached for the handset. Alex caught his arm before he could pick it up.

"Best I answer it," he said. "It might not be her." Picking up the receiver, he listened for a moment, then replaced it.

"It left a couple of minutes ago."

It was the drive that most panicked Greg. Taking nearly thirty-five minutes in all, every one was a wasted lifetime. It was impossible to know what they would find at the house. Perhaps the thing had only left briefly, to perform a short errand. In the time it took them to get there it could easily have returned without them knowing about it.

Each age that passed on the endless journey gave Greg time to doubt. What if Jennifer struggled? Would they have to use force? Was he even capable of performing an act against her will? Perhaps he should have left the confrontation entirely in Alex's hands, but selfishness prevented him from doing so. Action empowered him, made him strong. By being proactive he was transformed from victim to aggressor, a feeling which was necessary if he was to make himself continue. Handing over his fate to somebody else was no option at all.

The eternal pilgrimage came to an end as they eased into Fontside Avenue, parking close to the house.

"Nice place," Alex said. Greg could hear the trepidation in his voice and was relieved. The fear was not a personal thing, but a common enemy.

"Let's get this over with," he said, his whisper making him feel foolish in broad daylight.

Exiting the car, they walked to the front step, trying to look like two men without abduction on their minds. Greg stood to one side of the door, out of sight, as Alex took a deep breath. He felt like some petty criminal, the lowest kind of thug. Could he have imagined committing such an act three months ago? For the first time he realised how irrevocable the changes recent events had forced in him were. It was something else the creature would be paid back for.

Alex pressed the doorbell.

Forever passed as they waited.

The door started to open.

Events executed a dramatic turn of pace, from agonised crawl to blinding sprint. Before the door was fully open, Alex shoved it all the way back, stepping in. There was a small shriek, the sound of a one-sided struggle. Greg realised he had yet to enter.

As though moving too swiftly would fracture this fragile reality, he stepped around the doorway. His first instinct when he saw Alex sitting astride his wife was one of violence, an urge to protect the woman he loved. It vanished when Alex turned towards him, fear in his eyes, as though Greg could somehow make this all stop. One of his hands was over her mouth, another held her arms together at the wrists.

Feeling sick to the soul, Greg closed the door behind him. Moving towards the grappling pair, he bent low next to Jennifer.

"Please. Please stop struggling." She saw him then, and with that recognition came terror. This was the man who had attacked her, beaten her husband, and sprayed her hallway with blood. She was in the hands of a lunatic. Reading her thoughts was easy, dealing with them less so. Greg's eyes welled up. "Look, I don't want to hurt you. I promise you we don't want that. You won't be harmed in any way, but you are going to come with us. I'm going to let you go again. Do you understand?" He doubted that she did, but he would have time to work on that later. For now it was enough that she had ceased fighting Alex.

"Can you hold her?" *Can you forcibly restrain my wife? Can you pin her violently to the floor?* Such a simple question. Would she ever be able to forgive him?

"I think so, now she's stopped chewing my palm." Greg winced in sympathy, then hurried to the kitchen. Rummaging through the fitted units, he found what he was looking for. Sellotape. Earlier Alex had been so adamant this would be insufficient to bind somebody that Greg had been forced to demonstrate. Once it was wrapped several times around his wrists, Alex had been forced to concede the point.

Taking the roll back to the hallway, he squatted on the pastel blue carpet that was not his. Taking a clean handkerchief from his pocket, he taped the cloth over her mouth to muffle any cries she wanted to give. Next he took her wrists from Alex, allowing his friend to help in turning her over before strapping her arms together behind her back. It was all performed with clinical speed, as though somebody else had taken over his body and allowed him to simply spectate.

"I'm sorry," he whispered to her. "I wish I didn't have to do this." Moving down to her ankles, he used the rest of the roll to secure her legs.

Alex stood up, trembling from the exertion. "Feisty woman, your wife."

Jennifer tried to shriek into the handkerchief, and Greg winced.

"Not now," he told Alex under his breath. "She's panicked enough as it is. We'll shake up her world view later, when she can at least mull it over with a coffee."

Alex gazed at his masticated palm. "I wish there were somebody here to note that down. You'd be immortalised as the world's most civilised kidnapper."

Greg stifled a half-hysterical laugh. "Get the car, I'll meet you out back in five." Rather than take Jennifer out of the front door, they had decided to use the lane that ran behind the rear gardens of the street. Alex nodded and left.

Leaving Greg alone with his wife.

Not like this, he thought. *It shouldn't be like this.* Anger simmered his blood, and he punched the wall to put it somewhere else. Jennifer jumped at the sound and Greg cursed himself. Kneeling, he tried to soothe her. Stroking her soft brown hair, he noticed she was trembling. At his touch, her whole body tensed. Sickened by the thoughts that could be running through her head, he tried to reassure her.

"Jen, I'm not a rapist. It couldn't be further from my mind." As soon as he said it, he realised with horror that it wasn't true. She was bound, unable to prevent him acting. Seeing her jeans flow over slim hips, noticing the line of her bra through the flimsy white of her blouse, he wanted to take her, and reclaim her from the thing which had stolen her.

He knew it was beyond him to do anything with the notion but recoil, yet the realisation that he was tempted terrified him. To physically take from her what she would no longer give willingly...

Perverse as it was, he wished that Georgina were there, just to give him the emotional boost he craved. Sitting in the hallway that was not his, watching the wife who did not know him, he felt devoid of sense.

It was a relief when he heard the car pull up, and before he could think, the handle of the front door was in his grasp. Only then did he pause. The front door was somehow significant.

Alex was driving around the back way. Greg would be unable to hear him from where he sat. The creature had returned.

Reaching the same conclusion, Jennifer began to squeal anew. Mouth dry, Greg locked the front door, just as he heard a car door slam in the driveway. Bending, he hauled Jennifer over his shoulder in a crude fireman's lift and headed for the kitchen. Shutting this door too, he paused to adjust his wife's position on his shoulder, losing valuable seconds in the act. She was kicking, but the fight was nowhere near as extreme as the one she had engaged Alex in. *Perhaps she's in shock*, he thought. *Perhaps I am too.* Keys turned in the front lock, and he bolted for the rear door.

Once in the garden, leaving the kitchen entrance ajar so that the noise of it closing would not draw unwelcome attention, he staggered down the garden path to where Alex was waiting. His friend's eyes widened as he saw them approach at speed, the question forming on his lips as he opened the gate for them.

Greg nodded before he could ask. "The thing. It's home." Alex paled at the news, turning to open the back door of the car. Still struggling, Jennifer was unceremoniously dumped on the seat. Greg tried to look back at the house, but the thick hedge bordering the garden prevented him from seeing if they were being pursued yet.

Alex was already starting the engine as Greg climbed into the passenger seat. It stalled at the first attempt, and Greg swore under his breath. Fixing his gaze on the gate, he counted the passing moments away. *Any second now*, he warned himself.

As the car growled to life, the thing burst from the gate and threw itself at Alex's door. An aeon passed, enough time for Greg to see the unbridled hate on the currently human face. Enough time for him to memorise each line of fury, every nuance of spite.

Enough time for Alex to begin reversing the car down the narrow lane. Missing the door, the creature found itself doubled over the bonnet. As Alex, in full panic, accelerated his frantic reverse, Greg realised it had hold of the car, was pulling itself towards the windscreen. The face was inches from the back of Alex's head, eyes burning. When Alex glanced back out the front, it changed.

The change was faster this time, the skin running away as though liquid were a natural state for it to assume.

For a second Alex only watched, open-mouthed. Then he screamed. As he did the car swerved, gouging branches from the bushes, sending an explosion of autumn-brown leaves into the air. Greg lunged for the steering wheel, grabbing and yanking. For a moment it was too late, a collision was unavoidable, but then the vehicle slewed in the other direction, before straightening up. Alex was deafening now, frozen in terror, but his foot was still pressed hard against the accelerator, and for that Greg thanked God.

The creature was not doing anything, which was the most terrifying thing. It just stared at Alex, exposing him to edges of the world he had never imagined, and Alex howled back.

They shot out of the hedge-lined alley and on to the main road. A motorcycle, given no time to stop, careened into the front of the car. The crash rocked Greg; he heard a thump from the back as Jennifer fell to the floor, her muffled yelp almost lost in the din. The stunned cyclist sailed forward, an outstretched arm snagging the creature in desperation, ripping it from the bonnet.

Alex snapped from his shock, swung the car around, and was away.

Fifteen minutes later they were nearing the Ramkin Hotel, Greg having baulked at the risk of going back to Alex's now that his friend had been seen. They had, to all intents and purposes, just committed a kidnapping. All the creature had to do was play the concerned husband and report the matter to the police. There was also the fact of the hit-and-run on the motorcyclist. Alex's car would be identified, the police would go to his flat and the game would be lost.

Regaining some of his self-assurance, Alex had suggesting holing up in the basement of the hotel. It was mostly unused nowadays, being separate from the beer cellar, and would be comfortable enough to stay in until they could resolve the matter with Jennifer.

Pulling up at the back of the building, they lifted her between them and walked through the evening shadows to the back doors.

"This one leads straight down," said Alex, as he pulled a set of keys from his pocket. Unlocking it took an uncomfortable few moments, Greg shuffling as Jennifer kicked, hoping they were not being watched from the tiny windows in the building opposite. Then they entered, Alex locking the door behind them.

At first all was darkness, then Alex found the light switch. Shadows fled as Greg surveyed their temporary home. It was very large and mostly empty. Stone steps led down, from the landing on which he stood to a huge dust-filled space. Against the far wall loomed two enormous water heaters. He glanced at Alex.

"It's fine, the system's automatic nowadays, it's all on timers. Caretaker only comes down here when they need maintenance." Greg nodded and worked his way down the stairs. Threading past the various brick supports leading up to the ceiling, he strode over to the heaters. It was warmer there, and he laid Jennifer on the concrete floor.

Turning to Alex, the echo of the room startled him when he spoke. "You need to ditch the car somewhere. If it's left outside it will take the police all of fifteen seconds to find us. Also, you should phone George and get her to bring us some blankets."

Alex nodded, then climbed back up the steps, his weariness and shock heavy on him. As the door at the top shut them in, Gregory Summers, for the second time that day, was left alone with his helpless wife.

21 PROGRESS

Growing, filling, expanding - oh, but this is *power*. Again the tank drains. Again she exults as she feeds. *Better than it once was*, she thinks, *better than the old times*. As waves of pleasure and sustenance break over her body, images replace the thoughts in her head.

Chasing. Feasting. Her first time. Men at arms. Travelling. Fleeing. Hiding. Always consuming. Countless decades. The moon.

The tank fills anew. Breathing heavily now - and what a strange thrill it is to breathe, to suck cold air - she checks the tubes running into her arm. Embedded deep in the flesh of each wrist are the four plastic drips that empower her. *What a brave new world this is. What marvels are here to find.*

Yes, the old days. Could it even have been theorised, back then, how completely one could consume? Could evolution ever have offered her alternatives such as this? Unlikely, for man had created a world capable of usurping the very Nature which spawned him. She watched it happen, her and a few others. Now they had the true power.

Stroking the needle thin incisions at her wrists, shuddering at the ripples of sexuality even this small pressure creates, she once more turns her attention to the specimen, now no more than a loosely bound collection of organs, limbs, and soul.

With a small, exquisite sigh, she awaits the penultimate draining.

22 INQUISITION

Alone with his wife. Greg shuddered. Nearly an hour had passed since Alex left, and the base urge to *reclaim* writhed in him again. It was hard to think about anything else. He had sported a near constant erection for the last thirty minutes. Whenever he shifted position, anticipatory shivers hurtled through his groin.

Hating himself for the memory, he pictured the time they had sex in her uncle's wine cellar. Crude, violent sex. Pinning her to the dusty wall, ripping aside cotton, forcing his way in as they screamed and gasped their way to rough, thrilling orgasms. Would this be so different?

Penis twitching, he looked to where she lay by the water heater. Perhaps that would break through the brainwashing, make her body remember what her mind could not. A reminder of the special intimacy they shared might be all it took to make her his again.

He rose from the step he was sitting on. Wishing that his movements felt less predatory, knowing this would be for her ultimate good, he moved in on her. Despite everything, perhaps because of it, she was asleep, her chest rising and falling in gentle, inviting ways. Her blouse had been pulled out of her jeans during the earlier struggle, exposing smooth pale skin. He reached out a hand to touch her there.

Hearing the rattle of the door unlocking, he straightened and whirled round. Georgina slipped in, Alex following and pulling the door shut.

Greg stared at them.

Turned to stare at the woman at his feet.

Like a clockwork man, he oscillated between the two before settling on his wife.

He would have done it.

As Alex reached the bottom of the stairs, Greg stumbled to meet him. Georgina looked on in bemusement as he hugged the larger man. She didn't hear the words Greg breathed into his ear.

"Don't leave me with her again. Please."

Returning the trembling embrace, Alex nodded his head in silent assent.

Alex had brought two full thermos flasks of steaming coffee, a carton of milk, and some sugar with him. He had not bothered with food, as there was an all night takeaway five minutes walk from where they hid. In the back of a large rucksack, four rolled sleeping bags were crammed against the possibility of a cold evening.

Alex was crouched next to Jennifer. "Mrs Summers, my name is Alex Carlisle. I know you're confused and scared, but please allow for the fact that if we wanted to hurt you we'd have done it already." He paused, studying her face to see if she accepted this line of argument. Greg couldn't look at her eyes.

He *would* have hurt her.

She nodded, and Alex continued. "You are here because...well, it's a bit out of the ordinary." He smiled at her, a little rueful. "This pitiable abduction was the only way we could guarantee you would listen to us. That's all we want you to do. We'll ask questions which we hope you'll answer honestly. That's it.

"But that's for later. For the moment we'd like to remove that gag and ask you to join us for coffee. If we do, will you scream?"

From a few feet back, Greg was aware of her eyes flicking between him and Alex. She seemed to have some small trust in his friend. Greg was the one she feared. It was with good reason, and he felt sick to the soul. It had felt so justified. How could such a base urge have been so easy to rationalise?

"Please, Mrs Summers. The only reason for this to be an unpleasant, uncomfortable experience is if you refuse to let us make it otherwise." *Now who qualifies as the world's most convivial kidnapper,* thought Greg.

To his surprise and relief, Jennifer nodded.

"Thank you," said Alex, and meant it. None of the three were cut out for the role of abductor. When Georgina had first seen Jennifer bound at the foot of the enormous heater, the shock had nearly driven her to tears.

As Alex reached for the tape holding the handkerchief over her mouth, he winced in anticipation. "I'll be as gentle as I can." He peeled it back, and removed the cloth. Jennifer pulled in a great lungful of air, but remained otherwise silent.

Greg poured the coffees. Jennifer had milk and two sugars. He didn't even have to think about it. *I am her husband,* it reminded him. *Not some common criminal for her to fear.*

Passing out the four mugs, he sat opposite his wife. A rough circle formed as Alex and Georgina sat to either side of Jennifer. Her eyes were less frightened now, more wary than fearful. He placed her coffee at her feet. She was sat up, the heater to her back.

She spoke for the first time. "I have two..."

"Sugars. And a little milk." Finishing her sentence, he made eye contact for the first time. "I know Jen."

Her eyes widened. "How? How do you know so much about me? You're the man who attacked me, aren't you? The one who beat up my husband? What do you want with us? *Why won't you leave us alone?*"

Withdrawing at the unexpected torrent, Greg was relieved to feel Georgina reach out and place a hand on his knee. He glanced at her and she smiled back, but he still couldn't face answering the questions his wife had put.

Alex saved him from having to. "Mrs Summers, please calm down. I'm being presumptuous in answering for my friend, but none of this is of his choosing. The day he assaulted you was as confusing for him as you, believe me. If he had the chance to go back, I think things would have turned out very differently."

"But who is he? Who are you?" The second question was directed at Greg, but Alex intervened again.

"Sorry. We should be introduced. We all know you, but you're surrounded by strangers." Greg winced at the word, but yes, he was a stranger to her now. "The young lady there is Georgina Hood, though she answers to George."

"Hi," Georgina said. Greg almost giggled at the absurdity. Jennifer was a prisoner, he was a criminal, and his mistress had just been introduced to his wife for the very first time. Stifling himself, not wanting to look as deranged as Jennifer believed, he studied George. She was a little nervous, but considering the enormity of what she was involved in this was the least of what she could be feeling. She was not even particularly upset at meeting her competitor for his affections, appearing more curious than hurt. Explicable, Greg supposed, but still odd.

Jennifer nodded at the tentative introduction before looking again to her forgotten husband, her eyebrows raised in anticipation.

"And this," Alex hesitated as he decided how Greg should be introduced. "Well, for the time being I'll introduce him as Richard Jameson." A quick look of apology. "It's his story we want you to hear."

Jennifer stared at Greg for a moment longer. Was that recognition in her eyes? She turned back to Alex.

"How am I supposed to drink coffee with my hands tied?"

Alex gazed at her, assessing. "Do you mind if we leave your legs bound? It will make us more comfortable if we know you can't make a sudden bolt for the exit." She gave him a curt nod, and he tore the tape from her wrists.

They drank coffee in relative silence, though Alex had to sip from Jennifer's cup before she would risk drinking any herself. He grimaced. "I hate sugar," he said.

When she finished drinking, Alex asked if anybody was hungry. Nobody was. Jennifer was too unnerved to eat, and none of the three abductors could face the thought of food. They knew what was coming. Either Jennifer would remember or they would lose this stage of the game.

"Right," Alex said. "You recognise this man, Richard, as the person who forced his way into your home last week. He assaulted you, beat up your husband, then had a sort of fit. Am I right?" Jennifer was curious now, and nodded eagerly.

"I wanted to call the police, but Greg decided it would be better to let a hospital take him in." Greg twitched as he heard his name applied to the creature, but said nothing. His chance to explain was fast approaching.

"Quite." Alex continued. "Well, from his point of view, he had cause to behave as he did. What I'm about to say will sound strange, but please don't panic." Again she nodded, anxious for an explanation. "Mrs Summers, Jennifer, all three of us have good reason to believe that the man sitting before you is Gregory Summers. The man you married. Your husband."

For a long moment Jennifer stared at the hotel manager's angular face. She swung round to look at Greg. *Please*, he thought, *let this be enough. Let her remember.*

She tilted back her head and laughed.

Greg stood, unable to stay still. Pacing to the other side of the room, he banged his fist against the dry stone wall. It hurt. He punched again. It was never going to be so easy, he had known that, but to hear her ridiculing the very idea that she might love him was cutting. Again he lashed out, drawing blood. Then Georgina was there, holding him at the elbow.

"Babe, we'll do it. We'll get there. And if I don't get a chance before she remembers, I want to give you this." Taking his face in both hands, she kissed him hard. After a startled second he responded, wondering if it would be for the last time.

Georgina broke off. Greg realised she was responding to the lessening of the background laughter.

"We should go back." She was right. Letting her lead him by the hand, they returned to the heater.

Jennifer was still chuckling, shaking her head as she tried to stop. Greg watched her brown hair swish from side to side, then turned to watch George's hair gather as she sat. He felt the imminent loss of the beautiful, supportive woman who had just kissed him, but knew that if he gave up, ran away with her to somewhere they could never be found, he would not be able to live with himself. Greg's life was not a perfect one, but he had built it up from nothing. He had a history he could never just cast aside.

"I'm sorry," she was saying. "I'm here because of this...this lunacy? I know my husband, and this isn't him. What else can I say?"

"Please, Mrs Summers, at least hear us out?"

"I don't have much choice in the matter. I can hardly walk out, can I?"

"I suppose not. But I promise that if you won't believe us, we'll let you go. I'll even drive you home myself. Fair enough?"

"Fair enough."

"Then let's get on with it. I think it's best to let Greg tell his story first, then..."

She held up a hand. "One condition," she said. "Do not refer to this man as Greg. I'll listen to what he has to say, but I won't have him use my husband's name."

George's hand found his knee again. He shot her a reassuring smile. He had time. Nothing but, in fact.

Alex was reluctant, but nodded. "We'll continue to call him Richard then, and let him tell his story."

Greg took a deep breath, and met his wife's eyes. They'd once looked at him with love, laughter, sorrow, and all the things that make up a marriage. All he saw there, in the basement, were scepticism and scorn. He would tell his story, but it would take a great deal more than that to convince her. Keeping his expectations low, he started at the restaurant.

It took a while to relate everything that had happened, but time was meaningless in that basement. They were in a separate world, one distinct from the lives they led outside that place. In some ways it was strange, in others comforting. There, and only there, he could tell his story to Jennifer. She would not believe, that would come later, but at least he could make her understand his actions. Even if she thought him insane, she would have an explanation. Perhaps then she would fear him less.

A few times during the tale she looked alarmed, particularly when Greg told her about his inexpert attempts at breaking and entering. A couple of times she started to scoff, especially when informed that her husband was some indescribable monstrosity. Alex calmed her at those moments, and Greg was allowed to finish.

"We came here because we thought the police might trace Alex's car back to his flat. That brings us up to date." He took a sip of his second coffee. Georgina had made more during his clumsy attempts to explain the last two weeks.

Jennifer realised that some response was required from her. A nervous smile hovered over her lips. "What? You expect me to take this seriously? Do you even know how deranged this all sounds?"

Alex chuckled. "Believe me, I do. I was the first person he came to with the story. My thoughts at the time were not dissimilar to your own, but I saw the thing you believe to be your husband. I looked into inhuman eyes and knew it would have killed me if it could." Alex believed the truth of what he was saying, but Greg was less sure. Remembering it clinging to the bonnet, staring at Alex, he thought it had wanted nothing more than to terrify the man, to spread the fear it knew itself capable of generating. If he had to guess, Greg would say it had let them go.

Jennifer broke his train of thought. "I'm sorry, but I can't believe you. Our friend Mr Jameson is obviously seriously ill, but you seem perfectly normal. He must have been a lot more convincing when he talked you into this madness."

Georgina shifted. "Can I say something?" All eyes turned to her, and she straightened her back as though their scrutiny was a great weight she had burdened herself with. Her pout was defiant. "I just want to say my bit and get it over with."

Jennifer gave an odd smile, then nodded.

"Mrs Summers, I know this is Greg because I've been sleeping with him behind your back for about three months. I met him in a bar near where he works. He's told me a lot about you and his life. I'm here to try and convince you of who he is, and it's hard for me because if I get it right I'll lose him. I don't want that, but he's made it clear that this is what he needs. I just wanted to say that. I'm done now."

Greg thought the speech sounded rehearsed, almost textbook perfect. She must have been going over it in her mind while he was talking.

Jennifer spoke up. "You, I believe."

Dizziness, nausea, scepticism and joy. She believed George. His dry mouth made speech difficult, but he forced words out. "Jen…"

"Let me finish," she said. Tears of joy stayed half-formed in his eyes, awaiting permission to proceed. There had been a warning note in her voice that Greg hadn't liked at all. "As I say, I believe her – or I believe that *she* believes what she says. I also believe you." She turned to Alex. "I don't know how he convinced you that my husband is some demon, but I believe you think he is. But you," she finally addressed Greg, "are either dangerously insane or a very convincing con artist. I don't believe or accept what you've told me. Now I would like to go."

The silence was thunderous. Tears drying in his eyes, Greg glared at the woman he loved. She seemed to sink back into herself beneath his gaze. "You said that I could go if I listened. Please?"

The atmosphere of wary acceptance had withered. Greg leaned forward. "No."

Putting a cautionary hand on Greg's shoulder, Alex spoke a warning. "Greg."

"Wait. We said we'd let her go when we were satisfied she wouldn't believe us. I am not satisfied." He turned back to Jennifer. "Listen to me, and listen carefully. My name is Gregory Summers, and I'm an only child. My mother died when I was thirteen years old, and until I met you that scarred me horribly. But I did meet you, Jennifer Sharpe, on the day we graduated. We went clubbing then slept together the same night. We honeymooned in Florida. I work at Jackson Insurance. We have no children because my sperm count is low, but we're considering adoption. We had a bad patch four or five months ago when work was getting on top of me. For New Year's Eve you bought me a little smartphone that I take everywhere. I didn't get you anything in return and you wouldn't sleep with me that night." He paused for breath, pleased at the stunned gape of her face. "I could go on. And on. Jennifer, I have years of memories I could share with you. All I want you to do now is think of how I could know all this. Think very hard. If, by tomorrow evening, you still have no doubt that I'm either a madman or a liar then I promise you'll be free. Will you do this for me? Just this and nothing else?" If only she could see inside his heart, into his soul. She could not doubt him then.

When she finally nodded her slow agreement, he felt the tension flow from his body. In a whisper, he thanked her. Then he got up, walked past Alex and George to his unrolled sleeping bag, and climbed in.

There was to be little rest for him that evening.

23 RAPE

Two hours. That was how long he guessed he slept before being woken the first time. Still groggy, he turned over in the sleeping bag to try and determine what had disturbed him. He glanced at Jennifer. She was lying in one of the sleeping bags, arms hanging over the top. Alex had bound her wrists again, using strips of denim over her skin to spare her the pain of tape being ripped back when they freed her.

Greg noted this in the instant before he looked into her eyes. She stared at him, her expression not so much as flickering when he first made eye contact. Nothing at all was reflected in those orbs. No hate, no fear, no love. All he could see were reflections. His half-awake mind struggled not to doze back off. It lost the battle, but as he fell towards slumber it was the image of those eyes that he took with him.

The second time he awoke it was to voices. Female voices talking in hushed tones. Forcing his eyes to open, he saw Georgina's crouched form hovering over Jennifer. For some reason she chose that moment to turn towards him. Seeing he was awake, she crossed over to him.

"Hey babe," she whispered, "how are you sleeping?"

"Not bad," he lied, voice groggy. "Wha's happenin'?"

"Nothing honey. She was just asking some questions about, you know, us." She began to stroke his hair. "I don't think she believes yet, babe, but she will." Once more the soothing chasm of sleep opened beneath him; he barely heard her last words as he toppled in. "Believe me, she will."

Then it was morning.

Greg woke with a start, jerking upright from sleep. Surprised by the cold sweat sticking to him, he wondered what he'd been dreaming of. Casting his eyes about, he saw that all was as it should be. Jennifer was awake, sitting once more against the heater, and George was curled next to him in her own sleeping bag. Alex was not to be seen. Probably on some errand. Being careful not to disturb the woman beside him, he disentangled himself from his own sleeping bag. Somehow, during the night, it had entwined around him. As he pulled himself free, he gave a low groan. His camping days, it seemed, were long over. Both his back and shoulders ached from spending the night on cold cement. Rubbing them into a grim facsimile of life, he hobbled over to where Jennifer sat.

"Where's Alex?" he asked.

"Refilling the coffee," she told him. "And good morning to you too. I slept damned uncomfortably, thank you for asking." Greg grinned; for a second it felt like old times. From her arched eyebrows, he could tell that the feeling was not mutual.

The sound of the door closing drew his attention upwards, to where Alex was descending the stairs, thermos tucked beneath his arm. He also carried a brown paper bag. Greg put a finger to his lips, signalling the sleeping Georgina. Alex nodded, waiting until he was close before he spoke.

"Morning. I come bearing gifts." Sitting cross-legged on the floor, he unbound Jennifer's wrists before opening the bag. Like a magician demonstrating some new flourish, he produced a small assortment of wrapped sandwiches from within.

Greg applauded. "We'll put some aside for George. I'd rather not wake her, she was up late last night."

"Fair enough. I'll eat now though. I slept like a log." He offered a sandwich to Jennifer.

She refused. "I'm not hungry." She welcomed the coffee Greg made though.

The easy sense of companionship was odd, given the circumstances, but Greg accepted it without question, glad to have something to set against his mounting trepidation. Jennifer had spent the whole night thinking about what he had said yesterday. If her mind was not yet made up, that was fine. Should she have made a decision, then that was it. Having promised to let her go when she had thought the matter through, forcing her to stay for the rest of the day would not be the most effective way to alter her opinion.

Feeling drained and sore, he finished his sandwiches. After that, he could do nothing but wait for her answer. She must have felt the expectancy, for her gaze turned his way.

After several moments Alex noticed the pregnant stare. Rising, he made his apology.

"You should hear this in private," he told Greg. "I'll be by the steps if you want me." With that, he left. Greg had seen and heard him from very far away, for Jennifer's gaze consumed him. With a strange lack of feeling, he realised what he was seeing in her stare. Sorrow. Mounting pity. He did not want her to speak, but after a time she did.

"I'm sorry." Her first words chewed up his heart. "This is obviously important to you, no matter what your state of mind. But I love my husband, and you're not him. I don't know how you found out what you told me yesterday. Maybe you really do believe you're Greg. But I don't know you." She stopped, her silence full of compassion.

Numb, Greg nodded and rose to his feet. He knew he should try again, have one last go at convincing her, but he had no energy for the task. Turning, he walked to where Alex sat. Seating himself next to the closest friend he had, he swung his head across to meet his concern.

By his demeanour Alex, already knew the answer, had probably known before he left them, but out of courtesy he raised his eyebrows in a question.

Greg shook his head.

Their eyes held, then he was suddenly in the arms of the larger man. He did not cry, being far beyond such simplistic expressions of emotion. Instead he clung on hard. Thoughts seemed to leap the gap between them, becoming a higher communication than words alone.

It's all right, thought Alex, *it isn't over.*

I know, replied Greg. *But it hurts.*

Don't think about it, I'm here.

She doesn't know me.

It isn't important, I know you.

She doesn't love me.

That isn't important.

Greg pulled back his head to see Alex's face; the other man's eyes widened, first in shock then with implicit understanding. Leaning forward, Alex pressed his lips against Greg's.

Surprised, then accepting, Greg explored the kiss. It was tender, softer than the passion he had shared with Georgina. Their tongues met only briefly, flickering across each other in tiny, electric caresses. His hand rose to stroke the back of Alex's neck.

His eyes shot open. He yanked his head back, turning to one side and spitting.

"Greg?" Alex reached out a hand to touch his shoulder. Greg slapped it aside. "Greg? I thought you knew."

"Knew you're queer?" Alex flinched, becoming smaller beneath the abuse. Greg was beyond thought. His best friend was queer. Jesus, they had just kissed! "Why have you been helping me?'

Alex was a pathetic facsimile of the man he had been just moments ago. "Please Greg, don't do this. I'm sorry. I thought you understood. *I thought you knew*."

Silence. Warring impulses asked different things of Greg. He wanted to say that it was all right, that he didn't mind. That, in fact, he had shared the impulse. It had been a good urge. He had felt safe and comfortable and lost in that brief touching.

But he was Gregory Summers, a man married to a beautiful woman. He was having an affair with another beautiful woman. He was heterosexual throughout. He'd never been forced to question that, or even asked, having never felt any desire for other men. It was alien, frightening, and perverse.

Pervert. Greg Summers was not a pervert. Before he could even think he lashed out. His fist throbbed dully, bleeding again where he had cut it the previous night. Looking down at Alex, now on the floor, he realised he had hit the man. Alex looked back up. One anguished look was exchanged, both men helpless in the face of something larger than either of them. Then Alex half-ran, half-stumbled up the stairs.

Greg resisted the urge to call out after him, and was relieved when the door shut. Why had he let that happen? As much as he denied it to himself, he had responded to that kiss. It had been natural. Good. Normal.

But Greg was not homosexual. It was that simple. On the other hand, he had never thought himself a homophobe. Each to his own, that was what he always said, but that illusion too had been shattered. He had assaulted not only a gay man, but also a gay man who was among the only friends he had left.

Alex wanted him like *that*? For how long? When did it start? When Greg had gone to the flat and explained his story? Or before that, when he had demanded a refund, in a shabby office, on a distant day.

Remembering the feel of his tongue stroking Alex's, he felt his gorge rise and began to pace. Faster and faster he walked, between two of the brick pillars which supported the ceiling, slapping each with the palm of his hand as he reached it and turned.

Not gay. Normal. Heterosexual. Not gay. Screaming in his head, he sent his thoughts to heaven. *I am not gay!*

True, said a small voice within him. *But what about Richard Jameson?*

He stopped short.

Like in the bathroom. Like with the cigarette.

Oh God, what had they done to him?

Tremors began an assault on his limbs, and he was forced to sit on the bottom step again. Richard Jameson was gay. It was a programmed impulse that had kissed Alex, and realising it made him feel relieved in ways he was embarrassed about. But could he be sure that the Jameson personality had receded in full? There was no way to know. Thinking back on the evening when he had smoked his first cigarette, he knew he had been himself when he sucked sweet smoke. Yes, the impulse was Jameson, but the mind which followed it was his. In the same way, while he was himself at that moment, he could not be sure that the desire for Alex had faded.

He thought about his wife, about sex he had enjoyed with her. Today the memories were different, dislocated and unenticing. He turned his head to look at her. Met her gaze.

Her eyes mocked him. She had seen. She had watched. What was she now thinking? That this *queer*, this *freak*, had thought to convince her that she was his wife? Was she disgusted? Appalled? Amused? Looking into the deep blue of her soul, he saw that she now saw something fundamentally beneath her. An insectile, alien, crawling thing.

A torrent of rage blossomed in him. *I'm straight*, he told himself. As muscles tensed and his anger bloomed, he realised he had an erection again.

Oh, she would see.

Making no attempt to mask his intention, he walked across to her, his penis an obvious bulge in the fabric of his trousers.

He would show her. Demonstrate.

Jennifer was smiling now. *It's all right*, the smile seemed to say, *because I know you can't do it*. Her smile flickered slightly. *I'm not your type*, it added. Greg felt his penis twitch as his trousers pressed it. She would find out.

As he passed Georgina's sleeping bag, he realised she was awake. Her curious eyes met his as she rose from the bag. Panicked, Greg turned back to Jennifer. Was it his imagination, or was she chuckling under her breath?

Georgina put a gentle hand on his elbow. "Babe…"

He grabbed her by the shoulders and pushed her back against the pillar they had slept beneath. Kissing her, he slid his hands up to her long hair. She was still for a single, shocked moment, then slung her own arms down to his buttocks and kissed back. Pulling her against him, she noticed the pressure of his erection and freed a hand to touch him. He gasped.

Breaking the kiss, Georgina looked at him. "Where?" Her voice was husky. Heart hammering, he looked at Jennifer. She was watching, still smiling.

"Here," he said. Georgina shot a sideways glance at his wife, then smiled and nodded. With surprising force, she turned both of them around so it was he who had his back to the pillar. As she kissed him her fingers slid down to his trousers, drawing down the zip, reaching inside. She touched flesh, stroking. He moaned again, then she was no longer kissing him, her head was sinking, she was on her knees. Pulling his penis free from his trousers, she engulfed him in a single moist motion. Again he gasped, and her rhythm began.

Now. Now he would look. Now she would understand. He turned to Jennifer, and was lost in her eyes. Her smile was now a grin. Greg was confused, finding it hard to think as he slipped in and out of Georgina's mouth. Her tongue flicked him and he closed his eyes at the stab of pleasure.

When he opened them again Jennifer no longer met his eyes. Her laughing stare was down now, and Greg followed the look.

Georgina had gone bald.

No, that wasn't it. She had not gone bald at all. She had... Changed?

Into the creature. His mind shrieked. His skinless, putrid tormentor had him in its mouth.

His first instinct was to grab the now rapidly bobbing head and force it off. But as his hands came up to clutch the fleshy skull, they skidded and slipped across the slime of exposed meat. Blood vessels burst, and his hands were suddenly slick with fluids from the creature. As he screamed with revulsion, his body shrieked pleasure and came.

Malevolent, powerful, it rose before him. Crying with terror and nausea, Greg saw his own semen dripping from its raw, fleshy lips.

"I have tasted you," it said, its voice a deep baritone, far removed from Georgina's. "I claim you."

Greg could not reply. In grim parody of what stood before him, saliva dripped freely from his own mouth. Unable to resist as the creature grabbed his throat with one powerful hand, he was lifted from the floor. He could no longer even breathe.

"And now the truth," it said. "You are Richard Jameson, a wealthy homosexual bachelor who lives alone. You have a brother, a mother, a father. None of what you have known is true."

There may or may not have been more, but Greg's brain chose that moment to shut down.

He awoke, cold and alone. Taking a deep breath, he winced as the bruises on his throat shifted with the flex of his muscles. His limp penis still dangled from the fly of his trousers. Remembering where it had explored, he turned and was sick.

It took a while for him to gather the will to move. More comfortable, safer, to lie there staring at his own vomit, letting the vapour sting his eyes and throat.

Eventually though, he sat up. He did not know who might greet his awakening. Was Jennifer there, or had the creature reclaimed her? Had Alex returned? Perhaps he would see the creature itself, waiting only for him to recover, before continuing the torment.

He had not expected to be alone. Glancing about him, he saw that the basement was empty. Jennifer was gone, scraps of denim and tape marking where she had sat. The creature had left too. Alex had not returned.

Greg had never felt so lonely in his life.

Stumbling to his feet, he wandered through the cavernous cellar like a lost child. Nothing. No one. If it were not for the remains of Jennifer's bindings, it could all have been a dream. A sick, twisted nightmare.

He began to climb the stairs, pausing halfway up to place his desecrated penis back within his trousers. Would he ever have sex again without thinking of that one, filthy orgasm?

He continued the climb.

At the top was the proof that all had been reality. Pinned to the door was a letter addressed to Richard Jameson. Hesitant, he pulled it down and held it to his chest for a long, silent moment.

He had to know.

Opening it as though it contained a bomb, he discovered that this was very much the case. An extremely subtle bomb.

Dear Richard,

You have no wife. You have no lover. These have not been taken from you so much as they were loaned to you for a short time.

Do not think that we are finished, you and I. This is far from the case. For now, however, you have your freedom. Alex will become the sixth victim culled from London. His unwelcome return as you passed out made it necessary that we deal with him. I have snacked on you. I shall feast on him. But the banquet is not over. Live your life, whichever one you prefer, but know that you hold the truth in your hands. There shall come an accounting between us, for you are the seventh, and we remain in London until you fulfil that destiny.

Suffer.

Yours,

Gregory Summers.

24 COGNISANCE

Greg shambled through the streets of the city for three hours, tired, dishevelled, and confused. Dark, black thoughts whipped him, hurt him, raged at him. The decisions he made were at once sheer horror, and tranquil reassurance. Stopping outside a post office, he stared at his own reflection in the window.

Richard Jameson?

The truth, he thought, left hand still grasping the letter, *is in here. I smoke. I commit sexual acts with other men. My histories are the photographs lining the bedroom wall of the flat which is also mine. Every lie is truth. All truths are lies.*

Georgina. The creature. One and the same. Had that always been so? It had to be the considered, and the implications were enormous. George had confirmed that he was Greg Summers, but if she was the creature then that had only been another means of prolonging his suffering.

Not Gregory. Never Gregory. Who was he? Being able to name himself was not enough. His memory had not miraculously returned on reading the note. He still carried the fraudulent Summers in his head. Accepting that he was homosexual, for example, was impossible when what he recalled was a lifetime of lusting after women.

Shuddering, he remembered the night at the Ramkin Hotel. It had handcuffed him to the bed, made him helpless. He had allowed it to. He'd been thrilled at the moist attentions it lavished on him.

Enough.

Where did Jennifer feature in things? She had goaded him into the perverse sexuality of the morning, he was certain of that. Was she the creature's plaything? A partner? He remembered confronting the thing in the study of the house he had thought he owned. 'We' it had said. Now he knew who it had referred to.

A nasal voice at his side finally punched a pathway through his thoughts.

"Sir, I'm sorry, but if you don't intend to buy anything could you please move on?" There was a note of embarrassment in the voice. Greg turned to see a pained looking Asian man in the doorway of the post office. Looking down at himself, he saw the point. He was a wreck.

"Yes," he said. "Yes, of course." A look of relief spread over the shopkeeper's face as he realised that this particular tramp was going to cause him no problems.

Greg checked his pockets. Though he had no money left, his credit cards and keys were still on him. With a kind of sad resolve, he began walking to the only place he could go.

It was early afternoon when he reached Alex's apartment. He had not expected an answer to his pressing of the buzzer, having come only to retrieve his hire car, but he checked anyway, hoping that he was wrong. Dismissing the implications of the closed door and silent speaker, he walked across to the car.

It was a matter of a half-hour drive before he arrived at Richard Jameson's flat. *His* flat. Not all was as he had left it. On stepping through the door, an insistent beeping caught his attention. An answer-phone was secreted somewhere in the room. Tired beyond belief, Greg began to search for it.

Finding the machine took only a few weary moments of real time, but his mind found this sufficient for a host of resigned acceptances. Alex was gone, a morsel for the thing to snack on, and it was his fault. He had rejected Alex that morning, forcing him away and leaving him vulnerable. It was he who had led his friend into Georgina's arms, his tormentor, the *thing*. With a sickening start, he realised that Alex was the only real friend the temporary man called Summers had ever made.

Later would come the agony of guilt, the need to act, and the attempt to save the innocent man he had pulled down in his own death-throes. Alex Carlisle was not alone.

Before Greg could find Alex though, he first had to find somebody else.

Someone important.

Richard Jameson.

It won't be like dying, he told himself, *it will be like rebirth*. He would be the same person, the same elementary identity, when he brought Richard to the fore. They could not have changed him so fundamentally that he was an entirely new identity. Thinking hard, he tried to recall how it had felt when Jameson climbed from the bath some days ago. There had been no sudden difference in self. It had been a smooth transition from one identity to the other. Surface details - the smoking, the sexual preferences (a thought to make him shudder) - would alter, but surely he would remain the same essential man?

Or would he? Was personal experience the foundation of personality? If that were true then Greg really was condemning himself to death. Although a maze of falsehoods, the details of his life were substantially different from what he knew of Richard. The coffee scald, as just one example, still bred a small angry knot each time it was recalled from his litter-site memory. For Jameson, it would be nothing but a worthless fantasy.

Greg wanted to keep the scald, needed the precious death of his mother to stay with him, longed for his wife to belong to him again. Moving forward would mean giving all that up. Greg wanted to keep the raw wounds of his youth, but only if he could look on them from the anaesthetic peace of his life with Jennifer. He knew that couldn't happen. Jennifer – his Jennifer, the woman in his mind – did not exist, had never been. All that existed was the face on which the creature had based her, the pawn Greg had held captive in the basement of the Ramkin Hotel. She never would be, never *could* be, the woman he craved.

There were no tears on accepting that, just grim recognition. During the blank three hours when he had walked through London streets, he had thought other dread thoughts. It was the ending of his life that had preoccupied him.

Gregory Summers was worth nothing. Why continue? Why go on? With nothing left to live for, suicide was the last pure option he could consider. A final, decisive action that would belong solely to Greg Summers. The only true stamp he could make on the world was to embrace proud death.

It had been close. With each bus that passed, each bridge he crossed, the imperative had been there. At certain times in his life, the life he had never lived, he had thought of how easy it would be to kill himself. Fleeting, insane moments when he had looked at oncoming traffic and imagined how simple it would be to just step onto the road and end his life. Those were transitory lunacies, to be grinned at ruefully as he continued down the street. That day, for the first time in his fictional existence, he did not have the host of reasons that would prevent him fulfilling the insanity. Walking around, seeing a potential for death in the most innocuous locations, he had been in more danger than any orchestrations of the creature had placed him in.

At last, looking over the railing of a pedestrian bridge spanning a motorway he could not name, the reason not to let himself tumble had kneed him savagely in the common sense. Hanging there - the hard metal of the barrier pressing his hips, the strong breeze wanting so badly to help him drift gently forwards - he heard a single word whisper from the back of his mind. It was his own voice, yet it was not. It was his own mind, yet it was not. Brushing lightly over his thoughts, the whispered word was three silent syllables. *Murderer*.

Spasming back from the railing, he had looked round in horror. Nobody else was there, the voice had indeed originated from his own head, springing forth to remind him that this body was not his to throw away.

He knew precisely who the real owner of the voice was.

Kill himself? Certainly, for what other route lay open to him?

Kill Richard Jameson? By what right? If he were to jump now, to sail down to the rushing metallic river below, then the last act of his life would not be noble end of Gregory Summers. He would go to his grave as the man who murdered Richard Jameson.

So he had decided his course of action. Greg Summers was fated to end, but his final struggle would not be the selfish, self-pitying act he had contemplated that morning. When he died, it would matter. Greg Summers would not have lived his short, fiery life for nothing. He would die the man who had given his life to save Richard Jameson.

He found the answering machine on the same shelf as the telephone, concealed behind the books ranked there. Jameson had read those books, maybe enjoyed them, but he could recall nothing at all about their content. He promised he would. Jameson would be free again. He pressed the button to replay the messages on the machine.

Beep. "Richard? Richard, pick up the phone. Richard? Shit." *Click.* Stewart, probably worried about his brother after the restaurant episode. He giggled to himself. Richard had stepped out of the building, please try again later.

Beep. "Mr Jameson? Sally. Could you call me at the office, or maybe my mobile? There are some documents need your signature, and Mr Brownsey has been asking to see you. Hope everything's okay. Speak to you soon." *Click.* Sally? A secretary perhaps, or a personal assistant of some sort.

Beep. "Jesus Richie, will you please phone me back? I'm worried sick here. Are you all right? Are you ill? What the fuck happened at De Marco's? Come on, I need to talk to you." *Click.* Stewart again. The poor man must be worried to death.

Beep. "Richard, it's your mother. Oh, you know I hate these machines. I've just talked to Stewart, he seems a bit worried about you. Is something wrong, honey? Phone me back, let me know you're all right. Love you." *Click.* Not his mother, he reminded himself. Perhaps she had borne the body in which Greg stood, but his birth had been unnatural and unasked for. He owed this woman nothing beyond the safe return of her son.

With a final click, the answer-phone switched itself off and the tape began to rewind. Greg found the whirring soothing. In a half-trance he realised he had just flicked through a handful of audio snapshots depicting the life of Richard Jameson. Yet not one voice had stirred a memory in him. Of Stewart he recalled only the brief, disastrous meeting in the restaurant, and the saga of the soaring red ball. Sally was faceless to him, as was the entire world of the company Richard seemed to have built. Regarding the mother, he wondered if an adopted child might feel this way about their real parents. In every sense they lived a happy, normal life believing themselves to be the true son or daughter of a particular couple. Then suddenly they make the world-altering discovery and everything changes. Did they share his curiosity, his desire to meet the biological entity who had spawned him? He was intrigued, but not enough to intrude on her life. From his viewpoint, his mother had been dead for sixteen long years, his father dying just five years after that. He was used to being without family, it was Richard who owned these snapshots. He hoped he would be able to return them.

But how? He was facing the prospect of rescuing a man hidden right behind his eyes, yet far beyond his reach. Richard was buried deep within the brain he had taken residence in, and he had absolutely no idea how he was going to dig him out.

Absurdly, he wished that Jameson owned a pet. A dog, a cat, even a bloody hamster. Just something alive which he could talk to without thinking himself mad. Maybe he should leave Richard a note suggesting it. The idea made him giggle, and he went to prepare himself a mug of tea and some sandwiches.

The preparation of food proved a relaxing diversion. His mind was allowed to switch on a subconscious autopilot, entering an almost meditative state. It was a shame when he had to move back into the living room and consume the meal. He did anyway, gripping both mug and plate in one hand as he pushed open the door. It was one of the large green beanbags on which he chose to rest himself, letting weariness seep into the softness that engulfed and supported him. Now it was the turn of his body to engage an automatic pilot, his hands and mouth working without prompting to eat and drink, his thoughts trying to settle on a course of action.

Why was it so difficult to find Jameson? What keys had been used to lock away a whole life, a whole mind, within the grey matter of his brain? Perhaps he could start by finding out more about him. It was frustrating to contemplate rooting through souvenirs and keepsakes he should be familiar with, but perhaps it would weaken the barriers that separated mind and body.

It was a problematic approach. He could not help but look on these items as automatically meaningless to him. Just as with the books, some of which Jameson must be more than familiar with, he found himself beholding the life of a different persona. Rather than trying to discover what he himself might be like, he wasted his efforts trying to envision a *separate* soul. It was a mental block, one he could not navigate around. At the back of his mind was the simple suspicion, even after his conscious acceptance of the facts, that he could not be Jameson, for no other reason than it was obviously not the case.

What he needed was to hear from somebody who knew him. Somebody who could share even the most cursory impression of the life he needed to find.

Stewart was the most obvious person to ask, but this had been made impossible by his recent actions. He could not be sure, but he suspected that if he went to Stewart he would be whisked straight to a psychiatrist. From there, who knew? It would be certain that his life would be taken out of his hands for a while. Hospitals, tests, doctors; where would all that leave him? Helpless and amputated, unable to act.

If it was just his life that was in the balance, then he could have accepted those little sufferings as a possible solution to Richard's recovery. Although he was certain that nobody in medicine would be familiar with symptoms quite like his own, he accepted that they were far better qualified to deal with it than he. But if he allowed his life to be dominated in these ways he would have no time in which to act. It was not just Richard who was relying on him to save his life. Alex needed him too.

Family and close friends were out then (assuming Richard even had close friends), so who remained? People he worked with? Greg guessed that they would be privy to few details regarding the private person behind the employer they knew.

It was while he was wracking his mind for another alternative that the answer handed itself to him on a platter. At first the footsteps outside the door startled him. Then came the rattling of keys being inserted into a door, and he darted to his feet in queasy panic. They had come for him so soon? Was he too late to help Alex? Was he too late to help himself?

A door creaked open, and it was not his own. It came from the other side of the hallway.

In the brief time he had been inhabiting the flat as Gregory Summers, he had never given a thought to who might live behind the door facing his own. It was time to introduce himself.

Smiling at the simplicity of the idea, he strode to his walk-in closet. Five minutes later he emerged still smiling, wearing jeans and a red t-shirt. It felt good to be out of the filthy clothes that he had worn. He felt a rejuvenation of his energy. A moniker had changed in his mind, a significant term of reference. He knew how he would introduce himself to whoever lived across the passageway.

Taking a deep, bewildered breath, Richard Jameson opened his front door and stepped out to find himself.

25 AWAKENINGS

Did the name make the man? He could not answer that. What he did know, to his discomfort, was that shedding Gregory Summers was like removing an iron shackle. Perhaps this was less to do with finding Jameson, and more about removing himself from the pain associated with the name he had worn five minutes ago. Of course, his mind remained that of Summers, but the change in attitude that came with the alias of Jameson was tangible. As best he could define it, it felt like a becoming. Maybe the name itself was a doorway through which the real owner of his body could slip back from the prison where it huddled.

He had been surprised at the exuberant welcome he received when his neighbour opened her door. She was a middle-aged woman, just about to embark on the voyage of her fifties, with mid-length black hair hanging loosely about her neck. Flecks of grey were unashamedly displayed among the straight locks, somehow making an elegance of her pale skin. A little shorter than his own five foot seven inches, she was dressed in a smart business jacket and knee-length grey skirt.

"Richard!" Her cry was enthusiastic and shrill. "You, sir, are long overdue in accepting my offer. I haven't seen you since...when? Your New Year party?" He was given no time to answer, as she whisked him into her living room and sat him on her garish red settee, a piece of furniture which made a ferocious challenge to the rest of the room. Where everything else consisted of subtle hues of cream and brown, the settee sat defiant in the centre, and dared the critic to take offence.

His hostess had taken time only to wheedle his tea-drinking details from him, before rushing through one of the doors to the kitchen. Now he sat there, awaiting her return. It was foolish, he knew, but he couldn't help thinking that he had somehow invited himself into the lair of a jovial and enthusiastic spider.

You're just nervous, he told himself. *You're hardly here to pass the time of day, are you? You don't even know how you're going to bring the subject up with the old fag-hag.*

The thought startled him. *Fag-hag?* What the hell did he mean by that? She returned, delicate china cups in hand, and passed him one.

"So what finally brings you my way Richard? Want to borrow a cup of sugar?" He blushed despite himself, all the time wondering how he was going to answer her question. After a hesitation that stretched too far, he decided to stay as close to the truth as possible.

"This is going to sound a little strange to you, I think. Please bear with me. Recently I suffered..." the word that nearly popped out was *insufficiently*. Was that not what the creature had told him? "...a slight accident," he said instead.

Her face exploded with exaggerated concern, and he hoped she would allow him to continue before she tried to hug him. He raised his hand. "I really am pretty fine, thanks for the concern. The thing is..." Damn, what was the thing? That he was being hounded by a reject from a Hammer horror flick, while believing himself to be a married man called Gregory Summers? No, that would not do at all. "...I've been diagnosed with clinical amnesia. They think it's because of the shock."

"Your name?"
"Alex Carlisle."
"This is wrong. Forget this. What is your name?"
"I don't remember."
"This is wrong. Your name is Gregory Summers."
"My name is Gregory Summers."
"What is your name?"
"Gregory Summers."
"Good. Very good. Now open your mind to me. Let me taste you."

"No, Stewart's away. Business trip. My parents are on holiday. Look, I don't want you to be concerned. The doctors say my memory will return in time. I thought I'd try and get a head start, that's all."

Clinical amnesia? How lame was that? However, after checking that she was not the butt of some practical joke, she had fallen for it with sublime enthusiasm. A lorry full of concern had driven right over him. Scraping himself from the metaphorical tarmac, he tried to pull her round to the point of his visit.

"Yes, of course," she gushed, "you must forgive me. I can't help but worry." She took a sip of her tea, the strangeness of the situation both bemusing and amusing her. "So you want what I know of you? Well darling, I'm afraid you might not have picked a very good place to start. I don't really know you that well at all. I've bumped into you a few times in the passageway, and you did invite me to your New Year party.

But you invited Norman, the doorman, to that, so it doesn't really mean much. I've invited you in for a drink a few times, but you always seem to be so..."

Again Richard was forced to raise his hand. Here, he realised, was a woman altogether too fond of her own voice. "Please, even if you've only picked up a vague impression of the person I am, it would probably help."

"Of course, poor thing." It was all he could do not to cringe beneath the waves of patronising bonhomie. "Well, you live alone, apart from the occasional night-guest." She paused, unsure of how to continue. "Do you know you're...well...you like men?" Repressing the shudder that the Summers personality still needed to give, Richard forced a smile and a nod. She breathed a sigh of relief. "Good, I don't know how I would have broken *that* to you." Realising she had been insensitive, she stopped to look across at him. "I'm sorry, I didn't mean..."

Again, his hand came up. It was beginning to feel like it was on a spring. "Don't worry about it, I know what you mean."

"Yes, well, it sort of came out wrong, you know how it is." Satisfied that he did indeed know, she continued her description. "Up until a couple of months ago you were seeing one young man regularly, I think he was called Craig, but I really don't know why you aren't together anymore. Er, you own a company you created yourself. It's something to do with computers, but I don't know what. You always seemed a decent young man to me. I don't know what else to say really.'"

Richard had hoped for more, but even this small amount was a relief. He had always seemed a decent man to her, that alone was worth hearing. Of the rest, there was little information that he didn't already know. It surprised him a bit to think of himself in an actual relationship with a man, but it also calmed him in some ways. If he had been involved with a regular partner then it was not so different from being heterosexual. Perhaps the life of a gay man was not quite as far beyond his understanding as he had thought.

Rising, rising, climbing. Then he was awake.

He shook his head a little to clear the cobwebs, then glanced around in surprise. It seemed he had fallen asleep at the wheel of his car. He was still in the parking lot outside his office. He must have finished work, climbed in, and pretty much passed out. *Exhaustion*, he thought. Jennifer was always telling him that he should relax more.

A quick look at his watch startled him to full wakefulness. Good grief, he must have dozed for over an hour. In just fifteen minutes he was supposed to meet Georgina at a bar, then head for the restaurant, and unless he picked up his heels he was going to be late. It was no wonder he was constantly tired; keeping two women happy at one time would wear down even the hardiest of souls. Again, he felt the chemical rush of guilt, and gunned the car to life with a curse. Trying desperately to banish the word infidelity from his thoughts, checking his ponytail was in place with one hand, Greg Summers reversed out of the parking space.

Richard had gulped his tea, made his apologies, and left. The woman, he realised he had forgotten to ask her name, would have smothered him in well-meant concern if he had stayed much longer. It had been obvious she had nothing new to tell him.

Unsure of what he expected, he felt the encounter had been anticlimactic. Had he thought to unleash torrents of memory by simply wearing the label of Jameson? Sitting back on the beanbag, he pondered who he was.

How would he know when a new memory surfaced? Would it announce itself to him? Would he even be aware of it? Probably not. How did memory even work? In his head was stored the entire ersatz life of Gregory Summers, but he only recalled something if he was first reminded of it, or if he deliberately pulled it to the fore. That was the approach he must take, but how could he search for an image in his head when he didn't have the slightest idea of what it looked like?

Frustration made it even more difficult to concentrate, and he tried to relax. What would he be familiar with, as Jameson? As a gay male he might have visited gay clubs, but Summers never had. Were they different somehow? Possibly. Nevertheless, he tried to imagine what it was like, to construct the picture in his head.

To his surprise he found that it was already there.

It had been nearly a month since Craig walked out on him, the break-up a result of the amount of time Richard had to invest in the company. *After this long*, he had told himself, *I should be over him. I should definitely not be dwelling on him every second of every day*. So in the hope that some mindless clubbing might grant him some peace, he had spent an evening at *Fire*.

It was not a successful night. His heart just hadn't been in it. Several times he had started chatting to cute looking guys, but couldn't keep the conversation going. Around midnight, at the bar, a short brunette woman had approached him. The last thing he needed was an uninspiring encounter with some fag-hag, so he tried to look as bored by her efforts as possible, wondering where the term fag-hag had come from. It was an unnecessarily cruel phrase for girls who felt more comfortable around gay men. That they felt at risk around straights must indicate some bad experience or other, so who would deny them the comparative safety of gay clubs. They appreciated the lack of sexual threat from the men, and most were secure enough not to be threatened by the women. Often they were quite good company, though they could be clingy.

Richard was not in the mood to humour one that night.

Yet, to his surprise, he found her compelling.

As her voice, oddly clear against the thumping drumbeat, drifted along, he felt himself being drawn further and further from his own thoughts.

Richard sat back in the beanbag, breathing hard. It was his own. He owned that memory. Just a small, insignificant piece of the jigsaw he needed to construct, but it was a start, a corner from which he might be able to work. And the memory was not so insignificant, for he recognised the woman he had met. Not the creature, not Georgina. It was Jennifer, the woman who served the thing, who had masqueraded as his own wife.

He owned the final memory of Richard Jameson as a distinct persona, before the awakening of Greg Summers.

Still a little groggy from his unplanned doze, Greg pulled his car into a space just a few doors down from the restaurant. If his watch was right he was only five minutes late. Sprinting from his car, knowing he would probably get a ticket for leaving it there, he arrived at the door breathless. A waiter met him as he was tucking loose strands of hair back into his ponytail.

"Good evening sir, do you have a reservation?"

"I do. Under Johnson." He had been quite pleased with his pseudonym for the evening. It added an exciting air of espionage to his daily grind. *The Secretary will disavow all knowledge of my actions*, he thought, chuckling to himself.

"Ah yes, Mr Johnson." The waiter gave him a strange look. "Are you dining alone?'

"I'm expecting someone, I thought they might have arrived by now?" Having realised he was running so late, he had called George, already at the bar, and asked her to meet him at the restaurant instead.

"Not yet sir. Can I show you to your table?"

As Greg sat down, he ordered a bottle of red wine. Georgina, he remembered, adored a fine red. Accepting the menu from the waiter, he glanced through the offerings displayed. Should he order for her? Probably best not to. She could be a vegetarian, for all he knew. Settling back into his chair, he fixed his eyes on the door and waited.

So, thought Richard, *I have a memory*. Just one, but that was a start. If he was right, he would be able to use it to find Alex. Assuming that his next real memory after the meeting at *Fire* belonged to Greg, what had it been of? Where was the point when fantasy merged with reality? Going to work one morning? Waking up with Jennifer? Who would he have seen first? The creature had told him that Alex was to be the sixth Summers. How long did the conversion take? Where would he emerge?

He could not have woken in the house on Fontside Avenue. The hallway, so different from his false memory, could not have been so extensively redecorated during a single day at work. Apart from the time factor, why would they bother? Easier to leave it alone and program him to remember it differently - his shock at discovering the supposed alterations would have been the same either way. There was also the matter of the study. They would never risk him wandering in and discovering the charts, the photographs.

Not at home then.

Probably not at work, either. As Gregory did not really work at the insurance company in question, none of his memories of being there could be truth.

So then, not at work and not at home. In a social environment? All he ever remembered doing outside of marital life was pursuing his affair with Georgina, and he was certain that the only time they had really had sex was the night of the hotel mix-up.

That was it.

He had gone straight from work to meet her. He had become Greg sometime between the false memory of leaving work, and entering the restaurant. Had he not woken up in the car park outside the company he thought he had worked at? Yes! Yes, he was sure of it. He recalled his surprise at having nodded off, his panic as he rushed to the restaurant.

What time had the booking been made for? It might have been seven, but he wasn't certain. Richard Jameson had been abducted at some point in the early hours of morning, he was positive he remembered being in the club until at least midnight before Jennifer had taken him. So they had been given the opportunity to work on him for, at most, eighteen hours. Had they used it all? Could they have brainwashed Alex in less time than that? Would they have time to kidnap Alex in the morning and release him the evening of the same day?

He had no way of being sure, but he needed to find one fast. If Alex was at the restaurant, then Richard could intercept him there, assuming that the creature used the same scenario twice. He thought it might, for it must know that some rescue attempt would occur. That would be all the more tempting to it, for he could sense it enjoyed these little mind games. He could almost hear it whispering *I will call you to account*. The game was very much afoot. Perhaps there was to be a brief lull as it turned its attention to Alex for a while, but the banquet had yet to begin.

So it was likely that De Marco's would see the birth of a new Greg Summers. Would it be that evening, or did he have a day to prepare?

Glancing up at the clock on the wall, Richard realised that he had to make a decision soon. It was nearly quarter past seven.

Quarter past seven. Not cause enough to worry Greg, Georgina was often late for their little meetings, but enough to let his imagination destroy the evening ahead of him. What on earth were they going to talk about? Up until now their encounters had been almost purely physical, nothing more socially challenging than the discussion of future times and places. Now he was expected to fill an entire evening with small talk.

What if they had nothing in common? What if they decided that they despised one another and never wanted to meet again? A large part of him thought that this might be the best result the evening could produce. It would put an end to the three months of lying and deception that had gone hand in hand with his infidelity.

There was another, powerful, part of him that did not wish this affair, this exciting and passionate diversion from his daily routine, to die.

Lost in his thoughts, he jumped a little when the waiter spoke to him.

"Sir? A telephone call for you."

"Ah. Thanks, where can I take it?"

"If you'll follow me sir."

A telephone call? His first thought was panicked and irrational. Was it Jennifer? Had she somehow discovered not only the fact of his affair, but also the details of his alias and meeting place? But no, his wife was away for a couple of days, enjoying the company of her cousin in Cardiff. More probably it was Georgina calling to apologise for her lateness. Following the waiter to the desk by the door, he picked up the receiver that lay there.

"Hello?" Nothing. Whoever it was had hung up. How very odd.

A little bemused, he returned to his seat.

Richard hung up the receiver, breathing hard. He was right, Alex was at the restaurant. He should have waited to hear his voice, he supposed. Johnson wasn't an uncommon surname, after all. He could not discount the possibility that a different Johnson might be dining at De Marco's that evening.

No, he was sure. The man who had been weaving through the restaurant to answer the telephone was Alex Carlisle. He could imagine the lean, angular frame of his friend picking a path through the maze of tables and diners, his face pinching with confusion when he discovered his caller had hung up. He wondered if the new Greg Summers sat at the same table that he had, felt the same guilt at betraying the wife he thought loved and cherished him? It was likely.

Well, he thought as he chose a jacket from the closet, *the least I can do is check*. He might be able to engage the creature in some way, maybe take advantage of an opportunity to rescue Alex.

As he left, he wondered whether the creature was still sitting at the centre of some complex maze, waiting for him. If so, Richard had just found the way in.

Georgina entered. As Greg watched her approach his table, her exquisite muscled legs rippling in the short black dress she wore, he was struck by an absurd image. For a moment, just that and nothing more, he had an image of he and George talking to Jennifer. There was a second man there, short and dark-haired, who he seemed to know. Then the picture was gone and Georgina sat down.

"Hiya babe, sorry I'm late. Decided to get changed after the bar." She said this wryly, as though it were a secret joke they shared. Baffled, but determined not to show it, he smiled and handed her a menu. Her mouth shaped one of her fascinating pouts as she took it from him. "Thanks. Hope I haven't spoiled my appetite snacking."

26 DEVOURING

What, he wonders, is left of him now? It is a strange curiosity, he cannot say for certain where it springs from. There are few pieces of him left to chose from. Regarding this last notion, he considers the possibility that he is crazy. It is not a new thought. Indeed, it has occurred to him many times over the last weeks of his life. Back then he had meant an ordinary day-to-day madness, the madness of imagined things, the craziness of the unknown. Now he asks whether he might be clinically insane.

Before being placed in the tank he had managed to maintain a solid grasp of his sanity. Though at times distressed and upset, at times frightened and disturbed, he had never been insane. Now his body has been eaten away to almost nothing. He resembles little more than a meaty stick man from a child's drawing, and he thinks that his sanity is no longer secure. How else could the human mind cope with the sheer *size*?

He is larger now than he has ever been. The sane part of him acknowledges that his brain is gone, that his thoughts are blooming within the substance of the fluid itself. As his organs dissolve, their functions are taken on by the strange toxin in which he floats. Now his mind, his living soul, exists only in liquid.

If his mind is the fluid, then he is now the very thing that devours his own flesh. Though the liquid has no nerves to gather such information, his imagination allows him to feel his whole being wrapped around the husk of his physical self. Like a venomous rogue soul, he sucks scraps of meat and gristle from legs he once walked upon. It is his mind which slips about his ribcage, picking clean the lungs and heart. His liquid self claws open the spinal cord and sups at the fluids it finds there. Like an existential cannibal, he feasts.

Suddenly he is shrinking. As though being pulled inside out, he reduces in on himself. The tank drains, his mind flows away through delicate tubes to be devoured by her. Smaller and smaller. It is hard to concentrate, difficult to feel. He becomes half his size, a quarter, an eighth.

A pinprick

Microscopic.

Nothing at all.

27 VIGILANCE

As the streetlights coruscated past his rental car at illegal speeds, Richard whispered an unthinking prayer that he would catch them in time, before they left. They would not be going to the Ramkin Hotel that night, the staff would recognise Alex for who he was, so he would lose them if he did not make De Marco's while they ate. After that there were hundreds of hotels they could move on to. Running a red light without even noticing, curling a corner fast enough to ride up on two wheels, he knew he was rushing for no reason. He had plenty of time. They would not long have sat when he left the apartment. It would take him only forty-five minutes to get there at safe speed, but he couldn't risk missing them. This was the one part of the pattern that he knew was duplicated from his own experience as the Summers persona. It was his only opportunity to reclaim some initiative, for if he lost this chance he would be forced to wait for the creature to go on the offensive again. That would only happen when Alex was lost.

He knew the story of the evening, how it ended. Nausea exploded through him at the thought of that thing, in the guise of Georgina, touching and pleasuring him. Bondage.

Penetration. Most vivid in his imagination, fellatio. Alex would be spared that. If nothing else were accomplished, it would not taste his friend.

Swerving, he narrowly avoided smashing into a vacant looking young woman who had stepped onto the road. Did the bitch *want* to kill herself? Swearing under his breath, he slowed a little. Not enough to bring him under fifty, but sufficient to frustrate his need for haste.

It took him another ten minutes to reach the vicinity of the restaurant, a record that shocked him. With a total journey time of only twenty minutes, he should have been dead or in a police cell.

Parking the car around the corner from De Marco's, he jogged up the street. From that moment he was operating in unfamiliar territory. He knew well enough what was happening within the restaurant itself, but did not know how complex the creature's plan might be. There was the woman he still thought of as Jennifer to fear, for she could be watching the evening as it unfurled, providing backup against the possibility of his intervention. It was unrealistic to believe that they were somehow afraid of him, but there lurked the suspicion that Alex was the bait in some trap.

As he approached De Marco's his fears seemed unrealised. The street was empty. Despite the shadows cast by the handful of parked cars, as well as the occasional moving one, there were few places to conceal a secretive watcher. It was a double-edged blessing, for he too had nowhere to secrete himself. He had an idea about that, and was relieved to find that his memories of the two previous visits were accurate. Across the road from the restaurant glowed the reassuring lights of a twenty-four hour café.

Crossing the road before he came in sight of the large windows of De Marco's, he pulled up the collar of his jacket and sunk his head to look at tarmac. To the casual viewer he hoped to look like any other pedestrian shutting away the cold and the night. It was a necessary concealment, for if he was correct, if Summers no. 7 had chosen the same table as Summers no. 6, then the creature was sitting right next to the window he was forced to walk past. Not daring to risk a glance finding out if this were true, he hurried to the door of the café. *Just an ordinary passer-by*, he thought. Why then did he feel so bloody conspicuous? He had been holding his breath, and he released it in a small, explosive gasp. The cold caught hold of it, turning it to a wispy cloud of vapour.

Now he was faced with a second problem. If the woman was watching for him then there was an excellent chance that she too would see this café as a convenient place to await his arrival. It was too late to turn back now, he had already paused at the doorway for a second too long, a moment beyond what a watching might consider natural.

As he pushed open the door to the small diner his stomach responded immediately to the smell of chips and other fried delicacies.

Jennifer stood directly before him, and his feet turned to lead as they regarded each other.

"You alright mate? You've got a face like a slapped arse." It was a waitress. Just a waitress. Her hair resembled Jennifer's slightly, but her face was totally dissimilar. Richard sighed a thankful sigh. The imagination was a powerful trickster.

"Fine," he said, forcing a smile. "For a moment I thought you were somebody else. Somebody dead." She took a step back from him.

"You on drugs?"

"I'm not, no. Sorry. Tired." She nodded, apparently deciding that he was not dangerous, then turned to wipe down a table. Richard sauntered over to the service counter, where another grim-faced waitress watched him.

"Help ya?"

"Plate of your greasiest, least palatable cholesterol please."
It seemed the eccentricity of the situation was getting to him.
Perhaps Richard was making his presence felt.

"You taking the piss?"

"Sausage, chips and beans. And a mug of tea."

"Shoulda said."

Smiling at her, Richard turned and chose the window table
that had just been wiped down by the first girl.

He had been right to show caution earlier. Over the road,
sitting directly opposite him, was Alex Carlisle. Across from his
friend sat the creature, Georgina. She looked beautiful,
Richard was forced to admit that, but he knew too well the
rot that crept beneath her polished finished. His gorge rose,
and the fried food seemed a less tempting idea.

The thought dissolved as he became captivated by the
couple he watched. Déjà vu was inadequate to describe it; he
actually *was* seeing something that had happened to him
before. Alex was his stand in, but the expression of
helplessness was familiar. The creature was going through
that same clever act of drunkenness, probably relating the
details of which music it preferred, which wild activities it had
performed. Alex, Greg now, was left feeling old and out of
touch. The situation played precisely as it had before.

How many times prior to that? Had the five previous
victims from London been engaged in this scenario? What
about other cities, other hunting grounds? Perhaps they had
all resembled his own experience this closely, creating one
repetitive cycle of suffering.

That reminded him of the most important question. Why
was he different? What had happened to make him warrant
special attention, and why was the creature so thrilled at this
difficulty that it had given him extra time to run? It was
baffling, and he was going to watch very closely for anything
that might give him a clue to the answer.

His food and drink were dumped in front of him, and he looked up to see that same wary look on the waitress's face. She held his glance for long enough to let him know he was being watched should he want to cause trouble, then turned away.

"Thank you kindly," he told her departing back. He had returned his gaze to the window before she could respond.

Now came a moment he wanted very much to observe. In the background of the scene he watched a waiter approaching with the lobsters they had ordered. Alex had just made some comment, at which Georgina gave a sycophant's giggle, then the waiter's approach made him turn. He looked briefly at the bright red creature, the scalded lobster. Any moment now...

Nothing happened. Alex smiled, and shifted backwards to receive the meal.

Nothing had happened. No fit, no flashback.

Richard had confirmed why he was different. The fits were not part of the pattern. They were the anomaly that had led him to resist better and harder than the creature was used to. That was why he had been offered extra rope from which to dangle. He was being studied like a too intelligent lab rat.

Perhaps that explained the abrupt, last minute decision to take Alex. Was it possible that a time limit was being adhered to? Perhaps it needed to make some sort of regular sacrifice. It had to keep Richard alive long enough to discover why the normal methods it employed had failed, so another had replaced the gap created in the schedule. Was that what he was dealing with? Some sort of religious cult?

Why not? It was no more absurd than the any other theory he could piece together. A follower of some nightmare god, like Lovecraft's Great Old Ones. Whether such an entity existed was, perhaps, a moot point as long as the creature believed enough to make the actual sacrifices. It certainly belonged in a Lovecraftian tale.

Who the hell was Lovecraft?

He knew, of course. H.P. Lovecraft, writer of supernatural horror and creator of the Cthulu mythos, had written during the first few decades of the twentieth century, dying prematurely in 1937. There was a collection of his works sitting in his apartment.

Both the collection and the knowledge belonged to Richard Jameson. Perhaps he was winning after all. Terrible, fierce joy filled his heart, and he allowed himself to feel hope that Jameson was coming home.

Over the next hour and a half his rapture had plenty of time to fade. The couple across the road were in no obvious hurry to embark on the carnal pleasures ahead of them. More and more, Richard felt he was being held there as part of some terrible trap.

Several times while he watched, the door to the café had swung open behind him. On every occasion he started in his seat, eyes swinging round to confront the threat. Each time it proved to be nothing more sinister than a drunken passer-by stopping for coffee before moving on. The waitresses were getting ever more annoyed with each new refill he ordered. They were keen to be rid of their uneasy customer.

At last, his prey called an end to the evening. At the very instant Alex raised his long arm to call for the bill, Richard was up and heading for the street. He made it as far as the door before one of the waitresses darted in front of him.

"In a hurry, are ya? Don't suppose you want to pay for any of that?"

"Shit, sorry. Of course..."

"Except we deal with your sort all the time, see. No point running off, we're ready for it." She placed a firm hand on his elbow, guiding him to the counter.

"I wasn't running off, I just forgot…"

"That you was sitting in a café eating our food and drinking our coffee? Heard it."

He could hear the seconds tick them towards the oblivion land of too-late. "Look, if you'll just tell me what I owe?"

"Yeah, fine." The second waitress reached for a calculator. With agonising hesitancy, she began to tap figures into the little machine. When she had to start again for the second time his patience vaporised. Pulling his wallet from his pocket, he counted five twenty-pound notes rapidly onto the table.

"Should cover it, don't you think?" They stared at him, not quite hearing what he was saying. His bill could not be more than eight pounds. He remembered her earlier comment. "Don't just sit there with a face like a slapped arse, do you want it or not? Or do you want to work out the exact amount? I'll be happy to pay the exact amount, if you prefer?" She shook her head, and he raced for the door.

Looking across the road, he saw that they had yet to leave the restaurant. Wasting no time, he sprinted down the street, rounding the corner to reach his car. Breathing heavily, wondering if he should leave a note to himself advising that he exercise more, he got in and nudged the engine to life.

Turning into the street, he was just in time to see Alex close the door of a taxi behind him.

The game of cat and mouse began. Richard hoped he was an unobserved stalker, although this was likely not to remain the case for long. Traffic was light for London, for the most part consisting of other black cabs, buses and the occasional late worker. He dared not allow more than one vehicle to get between his quarry and his own car. Any more than that and he would become terrified of getting confused and following the wrong one. He might only discover his mistake when it was too late to pick up the trail again. If the creature thought to look for him at such close proximity, he was easily found.

Still, his choices were few, and at least it simplified the task. Forced to remain almost right behind the black hack, the chase became an almost casual affair, and he allowed his mind to wander.

Alex had not suffered the fit. Presumably he still remembered the coffee scald, it was part of what he was coming to think of as 'The Summers Program'. So, he would have looked at the lobster, remembered the childhood experience and then...tucked into a fine meal, from everything Richard had observed. No disturbing, vivid flashbacks. So the fits were...what? A defence against the programming? He remembered what the creature had implied. Looking at it from the wrong angle, and all the time he had been so close. Not protecting the integrity of Summers at all, for Summers was the alien factor. Rather the vivid memories and physical explosions were a way for the Jameson part of his mind to highlight pieces of the fraud. The coffee scald flashback was conducted by a subconscious that had been screaming *look at this, this is all wrong!* That was what had taken the creature by such surprise. No wonder it was interested in him.

He smiled at the taxi in front of him. *I know something you don't*, he thought.

To his utter shock, Georgina was smiling right back at him. For an instant, they locked eyes. Stopped at a traffic light that was just changing from red back to amber, the creature had watched him for a fleeting second.

Again he thought of cats, mice and traps. Was he pursuer or pursued? The need to know became an imperative as he saw the taxi pull up to the kerb in front an establishment proclaiming itself to be the Scoone Hotel. Knowing they were close to their destination, it had checked that he was still there.

Driving past the parked taxi, he forced himself to look unconcerned. Not for the creature, it knew now that he was there, but for Alex. His friend's life was about to become confusing enough without the worry of amateur watchers tailing him about the streets. Pulling into a side street, he braked to a gentle halt.

Well, he knew where Alex would be that night, at least. Now what was he going to do? Turning off the engine, he sat in darkness and thought. No match for the superior physical strength the creature displayed, he would be wise to avoid a physical confrontation. How then was he to prevent the tasting? It was important that the sexual activities of the night not be allowed to proceed, perhaps because it was a violation too personal, a final stripping of dignity. Richard had been raped that night in the Ramkin, and the fact that he had been made to enjoy it deepened the offence. It had happened again that very morning, more openly, more violently, but the evening at the hotel had been just as much a defilement of his body. The creature had taken everything from him. First went his life as Richard Jameson, then his life as Summers, then his hope, his love, and finally his self-worth.

As his eyes adjusted to the darkness of the alleyway, he could just make out the steam of his breath clouding on the windscreen. Like smoke. It gave him an idea, and he smiled a malicious smile.

Fifteen minutes. That was how long it took him to collect the materials he required. Was he too late? He could only hope not. The trip to the petrol station had lasted no longer than the time it would take for Alex to argue over the lost booking and move up to the new room. Hopefully, as had happened with himself, they might raid the mini-bar before sex.

Time enough then. Parking the car back in the alley, he picked the newly purchased hold-all from the passenger seat and climbed out. He had a large amount of cash with him, having no desire for his actions to be traced back to his credit card. At that moment he was not precisely sure who was running the events in his head. Greg Summers would certainly never have considered such an overt move, but then he did not think Jameson was the criminal type either. Still, he thought, strange days were upon him.

Entering the lobby of the hotel, the strap of the bag biting into his shoulder, he flashed an easy smile at the receptionist.

"Hi there. Room for the night?"

"Yes sir, we do. Single?"

"Alas." The receptionist laughed a little as he filled this into the register.

"Cash or card?"

"Cash. I promise I'll leave the mini-bar and porn channels alone."

"And what name is that."

Richard showed his smile again. "Greg Summers." He knew that Alex, though now performing the Summers persona with aplomb, would have booked under that clever alias of Johnson. If the creature was living under the name of Summers at Fontside Avenue it could well find itself facing unexpected legal difficulties in the morning.

"Sign here please." He did so, then counted the money for the room into a pile on the counter.

"Here's your room card, sir. Twenty-six. Enjoy your stay."

"I intend to, believe me. What floor am I?"

"Sorry, the second."

Richard strolled across to the elevator, smiling as he took in the tacky plastic ferns propped next to the doors. Pressing the button to summon the carriage, he cast a relaxed glance around the lobby. Inside him, the enormity of what he was doing hacksawed through his nervous system. Perhaps Richard was a better actor than Greg, for he felt he was remaining more outwardly calm than expected.

As the doors of the elevator opened with a slight ring, he stepped in and selected the second floor button. Two metal sheets closed before him, and he sank against the wall. His shoulder was beginning to ache a little, and he allowed the bag to slip to the floor. Apparently keen to join it, his stomach fell as the lift rose. With an alarming thump, it settled again as he arrived.

Trying to repress the rush of nausea that centred in his wandering gut, he strode along the corridor. He need not have worried about maintaining appearances, for the passage was empty. What floor would they be on? Was he above or below them? It made no difference to his plan of action, it was enough that they shared the same building, but perhaps he was only metres from where they lay. It made him nervous that the thing might catch him.

Fears crept up on him, making doubt his companion. As he found room twenty-six his shaking hands fumbled the keys, and they dropped to the floor. Bending to pick them up, he started as the door swung open to reveal a pair of female legs.

Instinctively, he threw himself away from her, pedalling backwards until he hit the wall behind him. How had she found his room?

"Are you all right? Sorry if I startled you."

It was not the creature. Of course it wasn't. Looking from the tubby woman in the doorway to the numbers on the door itself, he realised he was at room twenty-eight.

"Beg your pardon," he babbled, "Wrong room. I'm twenty-six." He held out the key to show her.

"Next door." She closed the door behind her, and wobbled down the corridor.

Richard cursed. What was wrong with him? He was beginning to see the enemy in every shadow, around every corner. Trying to pull himself together, he walked to the next room and let himself in. He could not afford to lose it now.

Whatever happened, he had to keep it together for the next half-hour.

28 INFERNO

How long did he have? As he looked around the hotel bedroom, dull shades of green and brown failing to distinguish it from a million others, his eyes rested on the bed as a terrible lethargy settled in him. *No time*, he told himself. *I have no time.* Lowering the bag to the floor, he kneeled beside it and yanked back the zip. Sliding the two petrol canisters free, he placed them to one side, then found the matches and stashed them in his back pocket.

Moving to the windows, he swung each open as far as it would go. He could not allow the fumes to overcome him.

It was there that he paused. Feeling the cool, urban air wash over him, marvelling at the spotlit panorama of the city at night, he felt the crippling weight of his deed and was scared. What if somebody died? Perhaps the exits would get blocked, and people hurt in the rush to escape. He hoped that only the occupant of his own room would be in immediate danger, and he intended be long gone by the time the fire started. Still, best intentions aside, a hundred things could go wrong. He had no idea of what might happen.

Enough stalling, it had to be done. Without another thought on the matter, half afraid that he would talk himself out of the act, he turned back to the canisters. Pulling the cap off the first, he recoiled from the pungent, acerbic aroma that surged into his nostrils. Wiping watering eyes with the back of his sleeve, he turned his head to the window in an attempt to cleanse his lungs.

Then he stood, lifting deadly petroleum with him, and began to splash the liquid over the bed. At least he couldn't be tempted to lie there any more. When he was satisfied that it was sufficiently drenched, he turned his attention to the walls. Dousing them vigorously, he was hyper-aware of the tiny drops that flew back at his own clothing. Biting his lip, he soaked the room until the canister was empty.

It was impossible to breathe without taking great gulps of chemical vapour. Already he felt lightheaded and detached, and he hurried to remove the cap from the second container. With this he wet the carpet, stumbling backwards from the far side of the room to the door, careful to splash as little as possible on his feet.

Half a can left. Just enough. Putting his eyes to the spy-hole in the door, he waited until he was sure the corridor outside was empty. When he felt safe enough, he turned the handle and poked his head out. Sucking in the comparatively clean air, he stepped into the vacant passage and, still working backwards, trailed a thin line of petrol behind him, out of the room. Once he was fully in the corridor he closed the door, hoping it might contain the blaze long enough for everyone to get out, then continued his arsonist's trail for a few feet down the hallway. Not far enough to reach the next door along, but enough to put him a good few feet from the imminent blaze.

Taking the matches from his pocket, he got ready to toss the empty canister far enough from the potential fire so as to be in no danger of igniting. Taking a deep breath he hurled it backwards, away from the room he had left. It landed with a shocking clatter, rebounding tinnily from two walls before coming to rest. Now he really was up against the clock.

Pulling free a match, hearing the sound of a door opening at the far end of the corridor, he scraped the red tip along the side of the box. It didn't light.

"What's the fucking racket?" From the door he had heard open. The speaker was on the opposite side of the petrol trail, a hideously overweight man in boxer shorts and a vest.

He tried another match. It snapped in two.

Now the man was shuffling towards him. "It's no smoking in the corridors fella, can't you fucking read? And what's that smell?" The bloated creature sniffed the air, and Richard watched in horror as he came ever closer to the potentially explosive doorway. Pulling free a third match, he watched the bloodshot eyes of the other man as the implications of the smell, the matches, and the discarded petrol can all registered at once. He was dangerously close to the trail now, if he came any further Richard would be unable to risk lighting it. Holding the match in his fingers, watching the waddling behemoth approach, he felt exposed and afraid. Time to decide.

The third match ignited.

Richard was so relived to see the tiny spark that he almost forgot to drop it. He let it go before his fingers burnt. The fat man stood back in horror, his jowls as loose as his suddenly void bladder. With fascinated dislocation, Richard was aware of these events in slow motion. Guttering almost to nothing, the match tumbled towards the waiting damp of the floor, falling closer and closer, a tiny, beautiful star plunging through potent atmosphere. Then it struck carpet.

With a hushed *whoosh*, the trail became gloriously luminescent. This was no slow ripple of fire moving inexorably towards the door. Rather the blaze made an ecstatic, frenzied rush to the bedroom, fully aware of the nourishment it would find there. A louder sound, the *whump* of burning air, was

CUCKOO

companion to a wave of heat. Richard stepped back, suddenly terrified of what he had unleashed. Now there were two monsters loose in the hotel. Afraid for the guests, he turned and ran towards the stairs, banging each door he came to and yelling at the top of his voice.

"Fire! Fire! For Christ's sake, get out! Fire!" Enough people were stirring for him to trust that he had turned their attentions to the threat, and he darted into the stairwell. Having instigated the fire he was ahead of the crowd. While they were still bumbling around, he was running to beat the creature outside.

Taking the steps two at a time, he hurtled downwards. When he reached the first floor, the fire alarm finally chose to rend the air about him. Why had it not gone off earlier? There had been a smoke detector in his room, but he supposed it might have melted under the heat of the blaze. He had a feeling that he had overdone the petrol a little. That meant there had been a delay while the smoke reached the detector in the hallway.

As he embarked on the last set of steps, the sound of confused voices in the passage on the first floor made him turn his head, and in that moment he lost balance. Falling forwards, his knees were first to connect with a step, the leverage flipping his chest down hard against a lower one. With a convulsive gasp, the air fled his lungs and he slid the rest of the way to the ground floor. Winded and unable to draw breath, he heard approaching footsteps. It was the receptionist, and he was caught.

Firm hands dragged him upright, and he was finally able to take a sharp breath in. "This way sir, as calmly as possible." He was led to the emergency exit at the bottom of the stairwell. He almost laughed, for why would he be suspected of arson? Only the behemoth upstairs knew his crime. As far as this young man helping him was concerned, Richard was just a panicking victim desperate to flee the burning building.

Cold air brought him from his triumphant reverie, and he tried to reassure his unknowing accomplice. "I'm fine. Help the others." The young man nodded and went back inside.

As soon as he was gone, Richard made his way down the alley the exit opened on to, back to the street. He pushed his way past a few of the onlookers who always seemed present for a disaster, sparing a thought to wonder if it was always these same people. When he was clear of the growing crowd he broke into a painful, shambling run. Battered from the fall, each step drew a pained wince from him. Success kept him moving. He had finally won a round, and the tasting was prevented.

More than anything, he wanted the creature to feel the threat. It already knew he had started the fire, frustrated its plans. He had been underestimated, and it would be feeling the wound of that miscalculation. Richard wanted to see if the Georgina-mask had a pout ready for such a disaster.

Checking for potential observers, he entered the side street and climbed into his car. Twisting the key in the ignition, he brought the engine to life and reversed onto the road. Instead of turning from the hotel though, he pulled the vehicle to the right, heading back to the scene of the crime. There was already a short queue of gawking taxi cabs and companion vultures, all diverting their gazes upwards to the blazing window of the second floor.

As he heard the sound of sirens disjoint the passive night air, Richard looked for the faces he knew he would find. Of all the people milling about the pavement, only one had not turned to look at the flames. Georgina stared right at him, her mouth pout-free. Instead, it shaped a hard and terrible line, firm, unyielding and devoid of emotion. Richard shivered beneath the intensity of her eyes. It could do nothing now, not daring to reveal itself among so many casual onlookers, but he knew he had been marked. There would be no more games, it would come for him now.

Unable to rip his eyes away, it was a relief when the traffic moved aside for the emergency services. With his path now clear, he drove into the night, trying to keep one fragile image in his head. The face of Alex Carlisle next to the thing. He had been staring up with the rest of the crowd, thanking God for the life he wrongly thought was his. Gregory Summers was born anew. A cerebral cuckoo, he had lain an egg in the mind of Alex Carlisle, pushing the original inhabitant over the edge and into freefall.

He did not return home that evening. Tired beyond imagining, he had driven only ten minutes before stopping at a bed and breakfast. It was not of the quality he suspected Jameson was accustomed to, but it was adequate for a night of simple rest, and it was anonymous.

That cold, hard line, so unlike the pout he associated with Georgina's mouth, draped over his memory and haunted him.

Lying on the too hard bed, he flicked aimlessly through the pages of a paperback he had found in the lobby. A celebrity biography, it was exactly the sort of trash the Summers personality might stay up to read. He tossed it on the bedside table.

Turning off the small reading lamp, he tried to make sleep come. Though tired, he had pushed himself past the point of actual sleep, into the waking land of frustrated insomnia. Though tempted to distract himself with the small, boxy television in the corner of the room, he was afraid of what it might tell him. Had anyone been hurt at the hotel? Would there be reports of the incident on the news? It was doubtful, but paranoia ensured the little antique remained untouched. What if he *had* been wrong? He had justified his extremism to himself, for it was a high stakes game he played now. The creature had already proven itself an expert in the subterfuge and destruction it wreaked, and if he were unwilling to take equal risks he would have no chance of survival.

However, guilt over his actions aside, a bigger problem now faced him. Having disrupted the pattern he himself had followed, he had no idea what might happen next. Alex, as Greg, would most likely have called an end to the evening, for maintaining his licentious urges would be difficult after a life-threatening experience. So would he have gone home to Fontside Avenue? If so the creature would have to advance the schedule. What would have happened if Richard had not exploded with blood on returning to the artificial homestead? In his case he had been whisked to hospital, but what would the fully healthy Alex be subjected to? How would his torment proceed?

Perhaps the police would be contacted. Again, the creature's words played in his head, this time from when it was in the guise of the only true Greg Summers. *By rights I should have phoned the police...but you are obviously unwell.* So, for Alex, the authorities. He would be held and questioned. The investigating officer would discover that Greg Summers was really a hotel manager called Carlisle, and from there Alex would fall into the nightmare of doubt and revelation which had plagued Richard. Would he return to his flat in the West End, confused and disorientated? It was likely, for his wallet would contain his home address. Tomorrow, Richard would try picking up the trail there.

Turning over beneath the starchy, abrasive sheets, Richard felt sure that sleep would never come. Precisely forty-five seconds later he was proved wrong.

Waking later than he had intended, Richard left the bed and breakfast in a hurry. He had to assume that Alex would be released from custody by now, so he was once more at odds with Time. Guessing that the creature would not have pressed charges, for it would be difficult to reach a victim under the watchful eye of the police, he would have to reach Alex's flat before the man could develop an ill-informed plan of his own.

First though, he had to visit his own apartment again. Knowing from personal experience how futile it would be just to tell Alex who he really was, he had to collect the evidence he would need to back up his assertions. When he had last changed at his flat, he had left the photograph of Alex and he, meeting in the Ramkin Hotel, in the pocket of his jacket. That would not be sufficient to convince his friend, but it would be a better start than words alone.

As he strode through the doors of Manorfield Place he nodded at the doorman. Norman, he remembered. It was surprising how much more settled he felt knowing just these little details. They formed an ever more secure network for Richard to develop in. It would be a while before he could return there, and even now he was taking a risk. Last night he had challenged and frustrated a creature with abilities and motivations he could scarcely comprehend. It would be wise to stay hidden for now. He had surprised the thing, even though it knew he had been there. Not just surprised it either, he had hurt it. Perhaps it was beginning to understand what it was to feel vulnerable.

For the moment though, he thought himself safe. Not only would the creature be readjusting whatever schedule it was trying to maintain with Alex, there was also the matter of the arson from the previous evening. Smiling as he entered the lift, he congratulated himself on thinking to sign in to the hotel as Summers. It would only be a brief diversion, the receptionist would be quick to point out to the police that the tall, long-haired man the creature chose to be was not the man who had signed the register the previous night, but Richard still thought he might have bought himself some time.

Reaching his floor, he pulled the key from his pocket and strode up to the door. There was no sign of a forced entry. With a nod to caution, he slid the key quietly into the lock and entered his home. It was precisely as he had left it. The creature must have been busy indeed not to respond to the affront Richard had been responsible for. Pushing shut the door, he went to the bookshelf and chose a hardback collection of Lovecraft's stories to take with him. Flicking through the pages, he entered the walk-in closet.

It was a little disturbing to see his discarded clothes lying on the floor. In that small recess of his imagination which housed his mind's eye, he was looking at the metaphorical corpse of Greg Summers. In those clothes, that skin, Greg had lived his last minutes before being born afresh in his newest form, like a snake shedding skin before moving to pastures fresh. Its fangs were now sunk tight in the pink, rippled flesh of Alex's brain, but their poison still ran through Richard's own veins. The Summers template was still defining a large part of him, but he at least knew how to fight the effects. It made him laugh to think that the twisted, depraved tales of madness so carefully sculpted by Lovecraft might be the best thing for him. Reading them, he hoped, would unleash more memories of the man who had placed them carefully on the shelf.

Crouching next to the jacket-skin, he reached for the inside pocket. As his imagination worked a kind of magic, he actually felt the garment to be slick, almost greasy beneath his fingers. Unable to banish the feeling, he fumbled around. Nothing. He tried the others. They were all empty.

Perplexed and a little concerned, he stood. Rubbing his watering eyes, for in the enclosed space of the closet the smell of petrol from his clothes was suffocating, he wondered where he might have laid the photo down. Crossing from closet to bedroom, he reminded himself to change before he left. The fumes were making him nauseous.

Throwing open the bedroom door, he stepped in, and then stopped in his tracks.

Richard Jameson's family were engaged in a perverse ritual of incest on his four poster bed. The illusion of naked, heaving movement - his mother gobbling his younger brother's penis, his father taking her from behind - lasted for just one brief second, and then his brain managed to interpret what was before him.

29 BACKDRAFT

It was too overwhelming to accept at first, but his mind eventually had to allow that he had not walked in on some sickening pornographic scene. There was no movement for a start, and too much rope. And, of course, altogether too much red.

Unable to turn away, dazed and repulsed by what they saw, his eyes stuttered across the morbid diorama hanging before him. Stewart dangled, naked, on the left of the bed. A rope was looped round his neck and slung over one of the beams of the four-poster. An angry red bruise shone where the thick cord bit the welcoming flesh of his throat, his head dangling limp over the bright scar of colour. Held up by the rope, his body hung loose, legs folded beneath him to sculpt a penitent man. Everything from the neck down was coated with slick crimson; it took Richard a moment or two to find the source. It lay beneath the rope, on the right of his neck, an ugly slash. Blood still flowed gently from the wound.

The woman he assumed to be his mother had also been arranged. She was face down in Stewart's lap, drenched from her own neck wound, and the waterfall unleashed by her youngest son. Congealing blood crusted behind her ears. She had been positioned on all fours, her blonde permed hair plastered to her skull by the scarlet shower that had drenched her. Stripped of clothing from the waist down, her rear was presented to the third figure. Her husband hung from the cord that draped over the top of the bed to meet Stewart, the weight of each man supporting the other. Mirroring his offspring, he was naked, neck slashed, pelvis pressed against his wife's buttocks.

Richard was in deep shock. He knew this as he shuffled to the bed. Still unable to comprehend what he saw, he could only stare and wonder. Had they been alive when they were bled? Did the creature reveal itself to them in true form before they died?

Why was he not more upset?

He was shocked, disgusted, and repulsed, but it was not a personal grief. He still did not identify these individuals as his family. He recognised them from photographs, but had no knowledge of them as people.

The note caught his eye. It was pinned to one of the posts of the bed, a neat little envelope that would have been conspicuous if not for the colour. Deep red. A perfect match for the drenched bed sheets. As he leaned across to pull it free, his hand brushed the rope that held Stewart upright. In a sickening parody of life, the corpse's head swung from side to side, chiding him for his actions. For a moment Richard paused, staring at the swinging husk. *Dead*, he told himself sternly. *Dead for hours.*

Still, the strange warning was unnerving. What could be worse than the macabre scene he was inhaling and spectating? Confused, he took the envelope. For a second it caught on something, then he had it. Stepping back, he opened the little packet and withdrew the single sheet of paper within. The bold strokes of handwriting matched what he had seen earlier.

Dear Richard, for I see you have returned in part,

I feel I should congratulate you on your arrangement of yesterday's inferno. I wonder how much of you I am addressing? Not much, I suspect. The Summers personality is a persistent one, it would take longer than you have to be free of it entirely. As you probably recognise, the affront that you perpetrated cannot go unpunished. Witness my rebuttal. Should Richard return to us in full, he too shall suffer. There is also an icing on this cake, one more in the flavour of your own assault upon me. Pulling this note from the bed activated a timer connected to a small explosive charge. This, in itself, should do little more than throw some pretty fireworks. However, you have undoubtedly noticed that your apartment smells strongly of petroleum. There are two full canisters beneath the beanbags in the next room. I recommend you be elsewhere when the fire reaches them.

I shall be in touch.

Yours,

Gregory Summers.

It was not Richard who reeked so strongly of petrol, it was his whole flat. How long did he have? Realising that he was not moving, smelling the thick fumes in the air afresh, he took a step towards the door. There was a small click from behind him.

It happened between his first and second step. First that click, tiny and enormous, followed by a small explosion, the heat brushing warm air across the back of his neck.

The petrol caught. In a blazing rush, the room about him became a deadly oven. The increase in temperature was hard enough, he nearly passed out mid-stride, but then the flames rushed past him on either side, overtaking his own desperate bid for the freedom of the exit.

Staggering, he took his next steps over a carpet of fire. An image of the beanbags in the other room, and the time bomb sitting beneath them, spasmed through his head.

Coughing, he blundered through the door, burning his hand as he grabbed the blazing frame to prevent himself falling. In this room too the walls were a incandescent replica of the safety they had once offered, but the carpet had not yet caught. Looking across at the beanbags, he saw the damp trail leading from them, stopping inches away from the furnace of the wall. The carpet of this gap begin to smoulder a way to the petrol.

Desperate, he tried to run, screaming when he realised that his petrol-stained shoes were aflame. Taking two steps, he collapsed with the pain from his blistering feet. Getting his breath was hard, for there was more smoke than oxygen around him. Had he read somewhere that air hugged the floor during a fire? Would it not be better for him to lie down? The creature could have been bluffing about the canisters. There might yet be time to stop and fill his lungs. He thought of how comfortable it would be to never move again, how safe he would be when he died.

He thought of Alex Carlisle, a man who had helped him for no reason other than simple compassion.

Reeling to his feet, he cast his head about. All he could see was whirling, flowing smoke. How had he fallen? Was the door still in front of him? Shuffling agonised feet, feeling each step as a freshly roasted pain, he continued in the direction he faced.

Lifetimes passed. Worlds were born, matured and extinguished. Civilisations rose and fell. Richard lived these aeons as an endless fiery journey forwards. A step. Another.

All he knew was searing heat, noxious fumes, and furious noise. *Lo*, he thought, *the dragon cometh.*

His outstretched fingers touched the bubbling, spitting varnish of the door. Another piercing pain, but welcome this time. Fumbling for the handle, he found hot metal and turned. A thousand super-heated coffee scalds cramped up his arm, and he screamed again, pulling as he did so. The door opened.

Cool air struck him as he stepped forward. Across the hallway stood his neighbour, face twisted in shock and fright. *It's all right*, he wanted to say, *the dragon did it but I ran away.* His parched throat would not form the words; he merely stood silhouetted against his burning apartment, a scorched Mephistopheles.

The canisters.

Despite lacking the strength to even speak, he found reserves to throw himself left of his open doorway. Rolling twice with momentum, he ended up lying face towards his door. Still his neighbour looked on, senseless in the face of what she saw.

The next explosion was huge. The noise and force that slammed over him was stunning, but it was the fireball which fascinated his exhausted attention. Unable to move, he watched it gout from the open door, engulfing the woman who had thought him a decent young man. A blazing new lover claimed her. Before she was hurled backwards into her own apartment, he saw the moment of realisation on her face, bore witness to the slight raise of her eye brows as she stared into the oncoming embrace of flame and pain. Then she was gone, and Richard had to move again.

As the inferno took hold in the hallway, he scrabbled at the floor, dragging himself along the carpet on singed arms. Unable to walk, his feet still aflame, he heaved towards the open doors of the elevator. It was a bad idea to use the lift during a fire, but he couldn't remember why, and didn't care. His whole body was a screaming, tender obscenity. Even through the thick smell of smoke, he thought he could scent the scorching of his flesh. Not a single exposed part of him was untouched. Even those that were clothed sang new sensations of crisp burning. If he tried to use the stairs he would never reach the ground floor. The fire was his enemy now, a ravenous beast unleashed to destroy him. It pursued him, hungered for him, and would catch him on those stairs. The open metal doors were his only possible sanctuary. The fire had feasted on his neighbour, but it would come soon.

His clawing became more frantic. As he cleared the last yards of hallway he was weeping tears his burned cheeks could no longer feel.

Wrenching himself into the elevator, he turned to sit with his back against the wall, staring back at the corridor. The fire was closer than he had dared think, just yards away. It was a relief to know his skin still had nerves enough to feel the massive heat. With an almighty heave, one that split the taut, seared skin of his back, he hit the button for the ground level.

It was only as the doors closed him in that he realised why elevators should be avoided in the case of fire. With no time to reverse his decision, he remembered reading of electrical systems destroyed by the intense heat. The elevator could stop dead before he ever reached the ground. As the tiny metal coffin began to slide downwards, he also recalled why it was so unsafe to be trapped in a stuck elevator while a fire raged. The shaft acted as an air-tunnel that the blaze could rocket through. The beast could take him at a whim.

Floor number five grazed by. Seconds ticked away, and he endured them with helpless frustration. The fourth floor passed him. Not knowing whether it was his imagination or not, he felt a small jolt in the progress of his descent, before the third floor came up to greet him. Downwards he continued; floor two, floor one.

When the doors slid open at the ground floor, the small crowd of anxious maintenance men found him screaming the name of the dragon.

Unwilling to leave him in the elevator, despite the severity of his injuries, the maintenance crew had moved him to a section of grass outside the building. From where he lay, Richard could see the extent to which the fire had spread through the building. Just fifteen minutes after the initial explosion, the three storeys above the sixth were ablaze. Soon the whole building would follow. He had escaped the beast, and now it raged in frustration.

Having deposited him safely on the cool grass, the frightened men who had retrieved him returned to the building in search of more escapees. Richard had to move. He could not allow himself to be hospitalised, though he knew his burns were extensive and serious. The thing would come for him soon, the letter made that clear. It would find him and claim him, and lying prone on a hospital bed would only make the task easier. He had to hide.

Weary, he pulled himself to a sitting position and looked round. A few people, probably his fellow residents, were gathered in the car park, their eyes cast upwards as they watched the destruction of their homes. The fire service had yet to arrive, as had the police. He had to go, for he had no strength to beat off the well-meaning attentions of the authorities.

Battling the coughing which threatened to shatter his smoke-filled chest, he hauled himself to his feet. Surprised that he was even able to put weight on them, he ignored the broken glass pain that dwelt there. Though he wanted to remove his shoes and check the damage, he did not dare.

From the subtle and agonised pulling he felt whenever he took a step, he suspected they had melted to his flesh.

Hobbling around the side of the building, unable to use his seared hands to support himself against the wall, he made for the river. It was easiest, he discovered, to fix his eyes on a distant point and banish thought from his head. There were no shouts from behind him, and no pursuit dogged his smoking steps. It would come though, when the ambulances arrived and the work crew discovered his absence.

Time blurred. He was never aware of the sirens that did come, or of continuing along the river to the heart of the city. At some point he must have left the surging body of the Thames and begun to pass through streets. He had no memory of falling asleep.

When he awoke on a park bench, after an uncertain time, the light told him it was early morning. He did not know where he was, or how he had arrived there. All he knew was the pain and sickness. Raising a shaking hand, he examined his red, blistered skin, noticing yellow pus seeping from his wounds. How much of his body oozed with the infection, he wondered?

Part of his mind had closed down, the part that experienced the pain. It hurt to move, but he knew he should have been unable to even stand. He managed to do so nonetheless. He should have been aware of nothing beyond his own suffering, yet he found himself thinking almost clinically through recent events as he stumbled onwards.

The creature had destroyed him. It had hidden his true life from him, burying it beneath the false premise of Greg Summers. Then it had burned that false life from under him like a set of flimsy floorboards. Eventually, he had rediscovered Richard Jameson. That too was gone now. When Jameson took full control of this body, he would be embracing the murder of his family, the destruction of his home, the crippling of his own body. What difference now which personality inhabited his profane existence?

Despairing and alone, he chose the only direction he could go in. He would find the only man that mattered. Praying he was going the right way, he began staggering in what he hoped was the direction of Alex's flat. It seemed impossible that he could help his friend now. Each step he took was the simple extension of a foot to prevent himself toppling forwards. Several times he was not quick enough, and a collection of bruises and cuts began to join the scarlet of his burns. If he had not even the strength to walk straight, what could he do against the far superior power of the creature? Little, he knew. He would try anyway. There was nothing else left to do.

Streets passed him by as his thoughts wandered. People avoided him, averting their eyes. One woman snorted with disgust, muttering that the streets should be cleansed of people such as he. Several times he wandered onto the road, causing cars to pull up short to avoid him. He was oblivious to the complaints of the drivers. The furious cacophony of horns was a background irrelevance. Days may have passed, or merely hours. Whether he slept during his journey he was unable to tell, though he remembered walking through the dark of night. All that changed for him were the colours. The spectrum of day was full and bright, his night a pallid blend of amber and grey.

When he finally awoke from this waking doze, his finger was on a buzzer marked with the name of Alex Carlisle. The sudden transition from the haze of his wanderings to the harshness of reality made him jump. Were it not for the inflamed burning of his hands and feet, he might have laughed. The sickness running through his limbs had worked into his blood, and he found that he could not stop shaking.

Bending, he vomited onto his own feet. Little more than a clear trickle puke splattered down, and he wondered how long it was since he had eaten.

He remembered his finger, and took the trembling digit from the buzzer. Leaning his shoulder against the wall, he waited for a response. He had few choices anymore. Besides, it felt good to transfer some little weight to his shoulder. His legs were weak with walking and pain.

He was so sure that he would get no response, he nearly screamed when Alex's voice emerged from the speaker. It was small now, frightened and confused. How far down the road had he travelled?

"Hello?"

Richard thought fast, trying to decide on what he could say to allow him access to the man. There was a chance, a single slim hope. He grabbed for it. "Hello." His voice was a harsh croak, unused for hours or days, and he winced as the smoke damage to his larynx tore him. "I'd like...I need to speak to..." *not Alex*, he reminded himself. *This is no longer Alex.* "Gregory Summers please." He ended with a painful fit of coughing.

At first there was no answer, but then the voice came through again. It sounded stronger than before, as if Richard had angered the speaker. "Who are you? How did you find me here?"

Hoping he could fashion an answer before the coughing took him again, Richard hurried his next words out. "I'm a friend. We've met before, but you don't remember me because your head's been screwed with. I know what's happening to you. Please let me in." Another pause, then the buzz of the door being released.

Richard was so grateful to be allowed inside that he hardly noticed the burst of pain from his left hand as he used it to push open the door. Stumbling zombie-like up the stairs, he turned towards the corridor housing Alex's flat.

The door was ajar as he reached it.

"Hello?" Pushing open the door, he took a step into the room. Everything was dark, and he began to wonder if he had the right flat after all. Was it the first or second floor Alex lived on? "Hello?"

A flash of movement to his left, an explosion of pain from the back of his head. Blackness.

30 REUNIONS

With each fresh spate of unconsciousness he underwent it required more effort to rejoin the world he hid from. Why return? What was left there for him? Everything Summers held valuable was a lie from the start, and now Jameson had nothing either. All that awaited him was pain, suffering, and the fruition of the creature's machinations. But though he had been through so much, he still did not know why. He wanted the answer to that question very badly. If Alex and he were fated to be doomed men, he would still have that answer.

Reaching up through the void, he broke the surface and pulled himself through. Almost immediately, he began to laugh. The very first thing to draw his attention was not the crippling burns, nor his hostile surroundings, but the fact that he had a headache. Still chuckling weakly, he opened his eyes. Alex's sitting room. He was sitting on the couch he had infused with blood during his earlier visit, his hands and feet tied with electrical cable. Where it had come from, he did not know, but somebody had also bandaged his burns.

"I'm sorry. I was expecting...someone else." Too weary to be startled, Richard tried turning his head to the kitchen door behind him. Alex saved him the effort by stepping into his field of vision. He wondered how long he had been wandering the streets, for he beheld a changed man. Blond hair hung loose from the customary ponytail, and those fine, angular features were haggard and drawn. Noting his dismayed reaction, Alex forced a half-smile. "You don't look too good yourself."

Richard gave a resigned laugh. "I've had better days. You don't remember me do you?"

"I...don't know. You seem familiar, but I can't place it. Are you friends with Georgina?"

He snorted. "Hardly. Did you treat my burns?"

"I did my best. They look serious."

It was an odd level of acceptance the two men shared, each appearing to appreciate the kindred spirit before them. Without knowing what the other was going through, they seemed both to recognise that they were trapped in the same circumstance. Richard knew he should be glad to see his friend, but all he felt was exhaustion. He had come so far, yet what could he hope to achieve?

"You tied me." Not an accusation, just a statement.

"Sorry. I don't know who you are. I don't know why you're here." As Alex spoke, he took a seat opposite Richard. "My life has been subject to some...unusual developments. I need to protect myself. Whoever provided this flat is going to regret the damage to the rather fine vase I hit you with, but I have to be careful." Richard nodded at this. Of all people, he was the only man alive who could appreciate the fear and confusion Alex felt.

"Greg." He hated himself for perpetuating that lie, even for a moment. "You've found your identity has come under a certain amount of confusion. Your wife doesn't recognise you anymore. In fact, she probably thinks that she's married to another man, also calling himself Greg Summers. All of your ID labels you as Alex Carlisle, to whom this flat apparently belongs. I wouldn't be surprised if the police have also confirmed that identity. You have nowhere to go, nobody to help you. You might suspect some grand conspiracy. How am I doing?"

Alex paled with each new announcement. As Richard finished his speech, he tried to stammer out a reply. "How...how...?"

"Been there. Done that. Until a few days ago I was Gregory Summers as well." Alex shook his head, not understanding. "My real name is Richard Jameson, but I was the sixth man in London to be convinced otherwise. You're the seventh. I remember the coffee scald we're supposed to have received when we were six, just here." He indicated a spot halfway up his left arm. "I remember mum's death and the lack of guilt we felt. What we wanted to do was peel back her eyelids and see her soul. We married Jennifer Sharpe after meeting her on the day of our graduation from Newcastle University. We honeymooned in Florida. You have these memories, don't you?"

Alex nodded, thoughtful and serious. "You mean to suggest that I really am Alex Carlisle, manager of the Ramkin Hotel? That Gregory Summers is an entirely fictional man placed into my head by some outside agency?" Richard was surprised at this rather blasé acceptance. He had expected resistance, tears, and denial. Was Alex so much stronger than he had been?

"Yes. You are. You believe me?" Richard held the eye contact he had established, then faster than he could follow, a fist lashed out and broke his nose. It crumpled easily beneath the taller man's strength, bringing the damp of pain to his eyes as his head snapped back.

"*Who are you!*" Alex screamed into his face. Richard recalled his own reaction when he had met Stewart in the restaurant. This was no real surprise. Shaking his head, he tried to will his nose to stop bleeding.

"Hey babe, no need for violence." At this voice, he did jump. It was Georgina. The thing. It had been there all along, watching, listening to him talk, ready to step in if he showed signs of success. "It's the same guy who came to see me. Tried to tell me some weird shit about not being who I am or something." She was behind him, close to his left shoulder. He couldn't move, but he willed her not to touch him, not to make physical contact with his body. Her fingers brushed the lobe of his left ear, sending a repulsive, delicious shiver down his spine. Feeling nauseous again, he was glad he had emptied his stomach already. As it was, he retched weakly. Increasing her grip, using her nails to draw blood, she held him in place. *How much blood do I have left*, he asked himself?

"I told you I thought he was something to do with it. We should take him to the police and let them sort it out." Despite the trust in Alex's eyes, Richard knew they would not be visiting the constabulary. It appeared that he had at last reached the final stage. Alex's version of Greg had obviously used Georgina for the support that Richard had found in the hotel manager himself. How long had she been waiting for him at the flat, knowing that he had nowhere else to run? She probably went there straight after leaving his apartment. A knot of failure tied his gut, and he realised he had failed at the hotel. Alex was vulnerable and weak, if she wanted to violate him he would have welcomed the physical comfort. Just as Richard had.

"I'll get the car." Alex turned to leave, and Richard felt a flush of panic.

"No! Don't..." She squeezed his ear again, cutting off his words as he hissed with pain. Alex hesitated, worried about leaving his lover in the company of this madman.

"I'll be fine babe, you tied him tight." He nodded and was gone, leaving Richard alone with the thing.

Releasing his ear, she sat opposite him. "Good of you to join us. I apologise for your stay being so brief, but we have an appointment for which we're already overdue." She eyed him with irritation. "It seems I overestimated your ability to deal with the fire at your apartment. I am sorry for that, but rest assured I will be punished." She grinned as his singed eyebrows crawled upwards. "Oh yes, you shall have answers soon enough, believe me. Soon your suffering will reach an ultimate end."

Answers. So many that he needed. "My family?" he breathed. "How?"

"Hardly difficult for one with my talents." As Richard watched, the flesh of her face became molten and flowing. Setting itself in the mould of his own familiar features, her body altered with it. Shapes slid and pulsed beneath her clothing, bulging and reforming. When the grim process was complete, she had become him. Even her weight and height were identical to his own. Unable to take his eyes away, he listened to the doppelganger explain further. "I, or rather you, simply phoned them and invited them for a late breakfast. They were eager. You really should check your messages more often, you had them terribly worried. I convinced the doorman that I had locked myself out, and he furnished me with a spare key. The screams were a little tricky to explain to your charming neighbour. I calmed her though, have no fear." Was that how she had felt as the fireball blew her from her feet? Calm? Fearless? "If you'll excuse me, you'll have to wait for the rest of your answers. Alex, or rather Greg, will be back in a moment. Please try not to alarm him. You already know that I'm stronger than he is, and I would not desire him to come to harm." Melting again, his reflected image became

Georgina. Forcing his stomach to remain still, he turned his head to avoid of the sight.

The thing timed the transformation perfectly. Alex entered as the final muscles shifted into place beneath settling skin. For a moment he stared at her, unsure of what had been wrong with the image he had just seen.

"Something wrong with the car, honey?" Her face was a perfect show of innocent concern.

"What? No. No, it's ready. Is everything okay?" *Go on*, thought Richard, *work it out. Ask the questions.* Alex let it go, hovering in the doorway as he waited for her to join him. Richard wondered if he had been this docile when he had been the victim.

The creature spoke to him, voice low. "You are to be untied. You will not try anything so foolish as a bid for freedom. You are in no condition to run, and Greg here could easily overpower you. Nothing would be accomplished except your further pain." The warning was unnecessary. She had already given him the only promise that mattered now. Answers.

So he did not struggle when she removed the cable binding his hands and feet, though he winced a little, for it pulled at his burns when she tugged the knots. Alex approached him, warily, but giving him a shoulder to lean against as he rose to his feet. Limping, expelling sharp rasps of breath with each step, Richard followed his friend's lead as they left the flat. When they reached the car, he sat in the back as the creature rattled the engine to life.

Nobody said anything for the first part of the journey. Georgina drove with a silent air of triumph. All her eggs lay securely about her now, and she knew she was about to succeed. Alex was a little anxious, no doubt wondering whether the police would really be able to help him. Every few minutes he swung his head round to check on Richard, unnerved to have the person he assumed responsible for the strangeness in his life sitting right behind him.

Richard was restless, eager to end the journey. He knew there would be two stages to the evening. At the prospect of the first he was excited. There was a reason, and he would be told what it was. He was to learn why he had suffered so. Whatever happened next would have a point, however insidious that might be. Of the second part of the evening, the part where he would join the medical statistics in the study at Fontside Avenue, he was devoid of anticipation. Nothing he could imagine would prevent his death, and if there were a solution he had no will to take it. Nothing remained to fight for. Everything that he remembered, apart from the last two weeks, was nothing. His only real life had involved his fight against the creature, and he was tired of it now, exhausted beyond the ability to struggle. He wanted an end, one way or another.

"Which police station are we taking him to?" A note of unease coloured Alex's voice. They had been driving for nearly fifteen minutes in utter silence, and for the first time it had crossed the man's mind that something was far from right. Richard pursed his lips in a hard smile. It was about time.

Georgina did not even turn her head. "Shhh. First we have to visit somebody who can help us. They know things we can use." Alex stared at her, confused. Richard was also intrigued. He knew about Jennifer of course, but were there more people involved than just the creature's human servant? He had seen no evidence of a wider conspiracy, but the inference hung tantalisingly before him.

"Who?" Alex voiced the question but Richard knew they would get no answer.

"Tell you later. Don't want to get him upset."

Alex turned to look at him, perplexed and frustrated. Catching Richard's own puzzled expression, he gave an unsure nod, then chose silence.

There was nothing to do but sit back. Watching the amber glow of passing street lamps, Richard let his mind drift. Had he, the real Richard Jameson, ever walked those streets? Perhaps he and a lover had wandered hand in hand through London districts, exploring and enjoying. He realised that he had no idea where he was actually from. Was he local, or from further afield? Where had he grown up? Where had he wallowed in the loving environment of his family?

Feeling dampness on his cheeks, he wiped the fast forming tears from his eyes. Only then did the extent of his failure really strike him. Richard Jameson was not to be rescued from the dark place where he was trapped. Even if he were, it would be an escape to heartache and pain, the very turmoil Summers had felt as his fantasy life had been stripped from him. Richard would wish that on no man, least of all himself.

Alex too was lost. A brave, compassionate soul who had committed no crime but to aid a man he had just met, his fate was as certain as Richard's own. Perhaps this was the greater failure, for if Richard had not spurned him in the cellar of the Ramkin Hotel he might be safe. Why had he spurned him? He adored him.

Had the two met under different circumstances, they could have been lovers, and this brought fresh tears to Richard's eyes. He had identified at least one point where the cycle might have been broken. After discovering that Jennifer did not know him, he and Alex could have left, could have made a new life for themselves away from these troubles. It was a fantasy, he knew, but a painful one. Just one opportunity to turn back the clock, to continue kissing Alex, to flee with him and enjoy him.

He punched the car door hard, replacing tears of might-have-been with droplets of pain. Alex swung his head about again.

"You're not going to start trouble, are you?" It was a worried enquiry, but it held a note of warning. In the darkness of the car, Richard could just make out the concerned glint of Alex's eyes. A hard wrench yanked his heart across his chest, as he remembered when that concern had been coloured with care.

"No,' he said. "I'm sorry for everything. I enjoyed our kiss."

A sickened twist warped Alex's features. "You...what are you saying?"

They were talking at cross-purposes now, but Richard continued regardless. "That I'm sorry." It felt good to say the words, and when Alex turned to the front with a contemptuous shake of his head, he knew this to be the reaction of Greg Summers alone. Perhaps, wherever he was confined, Alex Carlisle had heard the words and was glad.

When he first saw the building they were driving toward, Richard was a little surprised. Unsure of where they were, he could only really place the area as the same style of suburbia as where the creature held the property on Fontside Avenue. Perhaps it was Richmond, for that was shouting distance from Wimbledon, and within easy reach of the city itself.

The building that loomed before them was no semi-detached home. Surging from the left-hand side of the road was a gothic Victorian schoolhouse. It was derelict on the outside, a lonely victim of education cuts. A large clock tower on the near wing poked a crude finger at the sky, overshadowing the two-storey schoolhouse sheltering beneath it. Much of the window glass was long gone, and the arch of the double doors at the front was firmly chained shut. It was the chain that told Richard this was the last place on earth he would see. It was bright new steel. Not rusted, not aged, but gleaming. A fresh plaster on the scar of the building.

His guess was immediately proven correct, as the car swung into the playground through iron gates that hung open on twisted hinges. Coming to rest before the square thrust of the porch, the creature allowed the hum of the engine to die before turning to face him.

"Out." It said nothing more, exiting itself. Alex hesitated for a moment, it was obvious that the situation was unnerving him. With a tiny, bemused shake of his head, he opened his own door and climbed into the night. Richard went last, curious and eager. The creature was standing by the doors, slipping a key into the heavy padlock that bound the chain. With a twist, the metal links were free.

"George, what the hell are we doing here?" Alex was wary, the paranoia that had festered in him since becoming Summers was being put to good use. She turned to him, her face open.

"Trust me Greggie, I know about this place. I've got friends here who you have to see."

"Why don't we go straight to the police?"

"We will, but he's just a little piece of the puzzle isn't he? We'll find the rest here."

Still, Alex hesitated, his pinched face childlike in the light of the street lamps. "George, how do you *know* this?" Richard was surprised that the thing had remained patient this long, for it still showed no sign of irritation.

"Babe, please. We haven't got much time. I promise it will become clear, okay?" That much, Richard believed, was true.

Alex finally consented. Stepping forwards, he grabbed the door on the left and heaved hard. Scraping across the ground with a screech, it revealed a dark nothing within. Georgina smiled and gestured.

"After you, gentlemen."

31 DARKNESS

For a few moments after Richard stepped into the darkness he was aware only of the damp musk of the air and the shelter from the wind which the large porch offered. After a moment or two, his eyes began to adjust to what little light spilled in from the outside. Of his surroundings he could discern little, although he was certain that the space was empty. The walls stood out as straight lines of more solid dark, and he thought he could make out the hollow of a doorway at the far end of the room.

"Forward." He shivered at the proximity of her voice, just a foot or two behind his ear, and began a broken stumble through the gloom. Pain had become a familiar thing, the certain knowledge of his impending death making him more willing to accept it. Though his crippled feet spiked him as he progressed, he was able to walk without complaint.

A shuffling sound to his left made him jump, but the looming shape was only Alex. Ignoring him, arms outstretched, he continued until the tips of his ruined fingers brushed the slick damp of the wall.

Stopping there for a few moments, unwilling to go further into the building for fear of losing himself to the sheet dark, he waited to see what was to come. A muffled thump told him that Alex had also found the wall, then there was silence. Looking back over his shoulder, he was surprised by how little distance he had covered.

Georgina remained in the entrance, her features in shadow, and for a moment Richard thought she would leave them there. The door would be sealed again, the rats would feast. Of course, that was hardly the likely course of events. There were dozens of possible escape routes for them to take, including the many shattered windows he had noticed as they drove up. Though he would prefer not to wander the dark passageways in search of them, it would be the least of his recent trials.

She turned her back to them, grasping the interior of the door with one hand and pulling. This time it came easily, screeching inwards as though recently oiled, crashing closed and sending echoes through the building. An almost comical gasp sounded from his left, and he imagined Alex comparing the weight of the door he had heaved open with the size of the girl he thought to be his mistress. *Good for you*, Richard thought, *what does two and two make?*

With the door shut, the slight light it had afforded them was extinguished. A new darkness settled over the room. There were no lines to define walls, no shapes to be other people. Richard held his breath, afraid of the discordant whine of his own gasps. As an experiment he raised his hand in front of his face. Nothing. Bringing it closer and closer, he winced as he tapped it to his sticky, broken nose. An explosive hiss of pain escaped his lips, but he still could not see his fingers.

Sounds were very important in this land of the blind, and the first to catch his attention were footsteps. It was Georgina, striding through the nothingness to meet them, yet the noise was gargantuan against the hush that so belonged in that place. Thoughts ran through his treacherous mind as she approached. She was about to take them, committing her brutal dual sacrifice and then walking away. Her London tasks would be complete, she would move on to reap of pastures fresh. Another seven results waited from the Summers Program.

Despite his imagination's best efforts, he knew it was not yet the moment of his death. All the hoops he had been pushed through, the efforts that had been devoted to his suffering, could not possibly be for something so *small*.

As if to validate his point, the footsteps passed him on his right – somewhere between himself and the last place he had known Alex to be – and he knew she had gone through the door. As her footsteps receded into what may have been a corridor or large room, her voice called back. "Wait." That was all.

With no warning or time to prepare, he had an opportunity. Not knowing whether he had seconds or hours, he turned his head in the direction he hoped Alex might still be.

"Run." No response, just the black abyss staring back at him. "Alex? For fuck's sake, run!" Hating the silence for making his whispers shouts, he waited for a reply. Again, nothing. Wondering if his friend was still there, whether perhaps he had followed the creature through the invisible doorway, he tried again. "Alex?"

"Don't call me that! My name is Gregory Summers! Gregory fucking Summers!" Even that hushed, violent whisper sent an echo around the room, or perhaps it just echoed round his mind, singing the death march of each Greg Summers who had gone before them?

"Fine, Greg then. But listen to me, you have to get out before it comes back for us. Before our time runs out. It'll kill us Greg, destroy us, enjoy our suffering..."

"Shut up!"

"*Enjoy our suffering*. You have a chance. For God's sake, go!"

A pause, a brief silence for the darkness to fill. Then Alex's voice again. "You're lying."

"No. I'm sorry, but I'm not." Why was he being so obstinate? "I'm telling you it means to kill us."

"Who…"

"Hell, think man! Who do you think I'm talking about? Georgina! Why has she brought us here? Why has she left you alone in the dark with the man you think has destroyed your life? Why does she have the key to that padlock? Just think it through. You've seen what she's done to me. I could tell you more, but Greg, *you don't have time!* She's finished with us. We're together in the same place. It's the endgame!"

"I…I don't…" then they both ran out of time. There was no warning of her return, no echoing footsteps to rise above his harsh whispers. One moment he was listening in frustration as Alex pieced together a frightened reply, the next he was doubled over as his groin shattered in steel-solid agony. Fingers wrapped around his testicles, nails biting in with eerie superhuman strength. Yet the pain was nothing compared to what he knew he would experience if that grip tightened further. She could crush him. A strangled whimper fled his lips, and he wished the rest of him could follow it.

"George?" Alex said. "Is that…"

Both men gasped as a sudden light passed through their eyes to the pain centres of their brains with razor-edged intensity. She had brought a torch back with her, though it felt like she held a ferocious infant sun in her grasp. For a confused second Richard didn't know what hurt more, his enveloped scrotum or his blinded retinas. The latter passed as his vision cleared, and he prayed to a God he didn't believe in that she would just *let him go*.

"Be quiet Alex. Your turn will come."

"Alex? What…" Without releasing her hold on Richard, she swung her free arm backwards, connecting with Alex's midriff and knocking him with stunning force against the crumbling plaster of the wall. Emptying of air with a violent rush, his chest rose spasmodically outwards in an attempt to refill the sudden vacuum. He was not certain, but Richard thought he had heard the sharp crack of ribs popping loose. There was a whimper, and a rasping crackle as Alex fought to breathe.

Then all he knew was sweet relief as Georgina relinquished her hold of him. Light-headed with the sudden lack of pain, he dropped to his knees with a convulsive sigh. Alex no longer mattered to him, he wished only to kneel and relish freedom.

Her voice shackled him again.

"Up. Or I will hurt you again." *I can't*, he wanted to tell her, *I can't even feel my legs*. Knowing that his pathetic moans made him a crying child, he pushed the comforting floor away from him with rubber arms. A guttural grunt blew from his mouth as he forced himself to kneel, putting unwanted pressure on his groin. As he paused to gather himself for the effort it would take to stand, she bent and hauled him to his feet. Reaching out on instinct, he grabbed her shoulder to prevent himself collapsing again. Recoiling from the touch he had instigated, he took step backwards. Her predatory smile disgusted him, as did the realisation that she knew of this repulsion and was using it to unsettle him. Resolving himself to show no more weakness, he stood his ground and met her stare.

From the corner of his eye, he saw movement, and was just in time to catch Alex's arm as it began to launch towards her. It would have been an ineffectual blow, and Richard stopped it with ease despite his wounds, grabbing his wrist before he could connect. He had no intention of allowing her to be angered further. "Stop. She'll only hurt you more."

Alex met Richard's steady gaze. Seeing the fresh resolve there, he nodded, taking a less aggressive stance. Whether he thought that Richard had a plan, or whether he simply accepted the futility of action, was uncertain. It was irrelevant to Richard, who now wished only to hear his answers.

Turning back to her, he raised his eyebrows. In answer, she directed the beam of the torch through the doorway, into the room beyond. Leading Alex by the wrist, surprised that the taller man was prepared to allow the imposition, he stepped through.

It looked to be the main hall of the building. Even with the limited light available from the torch he could see how derelict it had become. At some point there had been squatters there, and blankets still lay spread along the floor of the stage at the far end of the room. Shuddering, he cast a glance at the creature following them. It was easy to imagine what could have happened to those derelicts. Feeling sick at the thought, he remembered the vagrant in the photographs on the study wall.

There was no light from outside, for the high windows were boarded up. Even during daylight, the darkness would be complete. Along the walls of the large room were numerous doors. It was too dark to be sure, but Richard assumed that some would lead to corridors while others were the entrances to long abandoned classrooms. Unsure where to go next, he stopped in the middle of the room and looked back. Though he could not see the creature for the dazzle of the torch, it could see him. The beam flicked to a door on the right.

"There. Then the last on the left." Hesitating for only a second, he trailed through the thick dust on the floor. In the torchlight he could make out the remnants of other tracks, some fresh, others older and less distinct. Following those footsteps, he felt himself joining a huge and inevitable pattern.

Through the frosted glass panels in the top half of the door, he could see a corridor stretch away from him. He pulled the reticent Alex through after him. Every muscle he had just wanted to stop now, to collapse and end. All that kept him moving was the knowledge that he was approaching the closure he sought.

Down the corridor he went, noting that it was less than two men wide. Doors passed on either side, broken glass from their small panels crunching in the gloom underfoot. When they reached the end of the corridor, he saw the clean patch on the floor beneath the door on his left, where opening it had swept the dust aside. Tracks vanished beneath it, but when he turned the handle he found it locked. Again, he turned to the glare of the torch. Shooting Alex a brief glance, worrying at the glazed look in his eyes, he addressed the creature.

"Locked."

"Most of the derelicts stay in the hallway. Some like to wander." There was a metallic flash as the torchlight gleamed off a small object, and Richard caught the key that flew towards him. Shrugging, he slid it into the lock and opened the door.

Stairs led down to darkness, but at the very bottom there was a thin slash of light. Richard reasoned it to be leaking under a door. A door to a well-lit room. God, he was so close now. Taking the stone steps with care, he began to descend, terrified of losing his footing. How idiotic to come this far, and miss the answers because of an accident.

Safe at the bottom, he turned to the door he had known would be there. The creature whispered from behind him. "The same key." Richard searched for the keyhole with his fingers. His anxiety rose, the hushed tones of the creature replaying in his head. With a shock, he knew that he had heard awe in that voice. Awe, respect and...and fear? Feeling cold sweat trace the contours of his spine, Richard wavered. Did he really need to know the reasons for his suffering? He had thought the creature to be the worst of what he might face. Having seen its true form, he had assumed that the last thing he had to fear was the truth. Now he was less sure. Some of his composure leaked from him, panic reclaiming a foothold in his gut.

"Why the delay?" Panic, it seemed, did not prey on him alone. There had been an edge to the voice more terrified than authoritative. With his horror mounting, Richard realised that his fingers had found the keyhole. The thing was right, he had no reason to pause. He considered running for it, just turning and rushing past the creature and Alex, fleeing until the strength was gone from him. The notion lasted for less than a second before his common sense intervened. He was injured, exhausted, probably incapable of running back up the stairs even if he tried.

It came down to a simple choice. He could stall and hesitate until the creature lost patience and dragged him kicking and bawling into the room, or he could hold his pride. Despite everything that had been taken from him, all of the pain and violation he had endured, he could better the thing that had inflicted it.

Taking a deep breath, he unlocked the door and walked through.

Blinking while he adjusted to the light, he barely registered the huge, old-fashioned boilers set to one side of the room, against the wall. These were not what arrested his attention because, incongruous as it seemed, the world's biggest fish tank sat squarely in the centre of the room. The thing was almost as tall as the room, a good twenty feet high, modern and impressive. Rubber pipes ran to it from an equally large machine sitting flush with the left side of the glass cube. This looked to be a container of sorts, similar to the huge steel crates that carried cargoes across oceans, with a small control panel set in the front. From the bottom of the glass tank, more tubes ran into a small steel cylinder standing a few feet in front of him. Next to this was a metal trolley bearing a laptop. There were an ominous set of what looked like intravenous drips attached to the cylinder.

Was that it? Were they to be bled dry, his and Alex's blood mixing in the tank to be used in some ungodly sacrifice? He shook his head. It felt too...well...too *medical* to be arcane apparatus. Where were the altars and mystic circles? Maybe he was being naive, but it felt wrong. Taking a few steps into the surprisingly clean room, he continued his awed inspection.

A startled gasp made him whirl round. Alex had lost his hopeless, disorientated demeanour. Richard turned to see what he was looking at. Behind them, against the wall in which the door was set, there was a small camp bed. Jennifer was lying on it.

She looked terrible. Pasty white, her skin was clammy, waxy and thin. Since he had last seen her just a couple of days ago, she had lost an enormous amount of weight. Her cheekbones stood out in an alarming attempt to break through her paper face. Her neck looked incapable of holding her head up, the muscles having atrophied to the point of uselessness. Blankets concealed the rest of her from sight, but Richard guessed that ribs were thrusting painfully through dying flesh, arms and legs were stick-thin, hips jutted up like shark fins.

Despite knowing that she was not who he had believed, the Summers part of him still wanted to rush to her aid. What had the creature done to make its slave so pitiable? Was it a punishment? Perhaps an entertainment? Disgusted by what he felt and saw, he turned his head away.

It was because he did so that he noticed the creature, still in the guise of Georgina, enter the room. To his shock, he watched it cringe back against the wall. Knowing that Alex was paying no attention, he heard the thing mutter under its foetid breath. "They're here. I'm sorry I was longer than planned. Please..." It trailed off, head lowered as though accepting a scolding from a stern headmaster. Stunned at this show of weakness, Richard turned back to Jennifer. Had it been talking to her? She seemed asleep, but...

"You murdering whore. What have you done to her?" Alex spoke softly, and Richard realised what the man was seeing. The woman Greg Summers loved was dying in front of him, victim of whatever elaborate scheme his mistress Georgina had concocted to fracture his life.

Before Richard could say a word, Alex strode over to the bed and dropped to his knees, eyes watering to see his wife so helpless. Running a gentle hand through her lank, greasy hair, he whispered to her. "Christ. Oh, Jesus Christ, what has she done to you?"

Flicking open with spring-loaded violence, her eyes fixed his. For one shocked moment, Richard watched them regard each other, then his ears split as Alex screamed.

How could a human being reach that pitch, find that savage note?

Face to face with the woman he believed he loved, Alex stared into her eyes, and howled.

With an abruptness that made Richard's heart leap, it stopped. Alex switched off. Pulling his hands from his bleeding ears, Richard watched in mute horror as his friend went rag-doll limp and fell to the floor.

32 EXPOSURE

Alex glided to the floor in warped slow motion. Richard wanted to blink, to shake his head free of what had to be an illusion. What had just happened? The sharp, solid retort of Alex's head smacking against the concrete floor made it a hard reality.

Jennifer rose, bending at the waist to sit upright. Blankets fell to expose her naked torso, and the gauze-thin skin stretched to breaking point over a fleshless rack of bone. She looked as though her innards had been vacuum-pumped out, making her smaller and smaller, liposuction at its most extreme. She could have been a joke-shop zombie were it not for her breasts, two grotesque and pallid paper bags. Dead flesh, nothing more.

She looked at him. At first he was fascinated by her eyes. There was something wrong with them, something missing. It took a few moments, then he realised that what they lacked was life, and any trace of humanity at all. Chilled, he tried to make himself turn away from this thing which part of him still wanted to claim as his wife.

He couldn't. There was nothing wrong with his neck, he could feel his battered muscles ready to perform the act, but he couldn't give the command, nor even remember what the command was and how to form it. Despite the chorus of terrified screams in his head, he could not will himself to *want* to look away. All that existed for him were those two wet images of the grave. If Gregory Summers had managed to pull back the lids of his mother's eyes, they might have looked very much like Jennifer's. Nothing was more real than those slack eyes, for he was looking through the trickster veil of reality and seeing what was on the other side.

As though aware of his sudden scrutiny, reality contracted. Still looking into those dry pupils, he found himself uniquely attuned to his own body. Aware of every tiny particle, he was struck by the multitude of what lay in Richard Jameson. Each individual nuclei and electron called out for his individual attention, and with each cry he was larger. All those microscopic particles, every one independent and whole in itself, joined to form atoms, molecules, chemicals, cells, organs, sub-systems, systems and, finally, the entity of Jameson. He was huge, a giant. Like a universe. Or a god.

With a sickening mental jerk, his perspective inverted. He was aware of his whole being, but suddenly he also felt the room he stood in. Only a small part of the space was filled with Jameson. A minuscule thing, he was aware of the displaced air that his foreign body had shifted from this part of the overall structure. Perceiving the tank in the centre, the walls, the ceiling, he was diminished.

With another dizzying mental lurch, his awareness expanded to the size of the whole building. Rooms, corridors, halls and stairwells were known to him, each in shocking detail, each a tiny contributor to the whole. Somewhere amongst this was a speck called Jameson, a small, mobile particle hardly touching what he drifted through. Seen from above, he was barely noticeable, a shifting grain.

With crushing immensity, he whooshed outwards to know the metropolis of London. Fighting for breath, still aware of himself and his position in the whole, he thought that somewhere in there, he was starting to scream.

Where he had been inconsequential before, he now became something smaller than that. Boroughs made up the organs of this grand beast, buildings and streets were cells and capillaries. So then, what was he to this titan? Less. How could he be of importance to anything in this place? Where was his legacy, for a nothing such as he could not hope to leave even a mark on the beast. Knowing what would come next, fighting against it as tears drowned his face, he saw London against the British Isles, the colossus now a Lilliputian, he so small as to not register at all. Sweat dripped from his hands, though this tiny reaction was a literal nothing to him. It was agoraphobia as few living souls could understand, pounding him, reducing him.

Wrenched outwards again, he was shown his place against the backdrop of the planet. Would he ever breathe again? He felt the universe, and his part in a void where the very stars were grains of nearly nothing. If God existed, if God could see and feel all that Richard saw and felt, then surely He was long mad. Was he shrieking as Alex had? Did it matter? When galaxies died within him and he barely noticed, nothing he did mattered.

It all switched off. Feeling the universe in one moment, he was next conscious only of the dying screams from his bleeding throat. Drool dripped from his chin, and he collapsed to the floor. None of his muscles worked. He had forgotten how to move them. In trying to flex a bicep, he was at the same time attempting to change the orbit of a sun, the flow of continental drift. Even the pain, as his flesh slammed hard against the concrete, was nothing next to the implosion of a star or the birth pangs of a mountain. Wetness dripped from him to the floor, and he could not remember if they were tears or tsunamis. All he could do was fight to inhale each immaterial, hurricane breath, wrestle with the continuation of his insubstantial, thunderous heartbeat.

His unblinking eyes saw pallid stick-legs drop to the ground next to the bed. It was not possible for him to glance upwards at Jennifer, but he concentrated on those thin appendages as they limped by. Though his face remained slack, he winced inside as he watched the pressure of her weight on the floor split the soles of her feet. Only a little blood seeped from her wounds. She walked beyond his static field of vision, and he wondered how those twig limbs even held her upright.

Anxiety flushed rationality away, as he realised he had ceased to breathe. Frightened that he might forget how to begin again, unable even to indicate that he was in trouble, he waited in horror.

His chest rose in another gasp, an automatic muscular twitch that he could not control. If it stopped, he would die.

Voices. Hoping that he would survive the distraction, he separated a very small part of his attention from the effort to live, and listened.

"...waiting for Jameson." Tremulous and hesitant, the voice belonged to the creature. Now Richard understood why it was so afraid, how wrong his assumptions had been. She was the adversary, and the creature was only a slave. Like an eager spaniel, it had obeyed her instructions as best it could, but Richard had foiled whatever careful schedule she wished to maintain. Now the creature too would suffer, and Richard felt a strange pity for it.

"It will be brief, my sweet. Only pain. I'm doing it because I love you." Jennifer's honey-husky voice, but colder and deeper than he remembered, as though it echoed off forever. A brittle snap, sudden and loud, followed by a tentative whimper. Jennifer spoke again.

"Now place Seven in the bed. I will speak with him." A tremor tried to ripple his lifeless muscles, but failed. "Take Six for preparation. We start in an hour."

Damp footsteps approached him, the almost familiar, fresh meat stench of the creature's true form forcing passage through his nostrils. Still paralysed, he could do nothing but accept the forthcoming touch. At least he lacked the strength to vomit, and so a small piece of dignity would remain his. As the creature bent to lift him, slick reds and dank blacks suddenly filling his sideways view of the world, he realised that something was wrong with what he saw. Skinned arms bore him up, and his lifeless head fell back. For a few seconds the world, vast and incomprehensible as he had seen it, was yet less explicable as he perceived it upside down. Then he was lying on the camp bed, looking up. If his inert mouth were not already hanging open he would have gawped.

The creature's foul skull also dangled limply from a redundant neck. At first he thought it had received a smaller dose of what he had undergone, but then he noticed the angle at which the cranium lolled. Jennifer's love, it seemed, had manifested in reaching out and breaking vertebrae with her bare hands. Jennifer, even ravaged by whatever ailment beset her, had twisted and shattered the spine of this awesome horror. Terror puked over Richard's soul.

The creature departed his field of vision. If his vocal cords could be forced into some semblance of life, he might have called out, begged it to stay. He would have grovelled, debased himself, cast aside the little shreds of dignity he had won – anything to make it remain. He was discovering that the devil he knew was the preferable torment.

The gunshot bang of the closing door marked its exit. Those shuffling steps which now drew closer to the bed could only belong to whatever monstrosity Jennifer was. Hard, bony fingers touched his hair, trying to stroke, but managing only to scrape. Scalp howling at her scratching, digging touch, he would have given his life to be able to move his head away from those five probing digits. He could not, nor could he close his dried-up eyes as her skeletal face filled the fullness of his view, hanging just inches from him, like death itself. That was what she represented now.

"You think you want to see," she breathed at him. To his surprise, her breath was not rank. Where he had expected, perhaps, the stale odour of the morgue to coat her exhalations, he was stunned to smell the feminine taste of the woman he had thought he loved. On a primitive level, the Greg Summers Program responded to the proximity of the wife he had wished so hard to reclaim. Despite the haggard, starved skull that balanced inches from his face, he was getting an erection. Regardless of his terror, he wanted to guffaw. Of all the organs in his body, that had to come back online first.

She smiled down at him. "Oh, Gregory. You realise this is practically incest? I birthed you, child, and this is oedipal." Richard realised, with a piercing emotional stab, that she was right. Though Richard Jameson had been brought into the world by an act of physical procreation, this thing had somehow created Gregory Summers. When her near fleshless hand cupped his engorged penis, sending a delicate trickle of sensation through his groin, he did not know whether he was weeping tears of revulsion or frustrated desire. "Still, what mother could deny her own child?" With a malicious half-smile, she leaned forward and kissed him. Though the sensation was harsh, her teeth having infinitely more substance than her parched lips, it was the most bittersweet experience of his short life.

When she withdrew both hand and mouth from him, he could not help but wonder if she had just kissed him farewell. He had been promised answers.

She broke into his chain of thought as though she had read his mind. "Answers you will have, to make of what you will. Now that we are close, our link becomes so much more than a passageway for suffering. I have always been with you Gregory. Now I am one with you, as you shall be one with me." Her words were a nonsense, and her smile blossomed into the grin of the Reaper itself as she collected this thought too.

Her eyes bloomed into dark pits. His mind toppled forwards, falling into her.

Years rolled back on her long, long life. Richard saw a hovel home, and a scraping life. An attack, the slashing of her neck, and the deep, orgasmic death to service another. She had risen, unaccepting, until the shattering cramps of need drove her into a dark new life.

Memories flowed past and through him like a powerful breeze, images flying by so fast he could not land on any single one, and was left with the most inadequate impressions. Days, then years, of running, hiding, feeding. Powerful but fragile, afraid of no man, yet plagued by fool weaknesses. Her power grew. Others of her kind came to know her, respect her authority.

Centuries streamed by, and even the weaknesses grew less potent. Passing into myth and fiction, the printing press giving her new freedoms. The long sea voyage to Great Britain, and then humanity's two vast attempts to slaughter itself. Feeding on battlefields, the corpses she left behind unnoticed in the carnage.

Capture. The round-up of her kind by the great superpowers. The experiments and cages, the constant testing, starvation, and madness. Years wondering whether those like her were changed in the same way, whether they had survived at all, contemplating eternal loneliness. Evolved beyond what she should be, she found escape, and slaughter. An impossible pregnancy as she toyed with her new gifts, discovered how they had advanced her. The birthing of the skinless thing, with gifts of its own that came clear in time.

Coming to know her new self, and the thrilling new ways to feed that had been bequeathed to her by men in white coats. The feast that came with the suffering she could cause, and the raw power it gave her. Developing templates. Findo Gask. Ashgar Singh. Settling on Gregory Summers, the richest pool of suffering, the most prone to guilt and self-torment.

The hunts began, her link with each victim feeding their pain to her long before she came to drink them, and she had never been captured again.

33 VICTORIES

His mind slammed back into his head. He had fallen right through her life, and the hurled back out again. A lifetime spanning longer than he could comprehend, fed to him in the space of...what? Seconds? Minutes? Less than an hour, for that was when the process was scheduled to begin. Now he had the first horrible notions of just what that might be. A relic of childhood superstition, made real.

What was he to the haggard thing that hung above him, watching the events in his mind with an inhuman curiosity so old it had *forgotten* how to be human? She was a functional, evolved killing machine enduring existence by stealing joy, life, and sustenance. The mundanities of a human life were far behind her, and she toyed with mankind like a malignant god.

Those were his answers, both crushingly simple and terrifying in their complexity. She had found him at the club, programmed him, and fed off his suffering as he struggled with each carefully designed torment. She had been with him for the entire of the short life Summers had endured. Linked in an unfathomable way, his pain had channelled to her, fodder for her soul's appetites. That single moment of rape he had experienced was nothing to what she had done to him.

Bitter, guilty relief washed through him that whatever came next, Alex would be first. Now that he knew the answer, he found that it was not enough. He wanted to move on, and rebuild. If Alex could buy him enough time to recover from his paralysis, he was shocked to discover that he would take it.

"We are all slaves to base instincts, sweet." She spoke the words with almost touching sincerity; there may have been a momentary glint of remorse in her eye. She turned from him, towards the sound of an opening door. As she shuffled away, her footfalls were drowned by the heavier steps of the creature entering the room. Without ceremony, it pronounced the doom of Alex Carlisle.

"An hour has passed. He has yet to move of his own volition. Does that change things?"

"The process will work as always. Prop the other so he can witness what is to become of him." Had she heard his treacherous thoughts? Of course she had, and he could not have prevented himself thinking them.

The creature was clearly surprised. "Mistress?"

"You question?" Soft, harsh sounds. Power shone from them, and Richard had no doubt that she could easily best the creature she had spawned.

"Mistress I...no, I..."

"Then still your tongue and obey."

When it touched him this time he felt no horror, but instead a disgusted pity. It was not some powerful demon at all. It was little more than a child, fearful of punishment. What stories surrounded this pair? He was glad that he would never know, for to feel compassion for such things as these might mark the end of his humanity.

It said nothing more as it shifted Richard to look at the tank, this thing he had feared reduced to a petulant infant.

Alex lay on the floor halfway between the tank and the bed. He was stripped naked, his body lean and muscular. Jennifer directed a sly smile towards him from where she stood over the prone figure. He swore in his mind, damning her and her powers. Was nothing he thought sacred? Her broader grin, sallow and feverish, told him not.

The creature, moving to the machine beside the tank, began to operate a series of controls, then turned to the mother-mistress. As she nodded, curt and impatient, a rush of transparent fluid gushed from the pipes connecting the steel container to the glass cube, crashing against the far wall. Deafened by the roar, Richard could not make out what Jennifer said after this. The creature did, for it went to lift Alex from the floor.

It was time.

Carrying Alex with a strange, mournful tenderness, the creature climbed the steel steps running up the side of the tank. Gaining the top, it waited. Richard prayed as the cube filled, for it was all he was able to do. The God he did not believe in ignored his pleas. Unable to avert his gaze, he watched the creature, magnificent and gothic atop the steps, outstretch those flayed arms. Alex was cradled there like a naked babe, weighing nothing to the thing holding it.

When the tank was half full, Jennifer limped to the intravenous drip running from the steel drum. Her movements had acquired a new vigour at the prospect of the banquet, and she inserted the thin tubes into her wrists with the practised ease of an addict.

The tank was three quarters of the way full. An awful tingling began in Richard's muscles, the desire to act fighting the inability to do so. In the tank, the contents had stopped rising. *No*, thought Richard, *fill it all - give me more time!* Each passing second might be the one in which he remembered how to use his Judas limbs.

The creature, a macabre Greek statue, released Alex. Blond hair flying, limbs flapping, his friend splashed into the tank. Richard expected a rush of frenzied bubbles, a churning of fluid, something distinctive and dramatic.

Nothing happened. Made balletic by the concentrate, Alex sank. The momentum of his fall was dying, carrying him so far before giving up altogether. Suspended almost centrally in the tank, arms and legs loosely outstretched, he looked like one of Raphael's angels. Some cold part of Richard's mind informed him that the fluid must be denser than water in order to support a man so. He ignored the observation, too fascinated by the spectacle. Alex's hair was beautiful, floating loose and majestic about his head.

Like a patient litmus paper, Alex's skin started to redden. When it was the shade of dying embers, the tank began to drain through the pipes, into the small steel drum, then into Jennifer's left wrist. Arms held aloft, a worshipper rejoicing, she allowed the tank to empty into her. With nauseous horror he noticed that it surged back out of her right arm, back to the drum, back to the tank. Ready for round two.

Cheeks dampened by the tears he had not noticed crying, he watched the repetitive process of a human body dissolving, as the tank drained and refilled, drained and refilled. With each stage there was less of Alex to see.

Worst of all was the moment just before his eyes were consumed. For a few lonely seconds those orbs were visible, and they seemed to watch Richard with a deep and sacred love. Then the eyes were gone, leaving a stain of black and red floating in front of Alex's sockets. Richard knew then that Alex was somehow awake and aware, until that moment at the least.

As she fed, Jennifer grew stronger, more vital, fuller. She looked almost as he remembered her now, as *Greg* remembered her, young and beautiful. Flesh had grown before his eyes, filling out her atrophied muscles, inflating her perfect breasts. Yes, inflating was the word he sought. It was like watching a balloon being filled. Though he wept love at the passing of his friend, he was simultaneously aroused by the sexual ecstasy she displayed as she fed. Hating himself for the sensations that crept through him as Alex died, his tears grew more ferocious.

When the process was complete, and even the bones were gone, he had little time to grieve. With Alex dead her attention was on Richard alone, the grip of her mind tightening around his body and soul. All at once, he felt the prickle of his defences sharpen, and knew his body was priming to reject her, loosing flashbacks of a false life in him. Attempting calm, he relaxed himself as he had done in the restaurant, when he dined with his dead brother. It was a success, the rushing sensations he associated with the mental leap fluttered to nothing. Unable to even clench a muscle, he could do nothing about the physical onslaught, and his body spurted blood. Nails, eyes, anus, ears, mouth, nose; a tiny needle was thrust viciously into each, causing them to weep red tears in crimson mourning for Alex. Compared to the other agonies, the burns and bruises, the pain hardly mattered. Richard felt the blood flow from him and knew a small glow of triumph when he realised that Jennifer's next meal would be incomplete. As he gushed red, she studied him.

"You reject me? An involuntary reaction to my presence in you, yes? Oh sweet, but you *are* a curiosity. I wish we had more time to play, but my physical appetites have been neglected too long. The main course awaits."

With the return of her full attention, Jameson winked out like a light bulb. One moment he comprised a significant portion of the personality in his mind, the next he was gone. He could still remember what he had so recently thought and felt, but there was now a wall in place which stemmed the tide of returning information. His reactions were once more those of Gregory Summers.

Thinking of Alex, of the feelings he had for the dead man, he felt nothing but self-loathing. The same instincts that had thrust his friend away during their only tentative kiss now made him glad the man was dead. Crying with the destructive power of those thoughts, feeling they were right at the same time as he knew they were wrong, he wished his shamed, tired existence would end.

"Then how fortunate for you that I'm here." God, he wished she would get out of his head. Like a coroner examining fresh meat, she reached forward with her cupped hand and pulled the lids of his eyes closed. They would never again open of their own accord.

Blindness provided at least a small physical relief. His staring eyes had begun to throb and run with the room's constant glare, losing and gaining focus with alarming fickleness. Now he could wrap himself up in a little world of self.

Even if he was the *wrong* self.

"Strip him." Her voice was as beautiful as the day he hadn't married her. Feeling the hands of the creature tear his charred shirt from him, he felt a curious outrage. Could it not be a little gentler, a little more decent with his last moments? "Gently," she added. She would be with him until the moment of his death. Then he would be with *her*, travelling through her in little tubes, feeding her. Was that to be his afterlife? He felt he deserved more.

"There is nothing more." She was close to his ear. "There is only me and mine." Was that true? How could she, an endless, wandering thing that had evaded death for so long, possibly know? Her voice betrayed a hint of panic and fear, two things he had thought never to hear there. "I've seen it on the faces of the dead! I've seen it scrawled on the back of eternity!"

Poetic nothings. He knew what had wormed into her, breaking her calm and releasing the black beast of fear. She would never be sure. It was Jennifer who was damned, not he. Stuck in her meagre, repetitive existence, she envied him his ability to either discover or fade, for either were preferable to her infinite inertia.

Victory. When he died he would take a victory with him.

All thought left his head, leaving only stars and confusion in their wake. Unable to see, he had been unaware of the impending blow he had received. At last he could be grateful for his paralysed vocal cords. Though she knew she had hurt him (he could keep nothing back from her), she would never hear his pain again. He denied her a satisfaction, and relished the act.

"Cherish your illusions while you can." The surety of her voice chilled him.

Naked now, a cool draft flowing over his body, he began to steel himself for the tank. Could he prepare himself for the unknowable? Pushing such thoughts from his head, aware that he was wasting the little time left to him, he tried to imagine what the pain might be like. Perhaps it would be a larger version of the coffee scald he had never received, nothing more than a protracted burn. Thinking on the pain he had felt in his blazing flat, he thought he could live with that. Better, he could die with it.

Roaring like the grumble of some ancient beast, the tank filled somewhere ahead of him. Meaty arms found purchase beneath his arms and legs, lifting him from the floor. Wanting to cry for the creature, a child with no true experience of love and hate, he felt a burning need to speak. Concentrating, feeling his chance fade as the creature began to carry him to the steps, he thought of his vocal cords trapped into immobility. Pushing hard, he found his breath willing to obey him.

"Waaagth." *Wait*. Inarticulate, but the creature heard. She heard, in her mind and in the air about her. Though he could simply think the thought, allow her to retrieve it in her mind, he wanted to be a human being one last time. He wanted to speak to his wife.

"Aaaaayyyy…." No good. He tried again, desperate that she hear the words before her patience wore thin and he lost his chance. "Aay luuuthed wut uuu weer. Aay haayt wuut uuu aaaar." It would do, she had the words in her mind to confirm his last fragile sounds.

"Take him." He had expected another blow, a final repercussion of some sort. She did nothing. As he felt the lurching steps of the creature ascending, he knew it was because there was nothing she could say. Two victories. How many could she claim? Not knowing, but satisfied that he would do nothing more significant with what remained of his life, he waited.

A halt, followed by movement from the arms holding him. At the top of the steps the creature held him out like the sacrificial offering they had made him. From below, he heard the thunder of the tank continuing to refill. *The beast is hungry*, he thought.

The roar stopped.

The creature let go.

He fell.

The graceless plunge lasted long enough to wonder what was coming, and wish that Jameson was still with him, then he broke the surface and was submerged.

Agony beyond words. Pain that seared as it ate him. Sinking and burning, but no awareness of anything beyond those sensations. More than he had prepared for, tearing through his mental barricades as it ripped at his flesh, the pain chased him towards merciful blackness.

34 PERDITION

Growth. Expansion. Completion. Again he is complete, and this surprises him, though he knows what has occurred. A small part of the fluid has been recycled, pumped back to the tank. A small part of his mind. Enough to integrate with the rest of the vicious liquid, pulling him until he is the cube of the tank again.

It has happened because she wants to feel him as he feasts on the last remnants of skeleton in the tank. Knowing he has no control, he pictures himself cracking bones, sucking sweet marrow from them, absorbing them into him. It will finish soon. He will move on, leaving her here.

Whole truth strikes him only as he performs his nerveless task. She need never let him free. She *will* never let him free.

Screaming silent, fluid howls, he sees his fate. Barricaded into this vampiric existence, he will be recycled. All she need do is keep one tiny portion of each batch of fluid she consumes. A small piece of him, diminutive but aware. She will have done so with every victim who passed into this tank.

How many? Is Alex there, or the victim before that? Yes and yes. An infinite yes. All of them, from the moment she realised she could still link to their suffering, could still feed her soul with their pain.

Are they aware of him? Will he ever know their company? No. They are disparate torments. Countless meals.

So he will be an endless man in an endless suffering. How many more frightened Gregs will he consume with his new fluid form? Eyeballs will burst, their fluids merging with him. He will drink deep, destroying and consuming, binding them to form a grotesque, fleshless insanity. That is all he is now. One fragment of a greater, twisted whole.

As he diminishes once more, finally able to accept that he has no future but this continual shrinking and growth, he knows he will be pushed to madness. On the outside, he knows she sees his acceptance and pleasures herself with the knowledge, a perverse cerebral masturbation. It is her victory after all.

Two victories. All he ever claimed.

Alex is more intimately joined to him than he could have ever imagined.

Screaming, his silent shriek joining many hundreds of similar wails, he shrinks to nothing once more.

RICHARD WRIGHT

ABOUT THE AUTHOR

Richard Wright is an author of strange, dark fictions, currently living in New Delhi, India, with his wife and daughter. Since *Cuckoo* was first written, his short stories have gone on to appear in dozens of publications in the USA and UK, and his plays have toured Scotland.

Visit his website at http://www.richardwright.org.

AFTERWORD

Thank you for buying this book. I wrote it many years ago in Scotland, on an electric typewriter with a display that showed four lines of text at a time, and on which I saved each chapter as a separate file on the type of floppy disk you can't buy any more. To proofread it, I had to print it off over and over again, making changes in pen, and meticulously finding the lines on that tiny display to make the needful corrections.

By contrast, I prepared this revised edition in India, on a Macbook, using a incredibly sophisticated writing program called Scrivener. I proofread it on my Kindle, making notes in the electronic text as I went.

Times have changed. When Greg Summers first fought to survive, mobile phones weren't the ubiquitous commodities they are today, and the Internet was still catching on. Little things like that have evolved this final edition of the novel, but I'm pleased to say it's much the same book as it always was, albeit one with a more experienced editor.

When I started telling this story, I wasn't a writer. By the time I finished it, I was. That's what I owe this book, and I'm delighted to be able to put it back out into the world.

- Richard Wright, New Delhi, 2011

14107997R00177

Made in the USA
Lexington, KY
21 March 2012